Destin's Hold:
The Alliance Book 5

By S.E. Smith

Acknowledgments

I would like to thank my husband Steve for believing in me and being proud enough of me to give me the courage to follow my dream. I would also like to give a special thank you to my sister and best friend, Linda, who not only encouraged me to write, but who also read the manuscript. Also to my other friends who believe in me: Julie, Jackie, Christel, Sally, Jolanda, Lisa, Laurelle, and Narelle. The girls that keep me going!
—S.E. Smith

Science Fiction Romance
Destin's Hold: The Alliance Book 5
Copyright © 2017 by S.E. Smith
First E-Book\print Published February 2017
Cover Design by Melody Simmons

Summary: A human rebel leader determined to rebuild the city he calls home must work with an alien ambassador to save the people under his protection even as a new war builds.

ISBN 978-1-942562-86-3 (paperback)
ISBN 978-1-942562-87-0 (eBook)

Published in the United States by Montana Publishing.

{1. Science Fiction Romance – Fiction. 2. Urban Fantasy – Fiction. 3. Action/Adventure – Fiction. 4. Suspense – Fiction. 5. Romance – Fiction.}

www.montanapublishinghouse.com

Synopsis

Destin Parks will do whatever it takes to rebuild the city he calls home, even if it means working with another alien ambassador. Her predecessor left him hesitant to trust the alien diplomats assigned to Chicago's rebuilding, but Destin knows that if he refuses to work with them, he will be replaced, and he won't give them the satisfaction.

Jersula 'Sula' Ikera is assigned to Earth by the Alliance and the Usoleum Council. The Councils hope her logical mind and calm demeanor will resolve the upheaval caused by the last ambassador. Sula has fought hard for her position, and while not pleased with her current assignment to liaise with humans, she will do her best to help rebuild the world its inhabitants have destroyed. What she does not anticipate is her reaction to the hardheaded human male who she has been assigned to work with. His ability to get under her skin and ignite a flame inside her is quite alarming, mystifying, and leaves her questioning her own sanity.

When Sula uncovers an alien cartel's plans to traffic human women and children, a near fatal attack leaves her unable to trust anyone but Destin. Together, Destin and Sula race to stop the aliens before anyone is taken off-planet, but the traffickers are not the only ones they are fighting against; the Waxian and Drethulan forces have targeted Earth.

Can Destin and Sula stop the traffickers and prevent the deadly forces of the Waxians and Drethulans from destroying the progress they have made? Will the Alliance be able to protect Destin when the enemy discovers his connection to a powerful Alliance family? The battle for Earth has just become personal.

Table of Contents

Chapter 1

"No!" a low, tortured hiss escaped Destin as he fought against the paralyzing memories holding him prisoner.

He struggled to free his mind, caught between the realm of nightmares and consciousness, but couldn't break free. After several long seconds that felt like an eternity, he jolted awake with a shudder and drew a deep breath into his starving lungs before slowly releasing it. Pushing up into a sitting position, he noticed he was tangled in the bed sheets.

Destin ran a hand over his sweat-dampened face before reaching to turn on the lamp next to the bed. It was missing. It took him a second to remember where he was and that the lighting system was still alien to him.

With a groan, he fell back against the pillows and drew in a series of deep, calming breaths, holding each one for several seconds before releasing the air in a slow, controlled rhythm. It was a meditation technique he read about years ago. He continued until he felt his pulse settle down to a normal rate.

A glance out the door told him it was still dark. He groaned and laid his arm across his eyes. He was up way too late last night or should he say this morning. Unfortunately, it didn't matter the amount of sleep he got, his body was programmed to wake early.

Destin dropped his arm back to his side and stared up at the ceiling. It was smooth and undamaged. There were no patched places, no cracks, and no bare metal beams. The architects and engineers back home were slowly making progress, but home was nowhere near as nice as Rathon, the Trivator home world.

Throwing aside the twisted sheets, he rolled out of bed. The jogging pants he slept in hung low on his slender hips. He ran a hand over his flat stomach and curled his toes into the soft, plush mat under his feet before he began his daily stretching exercises.

The taut muscles in his neck, back, and shoulders bulged as he tried to work the tension out of them. He might not be as tall as his Trivator brother-in-law, but years of hard work and targeted training had made his body the perfect fighting machine. Scars crisscrossed his flesh, each one a testament to the challenges he had faced over the past seven years.

His arms rose and he stretched, enjoying the cool breeze blowing in from the open doors and caressing his bare back. He could smell the fragrant aroma from the flowers blooming in the garden just outside and the tangy scent of salt from the nearby ocean. The weather here was a balmy seventy degrees if he had to guess.

He turned toward the doors and closed his eyes, blocking out the view of the garden and its high protective walls designed to keep out the wildlife. He tilted his head and listened to the sound of waves crashing against the shore. It was soothing last night, luring him to sleep, but now it felt relentless and violent, an echo of the adrenaline he woke up with.

Destin ran a hand down over his hard, flat abdomen again. His fingers traced a barely visible three-inch scar. It was a new one. He got it when a skittish street urchin fought to return to a building that was slowly collapsing.

Two years ago, he would have died from such a wound. He owed a huge thanks to Patch, the Trivator healer back on Earth. Patch had doctored him up, and after a few weeks of rest, Destin had been ready to travel off the planet.

He shook his head and opened his eyes. His travel through space to a distant world was unimaginable seven years before. It was hard to believe that Earth had received their first contact with aliens almost a decade ago. It was even harder for him to believe he was on an alien planet at the moment – at least until he looked around at the buildings and landscape. Twin moons, thick forests, flying transports, and bizarre creatures made him feel like he woke up in some alternate reality.

Destin turned and quietly made the bed. He grabbed a black T-shirt out of the drawer and pulled it over his head. He didn't bother with shoes; he wouldn't need them where he was going. Within minutes, he silently exited the house that belonged to his sister, Kali, and her *Amate*, Razor.

He crossed through the garden to the far gate. Punching the security code into the panel, Destin waited while the lock disengaged before he quietly slipped through. He made sure the gate was closed and the security system engaged before he turned along the path that led down to the beach. Both Razor and Kali had warned him to stay on the marked paths. He understood why after his arrival. From the air he got a brief glimpse of one of the wild animals that inhabited the planet. Destin was very glad the paths were secured against creatures like that.

The Trivators believed in living in harmony with the other creatures on the planet. They used only the areas they needed to live and kept large sections of green space. Most of the creatures were fairly harmless, but there were a few that were extremely dangerous – to both the Trivators and their enemies. Invaders would first face the dangers of the forests if they landed outside of the protected cities.

The roads and walkways were kept safe by specially placed security markers embedded into the paths. The markers were programmed with the animals' DNA. The embedded sensors detected when an animal approached the marked areas and a shield formed to stop the creatures from entering the path.

Destin didn't understand all the specifics; he just knew that he didn't want to tangle with that creature he had glimpsed from the air. The long tusks, six legs, and massive scaly body were formidable enough from a distance. He really did not want a closer look and was very happy that most travel on the planet was done by air.

The city he saw upon his arrival was magnificent. Large spiraling towers glittered with muted lights while transports moved along the ground and flew through the air. The tower on the far end spilled water from the top of the building in a dazzling waterfall into the Trivator-created reflection pond. Several of the transports disappeared under the reflection pool and reappeared on the other side. The more he saw, the more his excitement grew at the possibilities for Earth.

He paused at the top of the stone steps carved into the side of the cliff and looked out over the vast ocean. The sun wasn't up yet, but there was enough light on the horizon to see the waves break on the outer reef. He stood still, appreciating the beauty and peacefulness of his surroundings.

Destin couldn't remember the last time he had stopped to appreciate the beauty of anything. Death, destruction, fear, and responsibility had been his constant companion for as long as he could remember. He drew in a deep breath and released it.

No longer would that kind of destruction dominate his life. The Trivators' first contact had plunged the Earth into a panicked chaos, but in the past two years, he began to see a change. Progress was being made to heal the wounds. For him, the most important indication that life was getting better was seeing his sister Kali's glowing face and the living proof that there was hope for the future in his beautiful niece.

Originally, he had been reluctant to come, but Kali's quiet plea and Tim's, his second-in-command, assurance that the work Destin had done to restore a new Chicago would be carefully monitored by the team he had built convinced him that he needed the break. That reassurance, combined with his recent brush with death, reminded him of what was important – family. He felt like if he ever wanted a chance to see Kali again, and meet his niece, he had better rearrange his priorities. Until last night, he was convinced he had made the right decision. Now, he wasn't so sure after hearing what happened on another alien world called Dises V.

Destin shook his head at his musings. No, even with what he knew now, he was still glad he came to visit. Seeing Kali again and meeting Ami gave him a renewed purpose to return to Earth and fight for a better life for others.

Focusing on the stone path in front of him, he started down the stairs. He needed a good run to help clear his mind. He might as well enjoy the last few days he had here while he could. Once he returned to Earth, there was a city to rebuild and a lot of fires to put out, among other possible threats.

At the bottom, his feet sunk into the powdered, snow-white sand. He took off at a brisk pace down the long narrow beach beside the looming cliffs. For a brief moment, he was able to lose himself in the enjoyment of his surroundings and replace thoughts of his nightmares with dreams of something better – dreams of rebuilding his city and maybe, just maybe, finding someone to share it with.

* * *

An hour later, Destin walked back along the beach. Sweat soaked his shirt and he pulled it off. There was a secluded cove farther down the beach that he discovered on his second day on the planet. He would take a quick swim before heading back to Kali and Razor's house.

If he was lucky, Ami would be awake and waiting for him. His fourteen-month-old niece had taken a shine to him. It might have been all the toys he brought that put the hero worship in her eyes, but Destin didn't care. He had planned a new gift for each day of his stay. Mabel, one of the grandmotherly women that was with the rebellion from the beginning, suggested it.

Destin crossed the empty beach and entered a hole amidst the rocks that had been carved by centuries of wind and water. The narrow gap glistened with natural crystals found in the rocks. Lifting his hand, he ran the tips of his fingers along the rocks. The crystals lit up under his touch. He would love to take some back to Earth with him so he could study them.

His hand fell to his side when he reached the opening leading to the small cove. Out of habit, he glanced around to make sure the area was secure, then walked over to a large boulder protruding from the sand. He tossed his sweat-dampened shirt onto it and pushed his jogging pants down. He stepped out of his pants and shook the loose sand off before he placed them on the boulder next to his shirt. Afraid he might lose the medallion he wore, he slipped it over his head and slid it into the pocket of his pants. His hand ran along the waistband of the jockey shorts he wore, but he kept them on. Life had taught him to never get caught with his pants down. You never knew when you might have to fight and doing it in the buff could be a little distracting.

Destin walked to the edge of the water and stood looking outward. The gentle waves rolled over his feet and he curled his toes into the wet sand. A smile curved his lips and he slowly walked forward until he was waist deep. Drawing in a deep breath, he dove under the incoming wave, enjoying the refreshing feel of the water as it washed the sweat from his skin and cooled his heated flesh.

His arms swept out in front of him and his legs moved in strong, powerful kicks. The water was crystal clear and he could see the ripples in the white sand along the bottom. He swam as far as he could before his lungs burned and he was forced to surface for a breath of air. He turned onto his back and floated, lost in thought. The peacefulness of the moment, combined with the beauty and freedom of just watching the clouds, pulled the last of the tension he had woken with out of his body. For a little while, he was alone in the universe with nothing else to worry about.

* * *

Jersula Ikera stomped across the soft sand in a foul mood. The thin, dark blue silk cover she wore clung to her lithe body and floated behind her. If anyone saw her from a distance, she would look like she was floating across the powdery white crystals that made up the sandy beach.

Her long white hair was unbound and blew around her. Her icy blue eyes flashed with an uncharacteristic fire and her pale blue lips were pressed into a firm line of irritation. She had come down to the beach to escape for a while, at least until she could find her center and restore the calm mask she relied on to interact with others.

A swift glance up and down the beach showed it was deserted. Jersula – Sula to her family and her few close friends – breathed a sigh of relief. She could mull over the orders she received early this morning in private. They were distressing, but she knew she needed to release some of the anger she was feeling if she wanted to get through the day without making a mistake that could devastate her career.

"Why? Why are they sending me to that horrible place again? Wasn't once enough? Who could I have angered so much that they would send me there again?" she muttered under her breath.

Her mind flashed to the dozens of people that could be responsible. She knew her icy reserve and sometimes blunt attitude had angered certain members of the Usoleum Council, but she was always right in her assessments! It wasn't her fault that most of the political members of the council were sweet, confused people who couldn't think their way out of a wormhole.

Sula glanced back at her transport to see how far she walked along the beach. Not far; it seemed that stomping wasn't the fastest way to travel.

The small transport glinted in the sunlight. It was given to her when she arrived on Rathon six weeks ago. She had hoped to be appointed the new ambassador between her people and the Trivators. That hope was brutally crushed when her new orders arrived this morning before dawn.

"No, I have to return to that horrible, war-torn excuse for a planet brimming with savages! Those uncultured, hostile, brutal beasts who were ignorant of *any* life forms outside of Earth until a few years ago! They haven't even mastered space travel," she snarled under her breath in frustration before her footsteps slowed and she blinked back tears of annoyance. "That is what they are... ignorant beasts!"

Her anger boiled when she thought of her previous visit. The last time she had been to the primitive planet called Earth, her assignment was to assess the situation left by the previous ambassador who was killed, and it had been impossible to do anything when she received no support from the Trivators or the humans.

At the time, she was forced to wait two weeks before the Trivators would even allow her access to Councilor Badrick's starship. By the time she was finally allowed to board, the previous crew had been recalled, a new crew assigned, and all of Councilor Badrick's reports and personal files had vanished. The only things Sula was left with were a clueless crew, a Trivator named Cutter who had regarded her with suspicion, and a human male who had dismissed her with a look of contempt during their one and only meeting! It wasn't until much later that she unraveled the reasons behind the Trivator and human's animosity. Unable to blink back the tears of frustration this time, she lifted an impatient hand and brushed them away.

Sula had reported her initial findings on Badrick to the Council and her father, and within weeks of arriving on Earth, she was recalled to her home world, Usoleum. Believing she was being groomed to take over the Ambassador's position at the Alliance Headquarters, she had worked day and night on a variety of issues, but it had all been for naught. She had discovered a hidden cache of Badrick's files, and shortly after reporting the discovery, she was reassigned to Rathon. Here, she was to work with the Trivators to wring every bit of information possible from those files and to strengthen Usoleum's relationship with the Trivators after the damage wrought by Badrick's unconscionable behavior – a behavior that had mortified her family.

There were a large number of files to sift through, and in the meantime, she adhered to her assignment to grovel at the Trivators' feet for the past six weeks. It should have shown the Usoleum Council that she would make an excellent Ambassador to the Trivator Council here on their planet. But once again, her hopes were crushed. Sula was the only living Usoleum with experience on Earth, and she was now reassigned there to finish her original task, which is to clean up the mess Badrick left behind – almost two Earth years later! Her only hope for any kind of real success with the humans lay in parsing useful information from those files. To get even the slightest bit of trust and good will on Earth, she needed to be able to answer the question preying on everyone's mind: where were the rest of the missing human women?

Sula still had a couple of days left on Rathon, however, and part of reassuring the Trivators and the Alliance that everything was under control included attending some ceremony between a member of Chancellor Razor's family and a Trivator warrior. It would begin in a couple of hours, and if she was not able to gain control of her emotions before the ceremony, her career would be in even worse shape than it already was.

"This is an insult!" Sula hissed, discarding her maudlin misery in favor of the more empowering anger she felt earlier. "If Father thinks my brothers are so much better at diplomacy than I am, then one of them should be the one to attend the ceremony, not me! When they need a problem solved, they send me in to fix it. Father knows I am more than qualified for the ambassador position. Yet he gives the position to Sirius, the progeny who is least qualified. All Sirius wants to do is chase women that he couldn't do anything with and play at the gaming tables! He isn't even fit to be – to be – to care for the racers in the stables, much less be the Ambassador to the

Trivators," Sula muttered with a slashing wave of her hand in the air.

Sula released a long sigh and stepped through the narrow chasm in the rocks. She gazed out at the water protected by the small cove for several seconds before she walked toward it, drawn to the soothing waves. She missed her world. It was mostly water and her people were born within its beautiful seas. They live on land, but the water is where they find solace.

Sula's hand moved to the tie of the gown and she released it. The garment fell to the sand around her feet. Her body was covered in a form-fitting dark blue suit made for the water. She spread her fingers and the fine membranes between them spread like small webs. Stepping forward, she relished the first touch of the water against her skin. Pleasure coursed through her, cooling her fury and soothing her despair.

Her gaze scanned the water. The waves broke against the reef almost two hundred meters offshore. It would be a short swim for her, but she could do it several times before she had to return to her temporary lodging to prepare for the ceremony. Sula slowly walked forward until she was deep enough to sink down below the surface.

The two almost invisible slits along her neck opened and she drew water into her gills. The refreshing liquid filled the second set of lungs with life-giving fluid, extracting the oxygen trapped in the water into her blood when she exhaled. She loved living and working near an ocean. A shudder went through her when she thought of her next assignment. It was so far from the large oceans that covered most of Earth. There was a long, narrow lake, but it wasn't the same. She would have to make periodic trips to the coast to satisfy her body's craving for the salty water.

And I'll need to swim frequently to keep from killing that arrogant human male if he is still there, Sula thought. *Perhaps I will be lucky and he will already be dead, and a more reasonable human will have replaced him.*

Remorse swept through her at her hateful thoughts. It was so unlike her. She hated the idea of hurting anything or anyone. Her six older brothers teased her, saying that was why it was ridiculous that she would even consider becoming a member of the Alliance Council.

Sula pushed the negative thoughts away. She would lose herself in the pleasures of the ocean around her. Pushing off the bottom, her body cut through the crystal-clear liquid like a laser cutter through steel. All around her, colorful fish and plant life flourished in a world few could appreciate.

The cove was protected from the larger marine life that lived on the other side of the reef. She had researched Rathon's oceanographic environment and decided it would be best to stay within the protected barriers that sheltered the coast line. 'Nature's unique fencing' is the way Sula liked to think of it.

She was starting to feel more herself, more collected, but a wave of longing swept through her to just let go, to be wild for a few unadulterated minutes – not the frazzled, bitter release from the beach, but something… untouchable. To hell with her father's belief that she wasn't capable of dealing with the stress of being a leading member of the Usoleum Council or an integral part of the Alliance. She knew she could if she was given the opportunity.

Closing her eyes, she twisted until she was facing upward and allowed her body to slowly sink to the bottom. She relaxed her arms and a serene smile curved her lips. Maybe she would just forget about the ceremony and stay here all day. It wasn't as if it really mattered if she attended. No one, especially the Trivator male and his human mate, would even miss her.

Finally, the peace that Sula was searching for settled over her. Her body floated above the soft white sand. The light from the rising sun created shafts of glittering beams that reflected off the silver threads in her bodysuit and made them sparkle like diamonds. She was unaware of how ethereal she looked against the satin bottom of the ocean, or the fact that she wasn't alone.

Chapter 2

Destin dove beneath the waves and began swimming toward shore. As much as he hated it, he needed to get back to the house. He had promised Ami that he would make her some mouse-shaped pancakes this morning just like he used to do for her mommy.

He swam only a short distance when he caught a glimpse of something sparkling under the water. Surfacing, he glanced around with a frown before he took a deep breath and dove back down. He blinked when he saw the body of a young woman floating along the bottom. His heart thundered in dismay. He had seen enough death in his lifetime. The beautiful woman floating serenely near the bottom was too young to face such a fate.

Kicking downward with hard, powerful strokes, he reached for her. His eyes burned from the salt water, but he refused to close them. He grabbed her arm and quickly pulled her against his hard length, then changed his grip to hold her more securely around the waist as his feet pushed off the bottom.

Her slender hands clutched his bare shoulders, and her brilliant, light blue eyes snapped open. Destin and the woman locked gazes in mutual shock. Her delicate, pale blue lips parted, and Destin was afraid she would instinctively draw in a mouthful of water. Unsure of what else to do, he covered her lips with his. The moment his lips touched hers, a wave of heat swept through him and he couldn't help but wonder if he had captured a real, live siren.

Destin knew he should release her – or at least her lips – when they surfaced, but the fire that had ignited when he had pressed his lips to hers appeared to have short-circuited that part of his brain. She was not helping his resolve, either. Her hands tightened on his shoulders, but she didn't push him away and her soft lips trembled slightly as her breath mingled with his. It took several seconds before he finally forced his body to obey his command to stop. He reluctantly lifted his head, but still kept her firmly pressed against him.

"Are you okay?" he asked, blinking to clear his eyes of the salt water.

"I… You… Of course, I'm… You!" the woman sputtered before her eyes widened in recognition. "You aren't supposed to be here!"

Destin's lips curved up at the corners. "Where am I supposed to be?" he asked with a raised eyebrow, studying her face with a growing sense of dismay. "I know you…," he started to say.

"You should be back on that horrid, barbaric world," the woman snapped, pushing against his shoulders. "Release me!"

Recognition hit Destin hard. His arms slackened enough that the woman – Jersula Ikera – was able to pull away from him. She pushed at the water to put some space between them, her light blue eyes flashing with fire. This was a much different woman than the one he had briefly met back on Earth. This one was….

The sudden image of a siren flashed through his mind.

Trouble, he thought with a grimace, twisting around and striking out for the shore. The moment he was in shallow enough water to put his feet down, he did. He wanted to put as much distance as possible between him and the Usoleum Councilor he met back on Earth.

He ran the back of his hand across his heated lips. He could still taste her. It was a good thing his back was to her otherwise she would notice the physical evidence of his reaction to her. It suddenly occurred to him that she would have been aware of it when she was pressed against him.

Damn it! Well, he wasn't going to remind her by giving her a second look. He was sure that would thrill her even more – not.

Destin muttered a string of expletives under his breath as he exited the water. He strode across the beach, passing the film of dark blue material lying against the white sand. He kept his back to her while he grabbed his jogging pants and pulled them on with stiff fingers. He ran his fingers through his soaked hair. The dark brown strands were cut into a short, military style and would dry soon enough.

Destin grabbed his T-shirt off the boulder. It was still damp from his run and he decided it wasn't worth pulling it on. He drew in a deep, calming breath and slowly released it before turning around to make sure Jersula had made it back to shore. He would feel pretty rotten if she drowned while he was trying to hide the major hard-on he had. He could just see himself trying to explain that to Razor and the Trivator council!

A frustrated groan escaped him when he saw her emerge from the water in the form-fitting blue material that left very little to the imagination. Destin's gaze froze on the twin peaks of her nipples pressing against the fabric, and he swallowed hard. They were hard pebbles, perfect for....

"It has been too damn long since I've been with a woman," he muttered under his breath.

He forced his eyes back to her face. His lips quirked up at the corners when he saw her eyes were still shooting indignant sparks. She looked a hell of a lot different than she did when he first met her. He found her fascinating then, too, which hadn't helped his temper during their one and only meeting.

Her long silky white hair, glacier blue eyes, and unusual blue lips had made it difficult to look away. She was an ethereal ice queen. At the time, he was furious with himself for reacting like that to an alien. He had thought she must have been cast in the same mold as Badrick, but the woman angrily snatching up the silky fabric off the sand was anything but icy. He remembered her heated breaths and the softness of her lips.

She clutched the fabric in front of her and her long legs cut across the loose crystals, quickly closing the distance between them. He couldn't help but notice that her hair was the same color as the sparkling sand. Her cheeks were a slightly darker blue than before and matched the deep color of her eyes. He would have to remember that when she was angry, her eyes changed to the color of the ocean back home.

She was breathing heavily by the time she stopped in front of him. His gaze swept over her face, noticing the strand of hair stuck to her cheek. Without thinking, he tenderly brushed it back.

"I'm glad you are alright. When I first saw you floating along the bottom, I feared you were dead," he murmured.

Sula's lips parted in surprise. She swallowed and lifted her hand to touch her cheek, pausing when she felt his hand hovering near it.

"Why… Why did you kiss me?" she asked softly.

Destin dropped his hand to his side and he glanced over her shoulder to the ocean behind her. In his mind, the countless faces of those he had to bury over the years superimposed over her face as she lay so still under the water. He didn't look at her when he replied.

"I thought you had drowned. When I touched you, you opened your eyes and I saw your lips part. I was afraid that you would inhale water and choke. It was the only way I could think of to protect you," he replied with a shrug. "Anyway, I'm glad you are okay. I apologize if I offended you. It wasn't intentional. I've got to go," he added in a stiff tone.

"I…," Sula started to say, but her voice faded when he turned and started to walk away. "Human… Destin!"

Sula's soft voice called out behind him before he had gone more than a few strides. Destin slowed to a stop and partially turned to look back at the alien ice queen who had captured his attention over a year ago. He waited for her to speak again. She swallowed and lifted her chin.

"Thank you," she said. "... for trying to save me, even though it was not necessary."

Destin bowed his head in acknowledgement and turned away. As ghosts from his past rose up to choke him, he knew he needed to put some space between them. Sula was alive, not dead like so many others he had been responsible for. Over the past year, he had worked hard on learning to control the haunting thoughts that often tried to drown him. There were too many would've, could've, should've moments over the last seven years that could never be changed. Dwelling on those memories did nothing but pull him into a deep abyss that threatened to suffocate him.

Sula was in no danger at all and that should be the end of it. There was no reason to keep touching her. It threw him off balance that he had this aching need to feel her lithe body against his again, regardless of whether he had a reason or not.

This reaction was much more intense than the first time he saw her. At that time, he was still reeling from everything that had happened – Colbert's death, Kali being wounded and leaving the planet, the loss of the men who had fought beside him, and the realization that he now had what he wanted – Chicago to rebuild. That, on top of discovering how many women and young girls were kidnapped from Earth for the Usoleum Councilor's greed, made his physical attraction to the new Councilor too much to deal with at the time.

Destin focused on the narrow gap in the rocks in front of him. The moment he was on the other side, he broke into a fast jog. He didn't stop until he reached the back gate to Kali and Razor's home.

* * *

When Sula had called out to him, her gaze was focused on the maze of scars across his back. When he half turned, she noticed more on his thick arms and chest, but it was the one on his left cheek that had briefly frozen the words on her lips. Her fingers had ached to trace it. What happened to him back on the planet he called home?

She didn't move until he had disappeared. Glancing down, she shook out the silk cover and slipped it back on. A frown creased her brow when she saw a necklace in the sand near the boulder where Destin Parks had retrieved his clothes.

She walked over to it and picked it up. Her fingers brushed the sand from the small oval disk. Strange symbols, written in the language of the humans, were engraved on the front of it. The medallion appeared to be able to slide apart. Unsure if she should try to see what was inside or not, Sula bit her lip and looked back in the direction Destin had disappeared.

"What harm can it do?" she murmured with a shrug.

It took her a minute to figure out how to work the slide. A tiny catch held it closed. Once the catch was released, the rectangular metal piece slid open. On the side facing her was the image of a young, dark-haired little girl smiling back at her. Frowning, she turned the piece over and saw another image, this one slightly faded. It was of an older woman. She had the same dark hair and shining eyes of the little girl – and of Destin. A series of numbers were etched into the back of the medallion.

Sula knew this must be Destin's family. She carefully closed the piece and pushed the catch back into place. The long, leather cord had a clasp at the end. Destin must have taken it off before he went for a swim.

Her gaze moved back out to the water. For a moment, she could feel his lips against hers and his strong hands on her waist. Her eyelashes fluttered down and a soft moan escaped her when she remembered his body against hers. She had never felt such a reaction to a male before and it shocked her. Especially given who he was and how he had reacted to her when they first met. It was surreal.

Sula lifted the necklace and fastened it around her neck. She had no pockets and didn't want to take a chance of losing it. She would find out where Destin was staying and have a courier deliver it to him. She went through the gap in the rocks and retraced her earlier steps, this time at a slower pace. Her fingers trembled slightly when she lifted them to touch the medallion.

"Well, now I know that Destin Parks did not die back on his planet. What I would like to know is why he is here on Rathon," she whispered, staring down the long beach. "And will he be staying here or returning to his world?"

A growing sense of urgency filled her the closer she got to her transport. She needed answers. It might take her a while to find them, but she was very tenacious. She wouldn't stop until she found out what she wanted to know about a certain human male.

Chapter 3

Destin grinned when he saw Kali in a dress. This had to be a first since she was about... two years old! The brief glare she gave him showed she was well aware of his amused appraisal. He bent over and picked up Ami in his arms. She was wearing a pair of pink tights and a white dress.

"Doesn't your mom look beautiful, Ami?" Destin asked. There was definitely a radiance about Kali that he had never seen before. "She's as beautiful as your grandma was."

"You don't look so bad yourself, Destin," Kali murmured, reaching for Ami. "I wish you could stay longer."

Destin studied Kali's glowing face. He had missed her. Deep down, he knew he had done the right thing when he made the deal with Razor to take Kali away from Earth. She had almost died too many times. When he discovered she was pregnant, he was especially thankful he made the choices he had. Life had not been easy over the last two years. Yes, fighting for the city was pretty much over, but there were still issues with a few renegade gangs.

"I need to return. There is still a lot of work that needs to be done. Maybe one day it will be different and you can come back to Earth for a visit, see all the changes," Destin replied.

Kali's gaze moved to the open vee of his dark green dress shirt. "Where's your medallion?" she asked with a frown. "You never go anywhere without it."

Destin's lips tightened. "I misplaced it. I'll look for it when we get back," he said, turning when Razor came into the room.

"How is Saber doing today?" Destin asked.

"Cursing us all," Razor replied with a grin. "I never realized how much fun a bachelor party could be."

"What did you guys do last night?" Kali asked, setting Ami down when she started to wiggle.

"Destin showed us how to walk on walls," Razor chuckled. "It is easier if you have not had too much to drink."

Kali scowled and shook her head. "You're lucky none of you broke a leg. Speaking of which, how did Saber do it with his leg?" she asked with concern.

"He did fine. It was a chance for him to test out the new brace that Taylor developed. It worked very well. I can understand why you love doing this 'Parkour'," Razor said, wrapping his arms around Kali. "But, it also showed me how difficult and dangerous it is."

Kali leaned back and grinned at him. "And that is where you stop this conversation if your next sentence is going to begin with 'I don't want you...'" she teased.

"I think we should do it together from now on," Razor muttered, glancing at Destin with a rueful look. "Has she always been this stubborn?"

Destin chuckled and shook his head. "If you haven't figured that out yet, I'm not going to say anything. It will just get me into hot water with her, too," he quipped. "I think it is time to go. Ami, do you want a ride on Uncle Destin's shoulders?"

"Up!" Ami cried in delight, raising her arms. "Horsey!"

"One horsey ride coming up," Destin laughed, picking Ami up and settling her on his shoulders. He winced when she kicked him with her heels. "Ouch! She's going to be like you, Kali. Always kicking the sh...."

"Watch your language; she's like a parrot right now," Kali muttered under her breath after elbowing Destin in the side.

"I can see where that might be a problem," Destin agreed. "Last one in the transport gets to feed the monsters."

"Monsters! I wants a monster," Ami giggled, fluffing up Destin's hair.

Razor and Kali laughed at the pained expression on Destin's face. Destin held onto Ami's legs, making sure he ducked when he went through the doorways, though each was at least twelve feet high, so there was no actual need to, and romped out to the transport. He swung her down and placed her in the childseat in the back, then strapped her in and climbed in next to her. Razor held the door open for

Kali before he walked around to climb into the pilot's seat.

Within minutes, they were lifting off from the ground. The clear bubble on the transport gave them excellent visibility all around. Once again, Destin felt excitement grow inside him at the possibilities for not just Chicago, but Earth. If more humans could see and experience what he had by traveling here, they would have such a different perspective – well, most of them would. The groups of people trying to keep them in the dark ages were dwindling each year, but he knew some people would always cling to the past.

"It is unbelievable how far advanced in technology the Trivators are compared to humans," Destin murmured, staring out the window.

"It will be wonderful to do this on Earth," Kali replied. "Perhaps this is a chance for humans to start over and do it right this time."

Destin grunted. He didn't want to burst any bubbles today. Dreams and reality were two entirely different things. He knew better than most that it took all kinds of people to make up a world, and in almost twenty-eight years, he had seen the dark side more often than he had seen the light. The murder of their mother by a gang member just for a few lousy dollars and a chance for promotion within the gang had left him and Kali orphans at a young age.

He couldn't suppress the bittersweet thought of how different he and Kali had turned out from their mother. He clasped his hands together when he thought of the blood he carried on them. He had demons he needed to put to rest, and rebuilding Chicago into a modern, safe haven was one way he hoped to do it.

"What?" he asked, realizing that Kali had said something to him.

"I said maybe you'll meet someone here and you'll want to stay," Kali teased, glancing at him over her shoulder.

"I already have. Her name is Ami," Destin retorted, reaching over and tickling Ami when she turned to grin at him.

It wasn't the image of Ami that came to mind, though; it was a woman with long white hair, pale blue skin, and fire in her eyes. A flash of need swept through him and he closed his eyes. It had definitely been too long since he was with a woman. He would have to do something about that when he returned home.

"We're here," Razor said. "What is this ceremony called again?"

"A wedding," Kali replied, eagerly glancing out the window at the long garland of white flowers along the fence.

Razor gazed at Kali with an almost fearful look. "Are you going to want one of these?" he asked, returning his attention to landing the transport.

"No," Kali whispered. "I'm happy attending them, but I wouldn't want to have one."

"Thank you, Goddess," Razor muttered, shutting down the transport and opening the doors.

* * *

Destin didn't miss the look Razor shot the other men. They had all agreed that today they wouldn't discuss the threats that Earth faced. They did enough of that last night at Saber's bachelor party. While Destin arrived almost a month earlier, Razor, Saber, Dagger, and several others that Destin had not met before had only arrived two days ago.

"It is good to see you again, Destin," a large man with a wicked grin said.

Humor pulled at Destin's lips. He had met Lord Ajaska Ja Kel Coradon from Kassis last night. One thing he learned about the man in the short time he was in his company was to never challenge him to a drinking game. The man could hold his liquor more than everyone else in the room. He was a bear of a man. His black hair was tied back today, showcasing the long scar on his face that highlighted how dangerous he was. Destin resisted the urge to touch his own scar. It seemed that humans had a lot more in common with aliens than they would have guessed.

"A pleasure, Lord Ja Kel Coradon," Destin replied politely.

"Just call me Ajaska," Ajaska reminded Destin with a good-natured grin. "The other is a mouthful, or so I've been told."

"I can't believe Jesse, Jordan, Shana, and Charma did all of this so quickly," Kali breathed out in awe. "It is gorgeous!"

"Razor, Destin," Hunter called out in greeting, walking down the front steps of the house.

"Hunter," Razor greeted. "Where's Father?"

"He is practicing his walk down the aisle with Jordan," Hunter replied with a grin. "Mother and Jesse are helping Taylor prepare for the ceremony."

"For having only a few days to get things ready, this is unbelievable," Kali replied, watching Destin lower Ami to the ground.

"I'll watch her for you, Kali, if you would like to go see the other women," Charma said, reaching for Ami's hand. "The other kids are playing with my granddaughters in the garden."

"Thank you, Charma," Kali replied with a smile. "I'll go with you. I'd love to see what they've done inside."

"We'll be in soon," Razor promised, brushing a kiss across Kali's lips. Kali nodded and followed Charma into the house.

The home belonged to Hunter, but his parents, Scout and Shana, often stayed here when the men were gone. Hunter, Razor, Saber, and another Trivator named Dagger made up the core group of the men in the family. While Saber and Dagger weren't technically Razor and Hunter's brothers, they were as close as they could get. Scout and Shana often insisted that they had adopted the two men when Hunter dragged them home one day and announced he needed more brothers to fight with if he was going to be a warrior.

It didn't take Destin long to feel welcome here. Within the first few hours of his arrival, he had felt at home. Kali spent a great deal of time here with Jesse and Jordan. Not only did they have children close to Ami's age, but they had a lot in common – they were human like she was, and human's were rare on Trivator. But it was more than that, they had all fought for survival back on Earth.

"It will be hard to leave her and Ami," Destin said, watching Kali walk toward the house.

"You could always stay," Razor said. "It would make her happy."

Destin shook his head. "I can't," he replied, his voice laced with regret. "You know as well as I do that is impossible. I've fought too hard and too long. The people there have stood by me and fought beside me. I won't abandon them now."

"I understand. I have been in your position; it is not an easy one to make," Razor said.

"As have all of us, I'm sure," Ajaska agreed with a heavy sigh. "I just hope the humans who came to my world do not find out what has happened since they left. I have a feeling life would become very difficult for my sons."

"Why is that?" Destin asked, remembering last night when Ajaska told him about the group of circus performers who had turned his world upside down.

Ajaska grinned. "They are fierce and loyal. They would not hesitate to return to their world to fight. I've become very attached to them and have no desire for them to leave Kassis, not to mention that my sons would follow them," he stated bluntly, his smile fading and a serious expression settling over his face.

"We agreed to not discuss these things today. It is Saber and Taylor's day of joining. There will be a far worse battle to contend with if anything prevents it from happening. My *Amate* is determined to make sure Taylor has a traditional Earth joining," Hunter reminded them with a look of warning.

"Destin, do you know how to tie one of these things? Jesse and Jordan are busy, and Kali said she was not around males who wore such a thing," Dagger called out from the front steps.

Destin turned and chuckled, though his laugh had an edge of wariness to it. Dagger's expression was a mixture of irritation, frustration, and panic. In his hand, he held a red tie. Destin had to admit the black suit fit Dagger's broad shoulders perfectly. He liked Dagger, he really did, there was just something about the guy – as if he was always one step away from snapping – that made him leery.

"Yes, I know how to tie one. It's one of those things you learn when you're a teenager and never forget," Destin said, walking over to the front steps. He paused, looking at Dagger. "You guys are just huge," he complained, motioning for Dagger to trade places with him on the step.

Within seconds, Destin had the tie done. Dagger mumbled his thanks, turned to glance at the line of transports starting to arrive, and muttered under his breath that he needed to find Jordan. As Dagger passed him on the steps, Destin noted that small beads of sweat were forming on Dagger's forehead and his eyes were a little wild.

He must not be able to handle groups of people very well, Destin thought.

Destin turned when another transport landed along the curved driveway. His stomach clenched when he caught sight of the woman stepping out of it. Jersula Ikera was wearing a long gown that was slit along the sides. His gaze swept over her pale blue skin and snow white hair. Her hair was elegantly braided in an intricate hairdo that must have taken hours to create. The gown she wore clung to her form and was made of a shimmering material that matched the color of her hair. As she stepped closer, he could see the thin threads of silver and blue woven through the material, and they sparkled as she walked. The outer cover of the gown was blue, slightly darker than her skin, and was swirled with white and silver. The combination was nothing less than stunning.

A puzzling possessive feeling swept through him. He wanted this woman. He felt an attraction to her before, but this was different. This was a more primitive feeling combined with an urgency he had never felt toward a woman before. Oh, he had been horny, wanting to lose himself in a woman just as much as she wanted to lose herself in him, but he never felt this fervent desire to know more about her, to keep her close, and to protect her. Hell, most of the women he had known were more than capable of taking care of themselves.

As long as they weren't betrayed, he thought, remembering Maria, one of his lovers who was brutally murdered by someone she should have been able to trust.

Destin was vaguely aware that Hunter had walked up to stand beside him. Off to the side, Razor and Ajaska discussed the transports that were arriving, comparing the variations in the different models. He forced his gaze away from Jersula, his jaw tightening in aggravation. He would be leaving the planet in a few days. He had no business thinking such thoughts.

Not only that, there was still too much to do back on Earth and he would have no time for a long term relationship that *wasn't* long distance. He firmly believed that if a man was going to be in a real relationship, he needed to devote his time to make it work. At the moment, time was a very precious commodity, and every minute of it was given to rebuilding Chicago. Taking this time off to come see Kali and Ami had been difficult enough.

"What is she doing here?" Destin muttered.

Hunter glanced over at Jersula. "She is representing her people. The Usoleum leaders have been very apologetic after the revelation of Councilor Badrick's misdeeds. Most of the women and young girls who were shipped off your world were found and returned, but his disgrace runs deep for the Trivator forces and the Alliance," he replied.

"There are still eighteen of them unaccounted for," Destin reminded Hunter.

"Thunder and Vice will not give up until all are accounted for, Destin. You have my word on this," Hunter promised before turning to Jersula when she walked up. "Councilor Ikera, welcome to my home."

"Lord Hunter," Jersula murmured with a polite smile. "Lord Parks."

"I'm not a Lord," Destin responded. "You can call me Destin."

The corners of Jersula's mouth twitched downward before her features settled back into a pleasant facade and she bowed her head in acknowledgement. A shaft of guilt hit Destin. He knew his tone had been almost rude.

"On Earth, only nobility is called Lord and no one where I come from is given that title. We use greetings like Mr. Parks or Miss or Mrs. Ikera, depending on your marital status," he explained. "Only, if you were married, you would usually have the man's last name. For example, if you were married to me, your name would be Mrs. Jersula Parks."

"I… I will remember that. Thank you," Jersula responded, flushing a slightly darker blue.

"Charma is inside if you would like to go in," Hunter suggested in amusement, staring back and forth between Destin and Jersula. "There are refreshments as well."

"Thank you, Lord Hunter. Destin," Jersula murmured, stepping between them and continuing up the steps.

Destin couldn't help but follow her with his gaze. His breath hissed out when he noticed the back of her gown, which bared her all the way down to her lower back. Smooth, creamy, light blue skin shimmered, and his fingers itched to touch it to see if it felt as soft as it looked.

"She is unattached," Hunter murmured.

"What?" Destin replied, glancing at Hunter.

"I said she is unattached. I made sure to have a thorough investigation of her completed before she arrived. Razor and I did not want to take a chance of another incident such as the one with Badrick," Hunter explained. "She is listed as unattached. My sources also say she has not been in a long term relationship."

Destin scowled. "I'm not looking for a relationship. I have too much to do. Besides, I'll be leaving the day after tomorrow." Hunter's lips twitched at Destin's heated retort. Destin could feel his face flush and he quickly shoved his hands into the pockets of his jacket. He stared out over the driveway. His gaze swept over the other guests who had arrived. Compared to what he was used to seeing, they were all so exotic. "I'm serious. I'm not looking for a long-term relationship, especially with an alien."

"Our world is much different from what you are used to, but it is a good one, Destin. What happened on Earth was unusual. It was not the Alliance's intention to cause so much distress to your people,"

Hunter murmured, resting his hand on Destin's shoulder.

"How can we be so different, yet so similar?" Destin asked in a low tone. "You have homes, jobs, families – everything that humans do. How can our species have been the only ones to implode when we discovered we aren't alone in the universe?"

Hunter released a deep, long breath and dropped his hand to his side. "The Alliance did not realize until it was too late that Earth was not as advanced as we had first thought. The messages you sent out gave the impression that Earth was ready for this first contact. Once first contact was made, it was too late. We had no choice but to move forward."

Destin nodded and looked down at the tips of his boots. He knew that. He remembered the day that the Trivators had arrived. The shock and upheaval weren't something anyone would be likely to forget. It hadn't been the Trivators who struck out at the humans. It had been the humans striking out against each other. Fear could be a very, very powerful and destructive emotion.

"You're right. There was no turning back," Destin said with a shrug.

"Hunter, the ceremony is about to start," Jesse said in a slightly breathless voice.

Hunter and Destin turned toward Jesse. She was wearing a long, red and silver laced strapless dress. Her hair was styled in an elegant French twist with tiny silver and red flowers tucked in it. Around her neck, she wore a diamond and ruby pendant that matched her ruby stud earrings.

"Sweet Goddess, Jesse, you are the most beautiful female I have ever seen," Hunter hissed out in a deep voice.

Destin watched Hunter step toward Jesse and tenderly lift her inner right wrist to his lips, pressing a kiss over the markings encircling it. Destin had learned that was the Trivator equivalent of a wedding ring back on Earth, only far more permanent since it could not be taken off – it was a symbol of a Trivator's vow to his mate.

Destin started forward when he felt Razor and Ajaska walking up behind him. He entered the interior of the house, once again amazed by both the similarities and the contrasts to Earth. This was a home filled with family and friends.

His gaze softened when he saw Ami grin at him as he walked by. She was the spitting image of Kali except for the tiny row of ridges along her nose and her slightly sharper than human teeth. She was standing next to Lyon, Jesse and Hunter's oldest son, one hand wrapped around the handle of a tiny basket filled with flower petals and the other holding onto Lyon's hand.

Destin smiled back at her before crossing through the house to the courtyard out back. Before a long, shallow fountain, chairs were lined up with an aisle in the center. Destin's gaze immediately focused on Jersula. She was listening to another guest. Her gaze flickered up and locked with his. He watched her lips part, as if she were drawing in a deep breath. His body reacted to the thought of what those lips tasted like. A strong emotion briefly flared in her eyes. It looked like she wasn't immune to the attraction igniting between them, either.

Destin reluctantly broke the eye contact between them. He turned down the third row, crossed to the end, and sat down. A couple of minutes later, several other members of Hunter and Razor's extended family sat in the seats beside him. Hunter, Dagger, Razor, and Saber stood near the fountain. A sympathetic smile curved Destin's lips when he saw the nervous expression on Saber's face. The Trivator kept glancing back at the house. Dagger pulled at the collar of his shirt while Razor and Hunter quietly talked.

Razor suddenly glanced up when Jesse murmured, and he nodded. He stepped to the front of the group while Hunter and Dagger stood beside Saber. Across from them, Jesse, Jordan, and Kali all stood, waiting for Taylor.

Several minutes later, Destin heard the familiar song played at weddings back on Earth begin, and he turned to watch Scout escort Taylor down the aisle. Destin knew he should be focused on the wedding, but he couldn't keep his eyes or his mind off the unusual woman sitting a row ahead and across the aisle from him.

"Today we gather to honor the joining of two individuals who are family to me. I am pleased to join my new sister, Taylor, with a man I consider to be a brother, Saber, in both the traditions of her people and ours," Razor announced, standing in front of everyone. "Let the ceremony begin."

* * *

Several dark shadows moved through the thick forest. Their focus was on the house. Another transport flew overhead, and the four men froze. One of the men stepped closer to the heavyset man in the lead.

"The transports are heading in the same direction we're going. We will be outnumbered," the man stated with an uneasy glance at the sky as another transport skimmed above the tall trees. "Perhaps we should abort the mission

"I make the decisions," Kronos growled under his breath and shot the three men a look of warning. He considered their next step now that it was obvious their Intel was missing something as important as half the galaxy coming to visit at the same exact time the assassination was to take place. "We will wait until the gathering has finished. General Achler wants Chancellor Razor's family eliminated. There will be no aborting of this mission. If we fail, Achler would kill us, no matter what the 'mitigating circumstances' were. Once the guests depart, we execute anyone in the dwelling, just like we were ordered to do. I will contact Team One and inform them of the situation, but our orders haven't changed – there are to be no witnesses and no survivors. Unless you want to end up dead as well, I suggest you remember who ordered this mission."

The man reluctantly nodded and glanced at the other two men. There were originally six of them on the mission, but two had perished when they encountered one of the savage, six-legged beasts that lived in the forest. They had killed the huge creature, but not before it ripped two of the men apart.

"Understood," the man finally replied.

Looking up, Kronos glared at the sky when another transport flew overhead. He radioed the other team and warned them of the situation. According to the report they were given by General Prymorus Achler, Chancellor Razor and Lord Hunter were supposed to be off planet.

A sense of unease swept through Kronos. Something told him that not all their information was accurate and he wondered if that included the information about the Trivator warriors being off-world. General Achler was very clear in his orders – take out the family and leave no trace of who did it. The general also stressed that he would be the one to notify Chancellor Razor, personally.

Kronos couldn't understand why Prymorus Achler would want to enrage the Trivator warrior. There were few in the galaxy who had not heard of the Chancellor's reputation. Razor was just as brutal as Prymorus when it came to his enemies. Kronos had known when he was assigned this mission that it would probably be a death sentence… yet, at least there was a small chance of surviving.

The Waxian chosen before him declined the mission. General Achler made Kronos remove the body parts of the man before he turned to him and asked him if he had any objections to the operation. Still covered in the blood of the other man, Kronos had shaken his head and accepted the assignment.

He knew it would only be a matter of time before Chancellor Razor hunted down each of them. Death would not come swiftly or cleanly if the Trivator found them. Still, having a head start against a murderous Trivator would be better than what would have happened if he had said no to the Waxian warlord.

"Move out," Kronos growled to the others.

The men fell into step, moving forward again. It took them almost an hour to reach the tall barrier surrounding the compound. Kronos motioned for the men to spread out. Through the gate, he could see the large number of transports. He murmured to the men to settle in. They would wait until the transports left before attacking. Turning, he slid down along a tree several meters from the wall. He pulled out a small vidcom with the images of those targeted for termination and studied them while they waited for darkness.

Chapter 4

"Congratulations, Taylor," Destin murmured before he grinned at Saber and slapped him on the shoulder. "You made it!"

"No thanks to you and the others. I'm lucky I didn't break my neck last night doing some of the stunts we did. Thank the Goddess for the brace Taylor engineered for my leg or I would have," Saber grinned with a wave of his hand.

Destin couldn't help but notice the new markings around Saber's wrist. He had never seen tattoos created so fast or with so much intricate detail as the ones done at the ceremony. After Saber and Taylor spoke the vows they had written to each other, Razor pronounced them husband and wife. Then the couple began the Trivator ceremony where they each received the markings showing they were *Amates*.

"Trust me, that was mild compared to what it would have been like back home. I've been to a few bachelor parties that ended with trips to the emergency room, or worse, jail," Destin promised with another pat to Saber's shoulder. "You did good. I swear Trivators are a natural when it comes to learning Parkour. You guys do a great job jumping and climbing buildings, and aren't half bad at bouncing when you miss."

"We didn't bounce. We landed on our feet… most of the time," Dagger said, coming to stand next to them. "How do you get this thing off? Every time I grab one side to pull it free, it chokes me."

Destin chuckled and quickly untied the red tie from around Dagger's thick neck. Dagger immediately unbuttoned the top five buttons on his shirt with one hand. Destin noticed the man was more relaxed now than he was earlier. He suspected it had a lot to do with the little girl he was holding in his arms and the woman standing near him.

"Oh, I want to learn how to do Parkour," Taylor exclaimed, her eyes growing wide with excitement. "It's a lot like gymnastics. I bet I'd be pretty good at it. I sort of did it when I climbed out of the window at that old castle on Dises V."

Destin grinned and shook his head when Saber cursed under his breath. He half listened to Taylor, Saber, Dagger, and Jordan discuss the pros and cons of learning how to do Parkour, but his mind was on something – or he should say someone – else. A flash of blue out of the corner of his eye caught his attention and his gaze narrowed on the object of his thoughts. Like a magnetic force was pulling them together, his gaze caught and held Jersula's light blue one.

"Excuse me," Destin murmured, not caring if the others heard him or not.

A part of him knew he should be running in the opposite direction. The other part of him was determined to keep on walking toward the frustrating woman who had captivated him. He was fascinated with the fire he knew lay hidden beneath the icy composure she presented to the world. He had not only seen that fire in her eyes, but tasted it on her lips.

"Councilor Ikera," Destin said, stepping in front of her when she started to turn away toward the house.

"Destin," Jersula murmured, glancing at him before looking away. "I was hoping to see you before I left."

"You were?" Destin replied.

"Yes," she began, lifting a hand as if to brush away an invisible strand of hair. "I found something on the beach this morning, a necklace, near the boulder where you draped your clothing."

"My medallion," Destin murmured with relief. "I thought I had lost it along the path when I was returning to the house. Do you have it with you?"

Jersula shook her head. "No, I wasn't expecting to see you here. I left it in the quarters I was assigned to," she replied, her voice laced with regret. "I... I could bring it to you later this evening."

"I would appreciate it," Destin responded. "The medallion has a lot of sentimental value to me."

"I thought it might. I saw the images in it....," her voice faded and she glanced down. "It was not my intention to pry. I wasn't sure if it belonged to you, or...."

"Jersula," Destin murmured, taking a step closer and gently lifting her chin so she would look at him. "The medallion contains the only photo I have left of my mother and a picture of Kali. I'm glad you cared enough to find out who it belonged to. As I said, it has great sentimental value to me."

"I could see the resemblance between you and your mother. You have her eyes," she said softly, gazing at him.

"Destin, they are about to cut the cake," Kali called out. "Ami refuses to let me help her. She wants you, if you don't mind."

"I'll be right there," Destin replied, not turning away from Jersula. "Meet me later tonight."

She took a deep breath. "Where?" Jersula asked.

"On the beach, near the boulder," Destin said, brushing the back of his fingers along her cheek. "… When the second moon rises," he added, unsure of how to explain in Trivator time when to meet, but knowing that the second moon rose about ten thirty pm if he were to equate it to Earth time.

"I will be there," Jersula murmured before he started to turn away. "Destin…."

"Yes?"

Destin paused, his gaze moving from her face to her hand on his arm and back again. He could feel the muscle in his jaw tighten. A flicker of uncertainty flashed through her eyes and he forced his body to relax.

"I like to be called Sula," she said in a quiet voice.

"Sula…," Destin repeated, rolling her name off his tongue like a caress before he gave her a crooked smile. "I'll see you later."

* * *

Sula stared after Destin. A bemused smile curved her lips at the strange attraction she felt. She watched Destin as he knelt down and talked to the dark-haired little girl. Blinking, she turned back toward her intended destination. She had been in the process of locating Taylor and Saber to congratulate them on their joining before she left. She had spotted them, but she had also seen Destin.

At the moment, it appeared they were cutting a large, decorated dessert. She wavered, unsure of how to proceed. This was only the third joining ceremony that she had ever attended in a professional capacity, but it was the most unusual out of the three. Deciding that no one would notice if she disappeared, she turned back toward the house and quietly retreated to her transport out front.

It wasn't until she was alone that she released the tight control over her emotions and lifted a trembling hand to her throat. She carefully pulled the thin, leather cord from under her top. The dark metal of the medallion was warm from where it was pressed against her skin. She carefully opened it and stared down at the images inside.

"You should have given it to him when you had the chance, Sula," she whispered, running her fingers over the textured casing. "You are asking for trouble."

She swallowed and glanced back at the house. She still had time to go inside and give it to him. Shaking her head, she tucked the necklace back inside her top and started the transport. Within minutes, she was flying back to her living quarters with the memory of his kiss on her lips and his touch burning against her cheek. She had never been tempted by a man until now. The first time they met, there had been the shadow of Badrick's deceit hanging over them. This time she saw a different side to Destin Parks – a side that she wanted to explore.

* * *

"It's still deserted," the Waxian warrior named Bracin said, glancing at the screen in his hand.

"We wait," Zare stated, wiping sand from his laser pistol.

"For what, more of those beasts to eat us? You heard what Kronos said. His team is down two men," Bracin snorted, glancing warily up the cliff.

"Why do you think we are on the beach?" Zare replied.

"I wonder if they have creatures in the ocean as well," a third mercenary remarked from where he was leaning back against a rocky outcropping.

Zare grunted and nodded toward the water. "If you had researched the mission first, you'd know they do – same thing for the others on Team Two. If they had listened to me, they'd still have a full team. You should be thankful you are on this team and that we have the transport," he stated, rising to his feet.

"Are you sure it will only be the woman and child coming home?" the mercenary asked, ignoring his comrade's sarcastic comment.

"Chancellor Razor is trapped on Dises V. We follow our orders to kill his mate and child and get out of here before the other Trivators find out. If we don't, we'll wish we were the ones who were eaten," Zare said, turning when he heard the sound of a transport.

"The sensor has been triggered," another mercenary standing a short distance away informed them.

Bracin pushed off the rock. "I get the woman," he said with a grim expression.

"Whatever you do, don't play with her for too long or I'll leave you here," Zare replied, spitting on the ground and signaling to two additional men before he headed for the steps leading up to the top of the cliff.

* * *

"I not sleepy," Ami whined, yawning and rubbing at her eyes.

"Of course you aren't," Destin teased, reaching into the transport and pulling Ami out of her seat. Razor paused beside him, frowning.

"Honestly, I don't know how you kept her awake all the way back," Kali remarked, chuckling when Ami shook her head and clung to Destin.

"It was the tickle monster," Destin replied, rubbing Ami's back when she laid her head against his shoulder.

"Tickle monster," Ami repeated.

"She will miss you when you leave," Razor said. "Wait here."

"What's wrong?" Kali asked, glancing around.

"I'm not sure," Razor murmured, turning in a slow circle.

Destin felt the hair on the back of his neck stand on edge. He motioned for Kali to take Ami. The little girl must have sensed something was wrong as well. She went to her mother without a sound of protest. Destin stepped closer to Razor when he scanned the courtyard.

"What is it?" Destin asked.

"I need to check the security sensors," Razor murmured. "It is too quiet. We have several birds living in the tree near the far wall. They are normally very active at night."

Destin nodded. He remembered asking Kali about them the first night he stayed here. She said the flock moved into the tree shortly after the house was completed. They only grew quiet when a storm was approaching or if someone got too close to the tree.

"Maybe our arrival spooked them," Destin said, glancing over at the tree.

"Perhaps," Razor replied. "With the threat of the Waxian and Drethulans forces, I increased the security around the inside perimeter as a precaution."

"Surely they wouldn't be stupid enough to try to attack you here?" Destin muttered.

Razor released a deep breath and shook his head. "No, but I would rather err on the side of caution, especially with Kali and Ami here."

"The sensors would pick up anything unusual, wouldn't they?" Kali asked, cradling Ami tightly against her.

"Yes," Razor said. "It is probably nothing."

Kali looked at Razor and shook her head. "Destin and I learned to trust our instincts. It is one of the things that kept us alive. If you feel something is off, then there is probably a good reason. Why don't Ami and I stay near the transport while you and Destin check out the house?" she suggested.

"How about Razor checks out the house while I stay here with you and Ami? Or better yet, why don't you put Ami back in the transport and take it up into the air while Razor and I check things out. I'd feel better if I knew you two were somewhere safe," Destin said.

Kali opened her mouth to protest before she closed it and nodded. "I hate to say this, but I think that is a brilliant idea," she reluctantly agreed. "Razor…."

Razor turned and gazed down at her and Ami. He stepped closer and brushed his knuckles along Ami's small cheek before he pressed a kiss to Kali's lips. His eyes were dark with emotion.

"I will notify you when to return. If I don't, or you see anything, return to Hunter and Jesse's home," he ordered.

"I will," Kali replied, knowing that it was her responsibility to keep Ami safe. "Hopefully, it is just a bad feeling."

"Let us hope," Razor murmured before nodding for her to return Ami to her seat.

Razor reached under the pilot's seat of the transport and withdrew a laser pistol and a long blade. Destin shook his head when Razor started to hold a laser pistol out to him. Instead, he bent down and withdrew the knife tucked into the top of his boot. He had slipped the knife into his boot out of habit when he got ready for the wedding hours ago.

They both stood back and watched Kali guide the transport up out of the courtyard. As an added precaution, she guided it back toward the main road. Once she was clear, Destin turned to Razor and nodded.

He silently followed Razor to the front of the house. They scanned the area before Razor motioned him to take the back entrance. Destin turned and headed around the side. He paused at the gate. Disengaging the lock would make a soft noise. Instead, he took a few steps away from the house, parallel to the fence, then turned toward the house, ran and jumped. His feet hit the side of the house and he twisted as he pushed off, landing on the thick stone fencing separating the front from the back.

Crouching on the top of the fence, he remained frozen while he scanned the backyard. There was no movement. Destin dropped down to the ground and moved along the shadows. His fingers tightened around the handle of his knife and he stepped carefully along the path. Once he made a thorough sweep of the back garden, he stepped up onto the covered patio. He relaxed when he saw Razor step out of the back door.

"Anything?" Destin asked in a low voice.

"No," Razor replied with a grim shake of his head. "Noth...."

Destin cursed when he caught a flash out of the corner of his eye. He dove forward, wrapping his arms around Razor and driving them both back through the open doorway. A smothered hiss escaped him when he felt a line of fire rip across his left shoulder. The knife he was holding flew from his hand and skidded across the floor when they hit the hard marble.

Almost immediately, he rolled to the right while Razor rolled to the left. Both of them sought cover when several more bursts of laser fire scorched the interior wall. Destin searched the darkness of the room for the knife he dropped.

"I count two, but there are probably more," Razor said, glancing over at Destin. "How did you know?"

"I caught a glimpse of movement out of the corner of my eye and a flash," Destin replied, grimacing when he felt the sting in his shoulder. "Do you have any other weapons in the house? I appear to have misplaced my knife."

"Locked in my office. We didn't want Ami finding them," Razor muttered, glancing back out the doors. "Look out! They have RWDs."

"RWDs? What the hell are...?" Destin started to ask before he scrambled for cover when four small flying disks flew through the door.

"Remote Weapon Devices," Razor growled. "They have to be Waxians. They are known for using them."

Another curse escaped Destin and he rolled when one of the RWDs shifted toward him. A series of red lasers lit up the area where he had been. A second one came in and took aim at him. Destin rose to his feet and jumped over the long bar area into the kitchen.

Razor fired on the two weapon devices, striking the one turning toward Destin before striking the second one when it turned to fire at him. Destin barely saw the movement before he tucked into a roll. Pulling open a cabinet, he grabbed the lid of a large silver pot when a third RWD flew over the counter. He lifted the lid, using it as a shield when the RWD rotated and fired on him.

Surprise and triumph swept through him when the laser fire was deflected by the curved, mirror-like surface of the lid. The RWD spun when it was struck by the ricochet of its own assault. Destin's silent shout of victory was short lived because another device entered the room.

He scrambled under the kitchen table when it flew around the corner, then peered out from between two chairs, and remained still. He wasn't sure where Razor was now or how many more of those damn flying machines there were. He had caught sight of four so far. If that was all of them, then they should be down to one. No sooner had that thought flashed through his mind when another RWD flew into the room from the opposite direction.

"Shit," he muttered under his breath.

Destin scooted back across the floor under the long table, trying not to disturb the chairs. He could tell that one of the RWDs was the one that had been damaged. It was having trouble staying airborne. A grim smile curved his lips when an idea came to him. He waited while the undamaged RWD hovered over the counter, scanning the area where he had been.

Sliding out from under the table, he carefully crouched and watched the damaged remote wobble in the air. Gripping the lid, he reached for a piece of fruit in the bowl on the table. He wrapped his fingers around one of the pear-shaped pieces and slid back down. Almost immediately, the damaged remote turned back toward his end of the table. Destin waited until it was almost to the end before he rolled the fruit across the floor. Both RWD units turned toward his bait.

Destin rose up when the damaged RWD turned its weapon on the fruit. He grabbed the edge of the RWD with his left hand and swung it around just as the other unit refocused on him. Both RWDs fired. With his right hand, Destin lifted the lid, deflecting the burst of fire aimed at him, just as the damaged RWD's fire struck the other unit. The unit exploded in midair over the counter. Flaming pieces of the unit rained down into the sink. Destin swung the lid up and used the edge of it to slam into the bottom blade of the RWD in his hand, then lifted the sputtering, dying machine and smashed it against the thick stone pillar separating the kitchen from the dining room.

Destin dropped the unit when it started to glow a brilliant red. He ran the few steps back to the table and rolled over it. The RWD exploded, creating small, but deadly projectiles. The pieces cut through the air, impaling shards of hot metal into the cabinets and the wall behind the table.

Lying flat on the floor, Destin peered through the legs of the chairs at the molten remains of the RWD unit. He cautiously pushed up off the floor and stood up, making sure he kept his body hidden behind the wall. His gaze swept over the counter, pausing on a knife next to the sink that Kali had used earlier to cut up some fruit for Ami. His fingers closed around the handle and he turned back to the area where he had last seen Razor.

Chapter 5

Sula piloted her transport over the sea for most of her journey to the cove where she was to meet Destin. The twin moons lit the water below her, the light from them reflecting off the gentle swell of the waves. She enjoyed following the trails of bioluminescence that curved through the water behind several of the larger sea mammals that swam along the coast.

One of the females from the pod rolled onto her back and lifted her long, slender head out of the water. Sula could see the white underbelly before the female twisted back around. The vivid greens and yellows shimmered under the water, outlined by the tiny light-emitting organisms. Her large fins created a wake and the calves immediately swam forward to cavort in the small waves.

Turning back toward shore, Sula realized she had gone farther south than she intended. She retraced her path along the shoreline, approaching from the opposite direction than the trip she made this morning. She wasn't worried; she would still be earlier than she had anticipated. Within minutes, she was circling around the cliff and into the cove.

The beach at the cove was fairly large and she had plenty of room to land the small transport. As she slid out, the cool wind coming off the ocean welcomed her, brushing against her face and tugging at her hair. The sound of the waves lapping at the shore drew her, just as they had this morning. This time, a peaceful feeling washed over her as soon as she stepped on the beach. She bent down and removed her shoes, tossing them into the transport before she closed the door.

Her toes sank into the sand. It was still warm from the heat of the sun. One day she would have a home of her own on the water where she could spend her mornings and evenings swimming.

Sula wrapped her right arm around her waist while her left hand rose to touch the medallion she was wearing. She had changed out of her formal clothing into something more casual. The black leggings and body suit hugged her figure. She wore the traditional silk covering over it. This one was a dark red with black onyx beading. The red, slip-on shoes were comfortable, but she had always loved to go barefoot when she could. The feel of the sand against the bottom of her feet and between her toes had always been a joy to her. Her mother still despaired about her habit of abandoning her footwear when she was home.

"I wonder what Destin would think of such a thing? A woman from the royal house of Usoleum who hates to wear foot coverings," she murmured to herself with a smile as she curled her toes into the sand.

Sula turned toward the sound of a transport. It was hovering over the forest that lined the rocky landscape above.

She walked back along the beach to the narrow passage between the rocks to see if she could get a better view of it. Her fingers skimmed the rock on the inside as she walked through the narrow tunnel. She paused near the opening, peering down the beach before stepping out. She faced the narrow stone staircase leading up to the top, and her eyes widened when she heard a faint echo of an explosion and what sounded like laser fire.

"Something is wrong," she whispered urgently, stumbling a few steps back into the shadows. "That is where Chancellor Razor's dwelling is."

Sula glanced back up to the top, unsure of what to do. Her eyes widened when she saw another transport sitting farther down on the beach. This one was much larger.

She turned and flew back through the gap in the rocks to her transport. Her hands trembled when she pulled the door open and reached under the seat for the weapon she had stored there. Pulling it free, she reached for the communication switch.

"Emergency transmission. Request immediate assistance at Chancellor Razor's dwelling," she stated in a cool voice that belied her fear.

"State your emergency," a voice immediately responded.

"There is an unknown transport on the beach and I heard the sounds of laser fire and an explosion coming from the direction of Chancellor Razor's dwelling," Sula responded.

"Emergency personnel have been dispatched. Please remain connected until they arrive," the voice ordered.

Sula glanced back toward the opening, looking in the direction of the transport she had seen earlier. She shook her head and refocused on the control panel of her own transport. If the Chancellor was in danger, she was sworn to do everything in her power to help.

"Negative," she replied in a clipped tone. "This is Councilor Jersula Ikera of the Usoleum council. I will assist Chancellor Razor."

Sula gripped the baton in her left hand. With her right hand, she released the fastening of her outer cover. It slid off her shoulders and she tossed it onto the seat of the transport. She closed the door and pressed in the code to lock it, then retraced her steps to the narrow tunnel between the rocks. The first thing she would do is make sure that the other transport was disabled, and then she would do what she could to assist the Chancellor.

* * *

Destin paused in front of the doorway leading out into the back courtyard. In the far left corner of the garden, the gate that led to the path he had used this morning was open. Faint sparks still flickered from the destroyed locking device. Near the center of the garden, the shadowy figure of one of the intruders warily scanned his surroundings while moving toward the wall. Destin silently moved away from the door to the window.

A grim smile curved Destin's lips when he saw a brief glimpse of Razor. The Trivator rose from behind some shrubs near the wall. In seconds, both Razor and the man had disappeared behind one of the trees. Destin saw four more shapes moving in the darkness. It wasn't that difficult to see them considering the second full moon was beginning to rise.

Note to self, check the moon phases if you are going to try to attack at night on an alien planet, he thought as the man became clearly visible when he stepped up onto the covered patio.

Palming the knife, he decided not to risk throwing it. He had no idea if the man was wearing any protective gear. If he was, Destin didn't want to lose the only weapon he had. Instead, he moved farther back into the shadows near the door. He would take the man out when he stepped inside.

Destin remained motionless, controlling his breathing and waited. With the light from the moons, he would only get one chance to kill the man and get out of view from the others moving through the garden. He stared at the entrance, willing the man to look the other way when he entered.

A surge of adrenaline pulsed through him the second the man cleared the doorway. Destin reached out and pulled sharply on the arm that was holding the weapon. He kicked just above the man's ankle and twisted him around. Destin and the other man both raised their free hand, Destin's gripping his knife, and the man's moving to intercept the blade. A line of laser fire from the man's comrades cut a path across the man's chest.

Well, I don't have to worry about killing the bastard. Good thing, because he's about five inches taller than me, Destin thought.

The man's dead weight threw them both off center and then backwards. Destin grunted when the corpse fell partially on top of him. Once again the knife in his hand slid free and spun across the floor. Destin muttered a curse and awkwardly thrust the man's dead weight off his legs.

Razor must have seen what happened, because suddenly the interspersed shots Destin heard became the rapid staccato of cover fire. Out of the four men left, Razor struck two. The move gave Destin time to grab the laser gun from his dead attacker's hand and roll to pick up his knife.

"I'll be damned," he muttered when he found the first knife he had dropped as well. He quickly picked it up and slid it back into his boot, then gripped the other one in his hand. "Now that the odds are a bit more even, let's see what they've got."

Rising to his feet, he checked the laser gun. It was different from anything he had fired before, but similar enough that it didn't take him long to figure out how to make it work. He slid the kitchen knife under his belt, gripped the pistol, and moved into position beside the doorway. He leaned to the side to glance outside again, but jerked back when a blast cut through the opening.

Dropping to one knee, he swung around and fired in the direction of the blast. The gun blasts lit up the area. His eyes widened when he saw a small figure with a white halo of long hair cautiously enter through the gate. He pulled back, pressed his back against the wall, and drew in a deep breath. The silky white hair could only belong to one person – Sula.

Behind him, he could hear a burst of laser fire. Razor was trapped between the trees and the wall. In his mind, Destin mapped out the covered patio area. There was a table and chairs set up to the side and a brick planter along one edge. He could use it as cover, but he would be limited. If he went through the house and back around the way he had originally come, he could use the wall to access the roof and come from above.

Deciding that was the best way, he pushed away from the door and took off at a fast jog through the house. He pushed open the front door, staying to the side in case there were more unwelcome visitors waiting out front. When nothing happened, he swung out of the entrance and along the covered porch until he reached the end. He jumped up on the railing, braced a foot against the wall, and pulled himself up onto the roof.

In seconds, he was crossing the roof to the back section. From this angle, he had a vantage point. He kept low to the roof since there wouldn't be much coverage. Once he gave away his position, he would have very little chance of escaping.

Destin lay down and took aim at one of the men. He could barely see him through the branches of the tree. His finger was pressed against the trigger and then he saw a wave of light shoot out of the long rod Sula carried as she stalked toward the man. The light actually looked like a wave of miniature, blue and white transparent stingrays swarming toward the man.

The intruder turned toward the wave of energy. The moment he did, Destin fired. The laser blast struck the man in the center of his back and he collapsed.

His partner, realizing that he was now outnumbered, tossed a charge with each hand, one toward Sula and the other toward Razor. Destin saw Razor dive behind a large decorative stone planter.

Turning his attention back to Sula, he saw that there was nowhere for her to seek protection from the explosive. Horror gripped him and he started to rise until he saw her kneel down and slam the rod into the ground. There was a flash of white then the repercussion of the blast knocked him backwards on the roof. He slid down several feet before his feet caught in a gap between the tiles. Dazed from the impact, he shook his head and rolled to his side before he pushed up into a sitting position.

Almost immediately, he had to shield his eyes from the bright lights that suddenly appeared overhead. He twisted, covering his eyes to preserve a small amount of his night vision. Above him, he could hear the hum of several transports.

Destin kept his head bent and his eyes shielded as he searched the back courtyard for Sula and Razor. He blinked when he saw Razor stagger from behind the large stone planter. His gaze immediately swept across the yard again. Relief flooded him when Sula slowly rose from the ground.

"Remain still," a voice ordered from the transport above him.

Destin lay back against the roof and released his grip on the laser gun. It clattered down along the slant of the roof before it caught on the edge of a tile. Staring upward, he saw the transport that contained Kali and Ami coming in to land out front. A smile curved his lips. She had that fierce, determined look on her face that she got when she was ready to kick some ass. Kali was probably pissed that she had missed out on all the action.

"And I thought I was finally done with all this shit," he murmured, wincing when two Trivator warriors landed on a section of the roof a foot above him. "Hey, guys. Nice night for a fight. Too bad you missed it," he joked, grimacing when he sat up and lifted his hands into the air to show he was unarmed. "Oh, yeah, that burns."

"Razor!"

Destin's gaze found Kali rushing into the back courtyard. She was holding Ami tightly against her. His gut clenched when he thought of what could have happened if Razor had not sensed that something was off. He pushed back farther onto the roof to give himself a better footing and rose to his feet. Now came the fun part... getting down off the roof. He glanced up when a large transport flew over with a ladder hanging from it. The two warriors motioned for him to grab it.

Destin reached out, wrapped his hands around the bar, and stepped onto a lower rung. A minute later, he was being lowered to the ground. Four warriors immediately surrounded him. Destin stepped off the rungs and released the bar, keeping his hands raised. He glanced around and raised an eyebrow when he saw Razor standing with his arms wrapped around Kali and Ami.

"Ah, Razor, a little help here would be greatly appreciated," Destin dryly called out.

"He is a guest," Razor snapped, glancing up over Kali's head toward Sula. "Councilor Ikera as well."

"There was a transport on the beach," Sula informed Razor. Her expression darkened when she saw the torn, scorched material of Destin's jacket. "You are hurt!"

Razor's gaze turned toward Destin before he glanced at one of the warriors. "Get a medic and send out search teams. One of the intruders escaped. Check the beach and monitor the transports in the area. No one leaves the planet without first being cleared," he ordered.

"Yes, sir. We've received reports of another attack on Lord Hunter's residence," one of the warriors stated.

Destin heard Kali's shocked hiss. "Are they alright?" she asked.

"The last report I received stated there were minor injuries," the warrior replied with a bow.

"If you would step inside, I will examine your wound," another warrior stated.

Destin gazed at the man. The warrior was dressed like the other warriors, but he was holding a gunmetal gray case. Destin nodded and turned on his heel. He paused when he saw Sula's concerned gaze. He jerked his head for her to follow him. He wanted to ask her a few questions – starting with what in the hell was she thinking stepping into the middle of a battle!

"Come with me," he requested in a soft voice.

Sula nodded and followed Destin and the medic up onto the patio. They paused when two warriors came out carrying the body of a dead intruder. He didn't miss Sula glancing away from the man's ripped and bloody chest or the fact that her face appeared paler than he remembered.

"That is an interesting weapon," he remarked, trying to distract her as they entered the house and made their way to the kitchen. He noticed her bare feet and his lips quirked in amusement. "Did you lose your shoes?"

Sula glanced at the baton in her hand before glancing down at her feet. Her cheeks darkened slightly and she wiggled her toes. Her eyes were uncertain when she looked at him and gave him a half smile.

"I detest wearing foot coverings," she admitted ruefully. "I took them off while I was waiting for you.

I forgot to put them back on when I heard the explosions."

"Sir, if you could remove your jacket and shirt, I will evaluate your wound," the medic politely interrupted.

"Oh, yeah, sorry. I don't think it's that bad. It just stings a little," Destin muttered, carefully peeling his jacket off and tossing it on the kitchen table. He quickly unbuttoned his shirt and pulled it off. Once he saw the rip in it, he knew it was trashed. He tossed it on top of his jacket. "At least when you get hit by those lasers you don't bleed as much."

"It looks painful," Sula whispered, the blush that darkened her face moments ago faded, leaving her pale again.

Destin shook his head and sat down in the chair the medic indicated. He pulled out the chair next to him and grasped Sula's hand, pulling her down onto it. He leaned forward, holding her hand while the medic worked on his shoulder.

"Tell me about the weapon, and why you entered the garden," Destin murmured, stroking his thumb over the back of her hand.

"I... This is a Mylio-batoidei, Mylio baton for short. It is a weapon that is commonly used by royalty for centuries on my planet. We are taught from a young age how to control the energy waves inside it," she whispered, her gaze moving to the medic cleaning Destin's wound, then back to his face when he stopped stroking her hand. "There are pressure points on the weapon that allow me to create different patterns of energy."

"How were you able to protect yourself when the intruder tossed the explosive?" Destin asked, hiding his discomfort when the medic began sealing the wound.

"I… Did you give him something for the pain?" Sula demanded, looking at the medic with a frown.

"The sealant has an anesthetic that will numb the area," the medic assured her.

"Sula, how did you protect yourself?" Destin asked, lifting his other hand and caressing her cheek.

"I formed an energy shield around myself. This is a smaller weapon, so it was more difficult. The larger Mylio staffs are much easier to use, but more difficult to carry around," she answered, reluctantly pulling her gaze from his shoulder to his face.

"You said the members of royalty are trained to use such weapons. Does this mean you are royalty?" Destin asked.

"Yes…," Sula replied with a nod. "I am Princess Jersula Ikera, only daughter of the Royal House of Usoleum, Councilor Select for the Alliance representative to Earth."

"Councilor Select for…," Destin started to repeat with a frown when he saw Razor and Kali enter the house.

"I'm going to go lay Ami down," Kali murmured. She paused when she saw Destin without his shirt on and the medic standing over him. "How bad is it?"

"A minor wound, Lady Kali," the medic assured her. "It will heal within a few days."

"Good," Kali replied, giving Destin a small smile of relief. "I can't even begin to tell you how scared I was when I saw what was happening. I swear they need to add weapons to the transports."

"We have weapons on the transports that need them," Razor chuckled, brushing a kiss across her lips.

"It won't take me long to pack," Kali murmured, pulling away and walking through the kitchen.

"Where is she going?" Destin asked suspiciously, glancing at Razor.

"I am moving Kali and Ami to a safer location," Razor stated. "This was a coordinated attack against our family."

Destin murmured his thanks to the medic and stood up. He grabbed his ruined shirt off the table and pulled it on. He buttoned it up while he waited for Razor to continue. It took a moment to realize that Razor was hesitant to speak in front of Sula.

"What happened?" Destin asked in a grim tone.

"Hunter's residence was attacked as well," Razor finally said. "It was obvious the Waxians thought the women would be unprotected."

"Why do you think that?" Destin asked with a frown.

"They didn't have enough men with them," Razor stated.

"There may be information on the transport that was left on the beach," Sula suggested, standing up and looking at Razor.

"It is probably gone," Razor replied.

Sula shook her head and smiled. "No, it will still be there," she said.

"How do you know?" Razor asked with a slightly suspicious expression.

Sula lifted her chin and returned Razor's stare with a calm one of her own. "I assumed the transport must belong to those attacking you. Once I made sure there was no one else inside, I short circuited the main control panel. It would take even the most skilled mechanic at least an hour to bypass it," she stated coolly.

Destin couldn't contain the chuckle that escaped at her rather smug statement. This was the fire he had seen on the beach. Once again, he felt his body react to it and a curious feeling came over him. He wanted to know more about this royal princess from an alien world who liked to lie under the water, walk around barefoot, and could fight like a warrior. Destin reluctantly turned his attention back to Razor. He ignored the questioning look in Razor's eyes. Destin had given up answering to anyone a long, long time ago.

"What happened at Hunter's place?" Destin asked.

"Several men entered the compound. Ajaska and Father were still awake, talking," Razor explained. "Father received a minor wound when the men fired at them. The battle was short-lived. I do not have any additional information at this time."

"Chancellor Razor," one of the warriors murmured, stepping into the room. "Two transports were discovered on the beach. One is a long range vessel."

"One of the vessels belongs to me," Sula quickly interjected.

"The moment the remaining attacker is located, notify me. Also, make sure the main control panel is repaired on the transport and all information, including transportation logs, are sent to me," Razor ordered.

"Yes, sir," the warrior replied, turning on his heel.

"I need to meet with the Alliance council," Razor said. "This attack is unprecedented. They attacked the leading heads of the Trivator military and it was clearly a direct threat to the Alliance."

"What will you do?" Destin asked uneasily, noting Razor's cold expression.

"Eliminate them," Razor replied.

Chapter 6

It was well into the early hours of the morning before Destin and Sula slipped out of the house. Search teams and guards still patrolled the area. They nodded to two guards near the back gate and passed at least another six before they made it to the stairs carved into the cliff.

Destin paused at the top of the steps when he felt more than saw the shiver that escaped Sula. He quickly removed his jacket and held it out for her to slip on. His fingers were slow to release the edges of the brown leather. It was only Sula's glance over his shoulder, reminding him that they weren't alone that made him let go.

"Thank you," she murmured with an amused glint and stepped around him to continue down the steps.

"What's so funny?" Destin asked, turning and falling into step with her.

Sula shook her head. They continued to descend the staircase in silence. He paused when Sula stopped at the bottom and looked up. Overhead, they had a clear view of the beautiful galaxy that looked like a colorful river weaving drunkenly in and out of the stars above them. The soothing sound of the waves lapping at the shore, the muted voices of the warriors working on the intruders' transport, and the soft caress of the wind filled the night, making the earlier events seem surreal.

"So much has happened since yesterday morning. When I first came to the beach yesterday, I was angry," she admitted, enjoying the feel of the sand beneath her feet.

"I could tell," Destin chuckled. "You looked far different than I remembered."

Sula glanced at him and scowled before she laughed and shook her head. Destin swore the air warmed around them. He nodded to the warrior standing guard at the narrow opening to the cove where Sula left her transport. The guard looked at both of them before he stepped aside.

"I wasn't sure that you would remember me. You hardly spoke to me when I was on your planet. You and the Trivator warrior made my position very difficult," she replied with an indignant sniff.

"Yeah, well, it was a case of bad timing," Destin replied, shoving his hands in his pockets. "There was a lot of shit going on."

He vividly remembered his mental state at the time. He had just killed Colbert, and Kali had almost died. He had sacrificed so much, and with Kali gone, he had felt horribly alone. All of those emotions had erupted and left him in a deep, dark place inside his mind. Sula's sudden appearance had been too much, especially when he was just discovering the true depth of Colbert and Badrick's atrocities.

On top of everything else, he had been reeling from the monumental task ahead of him, which was to rebuild a city to house nearly a hundred thousand refugees. He had also been dealing with the an overwhelming feeling of relief that the battle he fought for so long was finally over as well as the pain of saying goodbye to Kali. The feelings Sula had awakened in him had confused him, and if he were brutally honest, scared the shit out of him.

He shook off the memories and pulled a hand from his pocket to touch Sula's arm. Murmuring for her to wait, he walked ahead through the narrow passage. Even though the beach was being patrolled, he didn't want to take any chances. As long as there was one attacker still alive and free, there was always a chance of danger. He scanned the area carefully before he turned and motioned that it was safe.

"You are very cautious," she observed, stepping out of the opening in the rock.

"I've had to be," Destin replied with a slight shrug, wincing when he forgot the wound to his shoulder. "It kept me alive."

"You are in pain," Sula murmured in concern, stepping closer to him. She raised her hand to touch his arm. "Your shoulder...."

"I'm fine. It's just a twinge," he assured her, pulling his other hand out of his pocket, and sliding it along her waist. "Sula, I'm going to kiss you. If you don't want that, you'd better tell me now."

"I was hoping you would," she admitted, stepping closer and sliding her hands up his chest. "You are different, Destin Parks. I have never met a man like you before."

Surprise and pleasure hit Destin before he mentally shook his head at his reaction. This woman continued to knock him off balance ever since the first time he met her. Maybe it was time he got used to it.

Desire hit him hard when he slid his other arm along her waist. Her shirt lifted when she slid her right hand upward to his shoulder. His left hand was now caressing soft, silky skin. A throaty moan escaped him and he bent forward, capturing her lips.

Her lips parted in a silent gasp and Destin took advantage. He swept his tongue inside her mouth, stroking the tip across hers, and pulled her closer to him. He tilted his head, sealing their lips more firmly together. Their breath mixed, growing hotter and faster when Destin deepened the kiss. Sula's response was tentative at first, as if she was unsure of how to respond, but within seconds she was matching him touch for touch, exploration for exploration.

Destin caressed the skin at her waist, wanting more. He had been with enough women on Earth to know that he was a good lover, but this felt different. He sucked in a breath when Sula's hands move up under his shirt and the cool breeze coming off the ocean touched his heated skin.

"Damn," he muttered, briefly closing his eyes and drawing in a deep breath.

"I do know that you like this," Sula stated with confidence. She slid her hand downward to press against the front of his pants. "The evidence of your desire shows that you do, unless you are built different from the Trivator and Usoleum men."

A hoarse chuckle escaped Destin and he pressed his hips forward so his cock, the 'evidence' that she was talking about, was pressed firmly against her hand. His eyebrow rose when he heard her startled breath and saw her eyes widen. Unable to resist, he captured her lips again, drinking deeply and challenging her to meet his desire with her own.

He pressed her back against the transport. His hips moved back and forth in response to their growing passion. Her legs parted and he stepped between them. Sula broke their kiss with a gasp and leaned her head back against the clear glass. He ran his lips along her jaw to her neck. His hands slowly moved down to her hips and he pressed up against her.

"Destin," Sula moaned, gasping for breath. "I have never felt this way toward a man before. What are you doing to me?"

It wasn't so much her words, but the confusion in her voice that broke through the haze of desire and need engulfing his mind and body. Closing his eyes, he continued to press hot kisses along her neck, peppering them with the tip of his tongue and the scrape of his teeth even while he forced himself to start thinking again.

This was neither the time nor the planet for this. Unfortunately, his body wasn't willing to listen to rational thought. It was ready and willing to do it now and up against the side of the transport. He pressed one last, lingering kiss against her throat before he drew back and gazed down at her with eyes he knew showed his internal struggle.

"You aren't going to make this easy for me, are you?" he muttered, drawing in a long, hissing breath.

"What… I do not understand. What is this easy?" Sula asked in a barely audible voice, blinking several times as if to clear her vision.

Destin raised his hand and cupped her cheek. His gaze moved to her face as his thumb caressed her skin. He never thought about the color of skin before, but the contrast between his dark tan and her light blue coloring was arousing to him.

"How many relationships have you had, Sula?" Destin asked, voicing a question he had never asked any of his previous lovers.

"I…," she frowned at him and shook her head. Her nose wrinkled slightly with an expression of distaste. "None. The men I have met are… not the type I have found to be attractive. They are generally crude, rude, and arrogant – what is the word I learned on your world? Oh, yes! Ignoramus! I truly liked that word when I learned its meaning." She pursed her lips together and glared at him. "Of course, that word also perfectly describes my father and brothers most of the time. How my mother ever tolerated the lot of them without suffocating them is beyond me."

Destin swallowed the chuckle that replaced the expletive he was going to say. Sula was able to coldcock him once again without even being aware of it. Why was he surprised? Didn't he already decide that this woman was different from any other woman he ever met? She was an alien princess, an innocent, and a fierce fighter – a lethal combination for his peace of mind. He had never met the first, had actively avoided the second and only knew the last.

"You are dangerous without even knowing it," he whispered, leaning forward to brush a tender kiss against her lips. "It has been a pleasure meeting you, Sula."

"You say that as if we will not see each other again," Sula said, tilting her head and searching his face.

Destin shook his head. "We won't. Perhaps if things had been different.... Goodnight, Princess," he said, stepping back and thrusting his hands into his pockets. "Make sure to safety-check your lodging before you go inside."

"I will," Sula replied, turning to open the door of the transport before she remembered she was wearing his jacket. "Oh, here."

"Thanks," Destin replied, reluctantly pulling a hand out of his pocket to reach for the leather jacket. His fingers brushed her hand in the exchange and he yanked the jacket toward him. "Be safe, Sula."

Sula nodded before she turned and climbed into the transport. Destin stepped back several feet, giving the alien vehicle room to take off. He saw her gaze down at him. He could see the confusion in her expression. Unable to stop himself, he raised his hand to wave farewell. She responded, her slender hand rising in response before she returned her attention to the controls.

Destin stood on the beach for almost an hour, staring out at the ocean, his mind filled with regret. In another life, it might have been different, but with the challenges and new dangers now facing Earth, it was better to leave love and hope for someone else.

"Someone who isn't an ignoramus," Destin murmured, tossing the word into the wind with a shake of his head and a chuckle when he remembered her saying she loved that word. "What a woman!" he added with a deep sigh.

Chapter 7

"What's the plan?" Destin asked Razor the next afternoon.

Razor studied the small group of men sitting around the dining room table. The men, namely Hunter, Ajaska, and Dagger's brother, Trig, had converged on Razor and Kali's house shortly after noon. Destin had remained at the house when Razor took Kali and Ami over to Hunter's place.

Kali, Ami, and the other women would travel with Scout, Dagger, and Saber to the mountain village where Scout and Shana had a home. It was remote, and Razor and Hunter felt comfortable with the other men staying there to protect them.

"I will journey to the Alliance Headquarters to report what happened here and reiterate the information we discovered on Dises V," Razor said, glancing around at the small group. "Ajaska will journey with me before returning to his own world to address the council there."

"I will stay here," Hunter replied, glancing at Trig. "The attack on our soil has shown we need to improve our defenses. Destin, Trig will journey with you back to your world."

"I've already alerted Cutter to the situation here. I've also dispatched additional Battle Cruisers to your world. We will not lose it now that we finally have peace and Earth's reconstruction is progressing,"

Razor stated with a grim expression. "Jag will command the deployment in space. The advanced technology of the Kassisans and the Elpidiosians as well as the added support of their military gives us a decisive edge over the Waxians and the Drethulans."

"I'm still set to leave tomorrow, aren't I?" Destin asked.

"Sooner. I've already alerted Jag," Razor stated. "You and Trig leave in an hour."

Destin whistled under his breath. "It's a good thing I told Kali and Ami goodbye this morning," he muttered, clasping his hands together when he thought of another woman he wished he could see one more time before he left. "You guys don't waste any time, do you?"

"Not when it comes to dealing with those bastards," Trig replied, sitting back in his chair. "I've dealt with both. I'd sooner kill them on sight. The females are just as bad as the males, so you can save any sympathy you might have. The Drethulan young have to be caged so they don't kill each other. They've been known to cannibalize their siblings."

"From the information our informant shared, the Waxians just teach their young to kill," Ajaska added with a shake of his head and rose from his chair. "I have to return to my world first, Razor. There are things that I must prepare for, as you know. I've given all the information that I have."

"I understand," Razor said, rising from his seat as well. "Thank you, Ajaska. Safe journey."

"Remember, what I told you," Ajaska murmured.

"We are taking precautions," Razor assured Ajaska.

Ajaska gave a brief nod to each man, his gaze lingering on Destin for a moment before he pulled it back to Razor. A strange sense of warning filled Destin and he regarded Razor's stiff face. Something was going on that the two men were not sharing with the rest of them. He glanced down at the table before peeking out of the corner of his eye at Hunter. The same tense expression was on Hunter's face.

"It was good meeting you, Ajaska," Destin commented, rising out of his chair and grasping the huge man's hand. "Safe journeys."

"You as well, Destin," Ajaska replied, staring into Destin's face as if he wanted to say something more before he nodded. "You are a good man, Destin Parks. It was an honor to meet you."

Destin gave Ajaska a puzzled smile when the other man shook his hand in a firm grasp before releasing it and turning away. Destin could tell the meeting was over when Trig stood up and stretched. He grinned. Trig reminded him a lot of himself. Both of them had a problem with authority figures and didn't like being cooped up for long. In fact, Trig was the only one of the group at Saber's bachelor party who could keep up with him.

"I'll grab my stuff," Destin said, turning to leave.

"I'll be waiting by the transport. We'll head to the port and take a military cargo shuttle to the *Star Raider*," Trig replied.

Destin stepped into the room he had been using and glanced around to see if he had forgotten anything. His hand automatically moved to his chest to touch the medallion before he remembered that with all the turmoil from last night he forgot to get it from Sula. A part of him regretted the loss of it, but another part was glad that she had it. Perhaps he could get Sula to give it to Kali or Razor.

At least he now had some new memories to replace it. Kali gave him a photo of Ami, Razor, and her. He could have a new medallion made. Kali looked so much like their mother when she was Kali's age that it would be like having her there. Destin grabbed his duffel bag, slung it over his good shoulder, and exited the room, shutting the door behind him. Perhaps one day he would come back again, this time to stay.

"Once the Earth is healed," he whispered, thinking of all the work in progress.

He would be damned if let another alien species tear up what he fought so hard for and sacrificed a part of his soul to achieve. Even though the humans did a pretty good job of destroying the Earth before the aliens arrived. Still, they certainly had plenty of violence left in them for the next seven years of massive fighting. The humans fought both the aliens and each other with a viciousness born from their tribal origins, seeking to conquer and retain what limited resources they could find instead of joining forces. In many ways, that helped the aliens win control, and once the humans were in hand, the walls between each human faction were broken down and they were forced to work together – for the most part. There were still battles left on Earth. Nothing could change human nature, after all.

For a brief moment he wondered if the fighting would ever end, then he pushed away the negative, depressing thought. He didn't have the time, the patience, or the luxury to dwell on the what-ifs. Still, he could not stop thinking 'what if' he had a beautiful, fiery, blue-skinned woman standing beside him? That was one what-if he would hold on to and tuck away for the long, lonely nights ahead of him.

* * *

Several hours later, Destin was gripping the bar next to the seat on the shuttle, trying to ignore Trig's grin. He was seriously thinking of putting the heel of his boot in the Trivator's mouth, but at the moment they were too firmly planted on the metal floor. He would have to wait until they were on the ship. If they had a workout room, he would give the grinning bastard a run for his money.

"Not much of a flyer, are you?" Trig asked over the noise of the engines.

"Yeah, at least not going into space," Destin replied through gritted teeth. "I like flying, but not in space."

"Your planet does not have space travel?" Trig asked.

Destin looked at the other man and shook his head. "We have it, but not like this. Well, sort of like this," he tried to explain before relaxing his grip when the shuttle quit vibrating violently after they broke through the atmosphere. "We had spaceships, but they just went to the moon and back or around the planet. Nothing like this. You guys are going up and down into space more like how our airplanes did from city to city. I've only been on a plane once and that wasn't until I was in college. I've always liked having my feet on the ground."

"Jordan told me a little about your world. It was not a good place for her. Though, ours has not been much better, it would appear," Trig muttered, glancing at several warriors when they unstrapped and began checking on the cargo they were taking to the ship. He and Destin were riding on the last shuttle before the *Star Raider* departed. "This will be my first trip to your world. It will be interesting to see what it looks like."

Destin relaxed against the seat and studied Trig's face. The other man's expression was calm, but there was an intense air surrounding him, almost like a storm building. Destin learned at a young age how to read a person. The Trivators were more difficult, but not completely impossible. The nagging feeling that there was something else going on continued to bother him, like an itch you couldn't quite reach.

"What are you guys not telling me? I know about the Waxians and the Drethulans and their plans to attack Earth. But I can't help but get the impression there is more to the story," Destin said, watching Trig's expression close and harden into an indifferent mask.

Trig regarded him, holding his gaze as if contemplating what he was about to say. Destin waited. He saw the brief flicker in Trig's eyes before the other man looked away. He knew then that he wouldn't get all the answers to his questions. What Trig said next, though, would help seal the Trivator's fate. If Trig tried to bullshit him, Destin would make sure the Trivator had limited access to anything going on. Trust was a delicate thread, especially when your life was connected to it. Destin was very, very careful who he allowed to hold it. Trig finally sat forward and rested his elbows on his knees. The intense expression was back, but so was the caution – and a small measure of regret.

"Whether you like it or not, you are stuck with me," Trig stated in a hard tone. "There are reasons I've been assigned to you. There are also reasons why I can't tell you certain things."

"Can't or won't?" Destin asked, his eyes narrowing with suspicion at the cryptic statements.

"Both," Trig retorted with a slight grin. "The first is an order, the second just to piss you off and keep you on your toes, as Jordan would say."

"So, what can you tell me?" Destin asked with a raised eyebrow.

The grin on Trig's lips widened and his eyes sparkled with amusement. "That I'm glad I'm not you," he replied, sitting back when the shuttle changed directions and the warriors returned to their seats.

Destin shook his head in disgust, but felt his gut relax when he heard the truth in the other man's voice and saw it in his eyes. "That tells me exactly nothing," he muttered, gripping the bar again and leaning his head against the hull.

"I know," Trig replied, folding his arms across his chest.

"God, I hate a smart-ass almost as much as I hate space travel," Destin muttered.

Several of the warriors chuckled at his sarcastic statement. Destin ignored them. Instead, he decided to focus on a mental vision of Sula's beautiful face. If he was going to die, he would rather her face be the last thing he saw instead of Trig's ugly and smug one.

* * *

Sula finished placing the rest of her clothing in the storage compartments. The quarters she was given were small but sufficient for her needs. Once again, her hand moved to the medallion around her neck and she absently stroked it as she picked up the tablet.

There would be plenty of time on the voyage to do more research on Earth. She did an extensive amount the last time she was there, but that was different. She was instructed by her father to find out what Councilor Badrick was doing and to report those findings directly to him.

She read through mountains of reports, many of them contradictory to the next. It was like trying to untangle a ball of string – every time she thought she was on the right path, she would have to start all over again. If not for the human nurse named Chelsea who she met shortly after arriving, she would not have known anything that was going on. Sula caught the human version of a cold and was miserable.

She finally stopped being stubborn and went to the medical unit in the former US Army National Guard building. Chelsea was on duty at that time. The human nurse had an infectious humor and a compassionate heart which encouraged confidences. Sula had poured out her frustrations, coated with a significant amount of nasal congestion, concerning her research on Badrick. She had broken down in tears and unleashed into Chelsea's sympathetic ear her frustration about the lack of cooperation from the Trivator forces, her annoyance with the human man that had glared at her like she was some form of pest, and admitted she just felt lousy. That was when she first learned of Badrick's true treachery.

Sula sank down on the bed in her living quarters. The file this time was not on Badrick and his betrayal; it was opened to Destin Parks. Before, she had only taken an ephemeral glance at his file. Badrick had made a few references to Destin that were less than glowing. After her initial introduction to Destin, she was more inclined to agree with Badrick – at least until she had learned the depths of Badrick's deceit. Unfortunately, she only had one brief, tense meeting with Destin before she discovered what Badrick did. She was recalled before she could see or talk to Destin again.

"You are a very complicated man, Destin Parks," Sula murmured, gazing down at his face on the tablet. "But, a very intriguing one."

She was about to slide her finger across to view the next page when there was a message flashing across the screen alerting her that another report was uploaded. Sula frowned. She wasn't expecting any additional reports.

Curious, she touched the icon. Her breath hissed when a vidcom activated and flashed a very vivid, disturbing image before it disappeared. Sula blinked, wondering if she had imagined it. She glanced down at the tablet, trying to reopen the file, but it was gone.

"No!" she groaned, searching for it in every possible way she could think of, but nothing she did worked. It was as if the file had never been there. "Ignoramus!" she muttered, rising off the bed in frustration.

Without thinking, she exited her quarters. Gripping the tablet, she muttered under her breath. She would find the Chief Communications Officer and see if he could find it.

"I see you've lost your shoes again," a warm, masculine voice said, startling her.

Sula's head jerked up and her eyes widened in surprise and delight. A smile curved her lips and she stared back in silence at the man she was just thinking about and who was suddenly standing in front of her.

Her lips parted when he suddenly strode toward her and wrapped an arm around her waist. The gasp died on a chuckle that was quickly smothered by his lips.

She didn't think twice. Her arms rose and she wound them around his neck, returning his kiss with a heated one of her own. She vaguely heard the soft thump of his bag when he dropped it. Pleasure swept through her when he wrapped his now free arm around her waist and pulled her even closer to him.

"Destin, your quarters are only two doors down if you and the Usoleum Councilor want to finish this there. If not, I don't mind a little entertainment, but I'd like to drop off my own bags first," a male voice said from behind them.

Sula broke the kiss and buried her face against Destin's chest. She could feel her face heating with embarrassment. Never in her life had she acted so impulsively or without restraint. A shiver went through her when Destin held her firmly against him, refusing to let her retreat.

"Go to hell, Trig," Destin muttered, glancing over his shoulder. "No one's stopping you from walking on by."

Trig chuckled. "I won't be the only one seeing what is going on," he said with a nod toward the security cameras. "I'll just warn you that this ship has very few women on board and the voyage will seem a lot longer than it is because of it. The other warriors wouldn't mind a little entertainment to help relieve the boredom, but I thought I should let you know, just in case you weren't aware that whatever you do would be broadcasted far and wide."

"Got it, Trig. Goodbye!" Destin grumbled.

"It's a lot more fun with a willing...," Trig's voice faded when Destin turned around and glared at him. "I'm at the end of the corridor. Let me know if you go anywhere," he finished with a nod of his head. "Councilor Ikera."

Sula murmured a greeting in a barely audible voice. Her hand slid across Destin's back, enjoying the feel of the muscles rippling under her palm. While she was embarrassed by her behavior, she was also thrilled that Destin was as happy to see her as she was to see him.

She stumbled back when he suddenly twisted, his hands splaying against the wall behind her. Her head lifted and their lips connected again in a long, heated kiss before he finally pulled back to gaze down at her. She swallowed at the intense expression in his eyes.

"Destin," Sula whispered, lifting her hand to touch his face.

"Come with me," he murmured, glancing at the camera.

Sula nodded, dropping her hand and hugging the tablet against her chest when he pushed back from the wall and turned to pick up his large green bag. Sula slipped her hand into his when he held it out. Two doors down, he released her hand long enough to press his hand against the door panel. It slid open with a slight swishing sound. Destin nodded at her to enter first.

Sula stepped inside and turned. The moment the door closed, he set his bag on the floor and she placed the tablet on a small table nearby before she threw her arms around his neck and captured his lips again.

Destin's arms wrapped around her, sliding down to her backside to press her against him. Their breaths mixed in a heated exchange. She was vaguely aware that he was moving forward, so she moved backward with him, refusing to break their kiss. At least, she didn't until she felt him gently lowering her to the bed.

She sank back, pulling him with her. Her gaze locked with his, her breathing just as fast as his. Her lips parted when he pressed his knee between her legs.

"Destin…," she whispered, reaching up to cup his face.

"I can't stop thinking about you. When I stepped off the lift and saw you coming down the corridor…. Damn it, Sula, I don't think I've ever wanted a woman as much as I want you," Destin muttered, bracing his arms on each side of her. "All I could think about was kissing you to make sure you were real."

Sula chuckled. "I feel very real," she whispered, touching his face. "You make me feel very real."

"Hallelujah for that," Destin muttered, gazing down at her. "What are you doing here?"

"I told you, I am the Councilor Select for Earth. I have been reassigned to your planet. It was one of the reasons I was so upset yesterday morning," she admitted, caressing the smooth skin of his jaw. "I didn't want to deal with a certain arrogant human man who refused to even say two sentences to me the last time I was there."

Destin's lips twitched and a mischievous twinkle appeared in his eyes. "Who said he was going to be doing any talking if you came back? Maybe a few moans and groans," he murmured, lowering his head and pressing his lips to her throat.

"I... I could... I could... deal with a... a few... Destin!" Sula moaned when he pressed his knee up against her. "Yes!" she hissed out, wrapping her legs around his and pulling him down to capture his lips.

Chapter 8

A soft moan escaped him when he felt Sula's response. Not only was she moving under him, her hands were unbuttoning his shirt. The muscles across his stomach clenched when she ran her soft hands along his skin.

His tongue swept between her parted lips. He could feel Sula writhing against his knee and knew that if they didn't stop now, they would not be able to later. Pulling back, he pressed a series of light kisses along her jaw down to her ear.

"If we don't stop now, I'm going to make love to you," he whispered against her ear, pressing another kiss just behind it.

Sula moaned and tilted her head so he could have better access to her throat. She moved against him and her fingers threaded through the dark trail of hair along his stomach. A shudder ran through his body when she gently tugged on it.

"Stopping is not an option that I am contemplating at the moment," she informed him, dipping her fingers under the top of his jeans. "Removing your clothing is an option, though."

Destin drew in a hissing breath and pulled back to study her face. She returned his gaze with one that showed she was not in a haze of uncontrolled lust, but very aware of what she was saying. A grin tugged at his lips. This was the serious, no-nonsense woman who knew how to control a situation.

His eyes widened when her hand slid farther down the front of his pants. The fire that she tried to hide from the rest of the world blazed in her eyes. He pulled back, and her hand slid out of his pants when he sat up.

He rose from the bed, shrugged off the shirt that she unbuttoned for him, and tossed it across one of the chairs near the table. Sula's blue eyes darkened with desire when he bent and untied the lacing on his boots. Straightening, he toed them off and kicked them under the bed. His hands moved to his belt.

"Let me," Sula requested, suddenly sitting up and reaching a hand out to stop him.

Destin dropped his hands to his side and waited. An expression of intense concentration settled over her face. He reached up and tenderly touched her chin.

"Enjoy it," he murmured, running his fingers along her cheek. "It is amazing how sensitive the tips of your fingers are, and how much pleasure comes from touching someone else. I enjoy the feel of your skin against my fingers – each caress makes me want to touch you more. Making love is more than about the act, it is about the experience and the connection with your partner. I want you to enjoy touching me as much as I'm going to enjoy touching you."

Sula gazed at him, while her fingers lingered against his hard, flat stomach near the waist of his jeans. He saw her swallow and her pupils dilate with desire. His breath hissed when she ran the tips of her fingers along his skin near the opening of his jeans. Perhaps he shouldn't have told her that, he thought when he felt his body reacting to the sensual caress.

"Like this?" Sula asked, tilting her head back and smiling at him.

"Oh, yeah, like that," Destin muttered in a strained tone. "Maybe… a little… lower…."

Sula's warm breath feathered against his flesh, heating it even more. Destin gritted his teeth and swore that she was enjoying herself far too much at his expense. He would have to show her that payback could be a bitch once it was his turn to undress her. He had a feeling the foreplay was going to drive him to the edge of madness and the loving part was going to take him over that edge.

His fingers flexed when she finally unbuckled his belt. They itched to help her, but he wanted to give her this time to explore. He watched, entranced, as she undid the button of his jeans before she pulled the zipper down with an agonizing slowness that had him mentally cussing.

He came damn near to losing what little control and resolve he had when she ran her fingers under the waistband of his underwear before gripping the side near his hips.

"I thought you said you'd never done this before," Destin gritted out between clenched teeth.

Sula's lips twitched. "I said with a man. Virtual vidcoms are plentiful and I've watched my share over the years," she chuckled. "They are very…." She pressed a light kiss to his belly button. "Very…," she murmured, teasing his flesh with her tongue. "Very…." This time she nipped him, causing his hips to jerk toward her. "Good at teaching ways to pleasure each other."

Destin closed his eyes and swallowed. "Now she tells me," he groaned when he felt the cool air against the heated flesh of his ass. "Sweet Mother of…."

His voice faded on a hoarse curse when she ran her nails along the crack of his ass. If he thought he was only near the cliff, he was vastly mistaken. He had gone over it and hadn't even realized it. Something told him he was about to achieve a level of pleasure he had never experienced before. That thought was confirmed a second later when his throbbing cock was surrounded by the moist warmth of her mouth.

His hands reached out to grasp Sula's shoulders and his eyes popped open in time to watch her slide his throbbing length – his barely-hanging-onto-his-self-control, throbbing length – into her mouth. His hands rose to tangle in her long hair and he gently rocked his hips back and forth. He could feel the slight scrape of her teeth along his sensitive flesh. A shudder went through him and he knew he had better stop her before he came. Her pleasure came first, then… then, he would find his own release.

"This is going to be amazing," he groaned, releasing her hair so he could pull away from her and kick his jeans and undershorts off. "Now, it's my turn."

* * *

Heat burst low in Sula's stomach and spread lower between her legs when Destin wrapped his arms around her and pressed his lips to hers. She could feel the slick moisture starting to flow and her body ignited with the need to mate. This was a new experience for her, but not one that she was ignorant about.

She had found moderate enjoyment in the vidcom files she told Destin about. It was a standard education for all Usoleum youths. In fact, being the only girl and the youngest of the group, she had plenty of opportunities to pillage her older brothers' collections that they carelessly left lying around.

She remembered the first time she observed the vidcoms. Her mother explained the necessity of such education and encouraged her to ask any questions she may have regarding the use of it when she started her fifteenth year of life. Sula always prided herself on being more observant, more studious, and a much faster learner than her brothers, especially Sirius, the youngest male sibling who was a mere five years older than her.

During her time on Earth, she witnessed some of the humans' strange behavior and actions. Her new friendship with Chelsea proved very valuable in learning more about the human culture and their habits. It wasn't like she had much else to do since neither the Trivator commander nor Destin would let her get on with her job. So, she spent her time learning about the humans. That learning had included their mating habits.

She had been fascinated the first time she witnessed Chelsea and her mate, Thomas, pressing their lips together. When she asked Chelsea about it, the dark-skinned female burst out laughing and taken her by the hand. They had retreated to a break room where Chelsea explained something known as *The Birds and the Bees* to a fascinated Sula.

Later that night, Chelsea delivered a large number of round, silver disks called movies and plugged a box into a large black video screen on the wall of the room Sula was assigned to. She told Sula to have fun and to let her know if she had any questions. Sula spent the next two Earth weeks binging on romance movies and the educational movies called PORN that Chelsea dropped off. She truly enjoyed the romance movies the most, but had saved several of the others for her brothers as gifts.

Now she appreciated the need to view both. The feelings and reactions from her body when Destin touched her made her think of the reaction of the women in the romance movies, but with the intensity of the humans in the educational files. Her breath caught and she briefly wondered if she had forgotten how to breathe when he remained still and she finally worked up the courage to pull down his leg coverings.

His penis was hard and moved up and down. From her vantage point on the edge of the bed, she could see the veins had filled. Her gaze locked on his 'mating stick' as her brothers called it. The memory of one of the women in the educational file leaning forward and swallowing the mating stick flashed through her mind. The man had immediately stilled, his expression twisted with pleasure, and he had encouraged the female to continue.

Licking her lips, Sula gazed at Destin. Her hands moved back up his legs and around the cheeks of his buttocks. A sense of delight washed through her at the feel of hair on them. Her hands caressed them, moving upward to the divide between them before she pulled him closer.

His eyes closed. Opening her mouth, she imitated the movement of the woman that was in the file. A wave of pleasure flooded her at the taste of him and she eagerly opened her mouth wider to swallow more of his length.

Flashing a glance up to his face to see his reaction, she was shocked to see him gazing down at her with a fiery intensity that threatened to scorch her. Her hands instinctively tightened on his backside, her nails scraping against his tight cheeks. He jerked forward before his hands tangled in her hair to keep her from releasing him. Holding her head steady, he began moving his hips back and forth, a guttural groan escaping him. That sound, combined with the grip he had on her hair to hold her to him, and the intense enjoyment of sucking on him, made her body react in an astonishing way.

Sula could feel her nipples harden and the moisture between her legs increased to the point she could actually feel the liquid soaking her underclothing and leggings. In addition, not only did her breasts ache for some unknown reason, but so did the area of her womanhood. A soft cry of protest escaped her when he suddenly pulled all the way out of her mouth, holding her hair so that she couldn't stop him.

His faint, harsh words barely penetrated the dazed fog of need threatening to drown her. She tilted her head, staring at him when he stepped back and kicked the clothing wrapped around his ankles to the side. Blinking, her hands rose to stroke her aching breasts as his words finally sank in.

"Now, it's my turn."

Sula wanted to protest that she was far from done, but those words faded when he stepped forward and pulled her top over her head. The cold air of the room felt almost painful against the throbbing tips of her hard, dark blue nipples. She had seen in the files the men stimulating the women by stroking them, but when Sula tried it on herself, all she felt was irritation. Now, they throbbed to the point she felt if Destin did not touch them, suck on them, do whatever needed to be done to take the ache away, she honestly thought she would scream.

How can something so small suddenly ache and throb so much? She wondered, lying back when Destin gently pushed her back against the bed.

Her hips rose instinctively when he reached down to grab the sides of her leggings. Instead of just ripping them off as she expected, he leaned forward with his hands under the edge much like she did to him. Confusion swept over her for a brief second before a hoarse cry escaped her. The world around her dissolved into mindless pleasure when he leaned down and captured one of her aching buds in his mouth and sucked hard enough that she arched upward into him, her arms wrapped around his neck, and threw her head back in ecstasy.

The fluid between her legs pooled and she desperately tried to seek relief from the heated agony starting to build inside her. None of the educational files from Earth or from her world prepared her for the intensity of the need that pulsed through her. It was painful to the point that she did not know if she would be able to control herself.

"Destin," she whimpered. "The other one... Please, it hurts... I need... more!"

Almost immediately, she wanted to scream. He had turned his attention to her right breast now, but her left one, bereft of his warm mouth, the slight sting of his teeth, and the deep pressure of his sucking – protested being abandoned. That feeling faded to be replaced by the growing ache between her legs when his right hand released her hip to slide between them so he could pinch her left nipple between his thumb and forefinger.

She cried out, writhing on the covers.

Destin released her breasts and moved down, pressing tiny, moist kisses along her heated skin as he worked his way down her body. Her hips rose again when he gripped her leggings and pulled them down. Sula's hands dropped to the bed and her fingers tangled in sheets, clawing to hold onto something when he paused to press a kiss where her womanly core was on fire.

He nipped her, causing her head to jerk up to stare at him. A mischievous grin curved his lips and he opened his mouth to run his tongue along his upper lip. She knew her own mouth had to be hanging open at his torturous teasing.

"I ache," she snapped in confusion. "You are making my body do things that were not in the files."

"Honey, we are going to be doing and feeling a lot of things that weren't in your files before the afternoon is finished if I have any say in the matter," Destin promised.

Sula's eyes widened and her curiosity grew. "I would like to experience that," she said, her eyes turning a darker blue at the thought. "Will the ache go away?"

"Not for long if I do it right," Destin teased and pulled her leggings off. "Will you trust me?"

Sula tilted her head when he paused, holding her leggings in his hands. She studied his intense expression for several long seconds before she nodded. She wanted to experience it all – with him.

"Yes," she whispered. "I will trust you. Can I make you ache like this as well? I think I would enjoy torturing you."

"You already have," Destin chuckled.

He tossed her leggings onto the pile of their clothes, never taking his gaze off of her. A shiver of need ran through Sula. His gaze was hot enough to burn away the vestiges of her control.

Her breathing accelerated when he rose up on his knees between her legs. She could see every proud inch of him. She could also see the scars that marred his darker flesh. The scars did not detract from the beauty of his body. If anything, they made her curious about how he received each one of them. She wanted to explore him and kiss each mark in reverence of his ability to survive so much. Sula knew she had led a sheltered life. That knowledge was one of the reasons she fought so hard to break free of the glass bubble her parents tried to cocoon around her. Destin was cut by the glass of the bubble he was born in. Each jagged scar was a testament to the challenges he had faced and overcome.

"Lift your arms above your head and hold onto the frame of the bed," Destin ordered, caressing her lower legs.

"But... I wish to touch you," Sula whispered, unsure of how she was supposed to pleasure him if she was holding onto the metal bar.

"You'll have a chance, but for now... just hold on and enjoy," he instructed, lifting her legs up and sliding them over his shoulders.

"Oh, are you going to...?" Sula started to ask before her head fell back and her eyes closed at the intense pleasure. "You have found the heat! Yes...," she gasped, trying to press up against him while at the same time unsure she would be able to handle the unspeakable pleasure swamping her body.

Destin's soft, warm chuckle feathered her sensitive flesh. She couldn't close her legs because he was between them. Her heels dug into his shoulder blades. The memory of the wound to his left shoulder swept through her mind. Worried, she started to lift her leg off of his shoulder, but he reached up and wrapped his arm around her thigh, stopping her.

She abandoned all reasonable thoughts after the first touch of his mouth against her swollen womanhood. She had seen this thing done on the files she watched, but the feelings were entirely different than what she expected. Instead of being repulsed by such an intimate touch, she craved to know more.

Closing her eyes, she focused on the explosions of pleasure bursting inside her. She pulled in low, gasping breaths when she felt his tongue caressing her. After talking with Chelsea and watching the files, she researched the differences between human females and her own body.

Physically, most of the differences were superficial. There were the obvious differences in skin color, and her facial features were flatter. She has larger eyes and a smaller nose. Her mouth was wider, though she saw some human females with mouths not much narrower than hers. She also has two breasts, though they tended to be smaller than the average humans.

Her feminine design was a little different. She did not have hair on her body except on her head. Like a human, a Usoleum female has one clitoris. It was highly sensitive to stimulation and was protected until the female became aroused by a male she chose to mate with; then it would swell, becoming accessible to the male. Without this stimulation, it was virtually impossible for a female to have a sexual relationship with a male.

At the moment, Sula was more than stimulated. Her chemical and physical reaction to Destin was unprecedented. The taste of his kiss, the way he pressed his tongue into her mouth and teased her, and the way his hands felt against her body released the mating chemical which now consumed her.

Her hips moved to the pace of his tongue. She could feel her body opening for him, ready for more, needing more. A hiccup of breath escaped her when he paused and she stiffened. It was as if he was waiting for that heightened sense of expectation before his hands slid up between her thighs and he exposed even more of her to his touch. A harsh cry ripped from her lips when he captured the swollen nub between his lips and touched it with his tongue. Intense pleasure soared through her body. Her hands gripped the top frame of the bed and her body arched in response. Destin's hands moved back to her thighs to keep her from pulling away while he continued to suck on her. Sula could feel the tidal wave building, growing more intense before it crashed through her, sending her into a convulsion of aftershocks as she came.

A low sob escaped her and she shook her head at the intensity of the feelings rushing through her. The stimulations she had performed on her body never prepared her for this. She was vaguely aware of Destin gently sliding her legs from his shoulders and moving back up her body.

Another loud moan escaped her when he captured her right nipple in his mouth and sucked hard on it. Already over stimulated by her orgasm, the added touch of Destin's almost painful attack on her nipple sent her back over the edge. It took her a moment to realize that an additional sensation was pressing against her. The hard, bulbous head of Destin's cock was slowly penetrating her now relaxed vaginal canal. The tiny muscles of her channel moved along his silken length, greedily drawing him deeper.

"Holy shit!" Destin muttered hoarsely, releasing her breast and rocking his hips when he felt the tiny muscles pulsing against him.

"Yes!" Sula moaned, feeling him sink even deeper.

She lifted her legs again, this time to wrap around his waist. The position connected them completely. Her body molded to his until they were one. Sula gave herself up to the utter abandon of pure pleasure. She had discovered her mate, an alien male unlike anything she had ever dreamed possible.

Chapter 9

Destin woke with a start, sitting up in the narrow bunk. A shudder went through him and he ran his hand down over his face. The nightmare still gripped him. He turned his gaze to the empty space next to him and frowned.

When in the hell did Sula leave? he wondered, dropping his hand to the covers.

He glanced around the dim interior of his living quarters. It did not take him long to realize that she was not in the room. Shoving the tangled covers aside, he twisted and sat on the edge of the bed. He was not sure how much time had passed. From experience, he imagined it had only been a few hours, because he never slept more than that at any given time.

He could only attribute his deep sleep to exhaustion from the previous night and his time with Sula. Hell, the way his body had melted after his orgasm, he was lucky he wasn't comatose! He couldn't remember ever having such an intense orgasm before – or being as satisfied afterwards.

"Get a grip, Destin. You're growing soft in your old age," he muttered out loud.

With a sigh, he pushed up off the bed and walked into the bathroom. It wasn't much bigger than the bathrooms he was used to on Earth. Bracing his left arm against the back wall, he quickly relieved himself before turning to the shower unit and giving it a skeptical look. If this was like the other showers, it was more of a heavy mist with a soap solution in it. He learned that the water was filtered and reused on board the ships. That was a necessity considering there was no rain or places to stop and refill the tanks.

He stepped inside, closing his eyes when the shower activated. Immediately, the image of Sula materialized in his mind. The feel and taste of her still lingered on his skin and mouth. A satisfied smile curved his lips when he remembered her smothered cry and her body arching against his hands. He bowed his head and opened his eyes. Staring down his body, he grimaced. It was obvious his cock liked the memory.

"Another first," he chuckled.

Wiping a hand down his face, he shook his head at his errant thoughts. Over the course of the trip to Earth, he needed to focus on some of the items he placed on his To-Do list but never had a chance to take care of. He would also check in with Tim to see how things were going back home.

No sooner did those thoughts flash through his mind, then his resolution to focus on them wavered, and Sula crept to the forefront again. With a growl of frustration, he opened his eyes and quickly washed the remains of the afternoon from his body. Once he was finished, he waited for the warm air from the dryer to evaporate the remaining water from his body and stepped out.

Striding back into the other room, he picked up his duffel bag and placed it on the table. He unzipped it and pulled out the clothes he was going to wear: a pair of well-worn jeans, socks, jockey shorts, and a dark blue T-shirt. It didn't take him long to get dressed. He quickly unpacked, storing his clothing in the drawers built into the wall, and slid the duffel bag under the bed.

He sat down on the edge of the bed and pulled on his socks and boots. Once he was finished, he stood, turned, and made the bed. His fingers lingered for a moment on the covers, thinking of Sula spread across them. His lips tightened in agitation. He was used to waking up alone. Normally, he and his partner had a mutual agreement that once their physical needs were taken care of, there was nothing else to keep them together. His time with Sula a few hours ago was different. He wanted to wake up with her in his arms, in his bed, just as he had held her tightly before he fell asleep. Waking alone now felt wrong.

A wave of irritation swept through him. This was uncharted territory for him and he wasn't sure he liked it. He wasn't delusional enough to think he was in love. Hell, he was not sure he even believed romantic love was possible for him. One thing he did know was that he was physically attracted to Sula in a way he had never been before. Still, that was a long way from something as undefinable as love. He knew and recognized infatuation and lust. Those two emotions he had seen and experienced. He experienced the first when he was a teenager with a girl in their old neighborhood. Now, that he thought about it, even that was probably more lust than infatuation. In the subsequent years since, he had purposely steered away from any woman wanting a more permanent relationship. The moment the 'L' word was mentioned, it was time to end the relationship. That was what he had liked about Maria. She had wanted him for his body and he had reciprocated. They had scratched each other's itch without wanting or expecting more. It was a good, working relationship until Colbert's insane jealousy made Maria a target.

Destin shook his head and quickly pushed the wave of guilt away. The fact that Kali had warned him and he had brushed her concerns away would always haunt him. If he had listened, he could have prevented the deaths and miseries of hundreds, if not thousands, of innocent people. It was a burden he would always carry.

Destin stepped close to the door and it slid open. A dark scowl crossed his face when he saw Trig standing outside of it with his hand raised. He didn't miss the inquisitive glance over Destin's shoulder and into the dim interior.

"What do you want?" Destin asked with a raised eyebrow.

"I was about to get something to eat and wasn't sure if you were still occupied or not," Trig replied with a slight smirk. "From your unhappy expression and biting tone, I will take it that things didn't go well with the Usoleum Councilor. They aren't known for their warmth, though you appeared to be defrosting this one. I've heard that Elpidiosian females are pretty aggressive. Ajaska warned they can be rather predatory if you aren't careful."

Destin shook his head. "I don't need a babysitter, especially on board the ship. If you are going to be a pain in my ass for the next couple of months, I should warn you that I'll probably try to stuff you in the disposal tubes," he groused, pushing past Trig. "And my relationship with Sula is off limits. If you so much as make one derogatory comment about her, I'll beat the living shit out of you before I eject your ass into space."

Trig's mouth tightened. Destin wasn't sure whether or not Trig was trying to keep another smart-ass comment from escaping, he was just glad when the other man nodded. Destin eyed the door next to his living quarters and paused. He wanted to see if Sula was alright, but he did not want to do it with Trig standing there pushing his nosy ass in the middle of a situation Destin wasn't exactly sure how to handle.

"I could find out if she is in there for you," Trig offered.

Destin glowered at the other man in exasperation and shook his head. "Please tell me you are not going to be a boil on my ass for the next few months?" he asked with a pained expression.

"What is a boil?" Trig asked warily.

"Look it up," Destin replied. "Let's go get something to eat."

Trig nodded. "If it is on your ass, that does not sound promising," he said with a grimace. "If it helps, this isn't something I volunteered for."

"Well, until you tell me why Razor and Hunter are so set on having you as my babysitter, don't expect any cooperation or sympathy from me," Destin retorted, stepping into the lift and turning to lean back against the wall.

"Noted," Trig muttered, following Destin. "Level Eight."

* * *

"Lesson sixteen," Sula muttered, staring at the screen. "No, that isn't it. Lesson twenty-one, lesson twenty-two."

Frustrated, she skimmed the contents, searching for anything that could explain what happened earlier. With growing aggravation, she closed the educational files her mother had given her. So far, she had not discovered anything that explained the intense physical reaction to Destin's touch.

Her people did not touch lips together. They showed their affection by pressing their foreheads and fingers together. While the files showed her how to relieve her own discomforts, they did not go into detail about the physical relationship between a man and woman like the human PORN files did. Even her brothers' files were only slightly more descriptive.

Deciding she had wasted enough time and energy on the subject, she opened the files pertaining to

Badrick's legacy and the current environment on Earth. The more she read about Badrick, the more she wished the former Usoleum Councilor was still alive so she could kill him. It was obvious the male had some mental issues that should have been diagnosed before his assignment to any position. Sula suspected it was only his family's high position in the Usoleum government that had shielded him. She would have to recommend some reform in that area.

Leaning forward, Sula rested her chin on the palm of her hand and stared out into space. The small, quiet room was nearly empty. There were only five others in the room set aside for relaxation; two couples who were talking quietly with each other and a male warrior sitting near the back wall, asleep.

Setting her tablet aside, Sula reached into the small bag she brought with her and pulled out the game Chelsea had given her. It was in the shape of a triangle and contained numerous holes in it. Opening the clear bag containing all the pieces, Sula inserted the colored pegs into all the holes but one. Over the next several minutes, she played the game, trying to leave only one peg remaining.

"I'm just plain stupid," she muttered with a sigh, gloomily staring at the three remaining pegs.

"Maybe for sneaking out on me, but otherwise I'd say you were pretty smart," an all-too-familiar masculine voice said, pulling her out of her reverie.

Sula's head jerked up and she twisted in her seat. Her gaze softened when she saw Destin standing beside her. Her lips curved when he glanced down at the game and grinned.

"So, that is where you learned the word you like," he murmured before returning his gaze to her face. The grin on his face faded and his expression grew more distant. "Do you mind if I join you?"

"Yes...," Sula started to say before she released a sigh. "Yes, I would like for you to join me, not that I would mind."

"Good," Destin replied, swiveling the chair so he could slide onto it. He sat forward, clasping his hands together, and gazed at her in silence for a few seconds before he spoke. "Why did you leave?"

Sula bit her lip and turned her gaze to the game in front of her. Her fingers played with one of the pegs, turning it inside the hole. She blinked when Destin gently placed his strong fingers over hers. The contact sent a wave of yearning through her. Almost immediately, she felt her nipples harden and her stomach clench in remembrance of the feel of his hands against her flesh.

"I needed time to think," she admitted, glancing at him. "What happened... It was very unusual for me. Everything about my reaction to you is unusual. I am trying to understand it."

"Do you have any regrets?" Destin asked, tightening his grasp on her hand when she started to pull away.

"No," Sula replied, staring into his eyes.

The corner of Destin's lips moved upward and his eyes glimmered with an expression of satisfaction. He released her and sat back in his seat. A wry expression crossed his face and he turned his head to stare out of the window into the blackness of space.

"Good," he finally said, turning back to look at her. "I was ready to fight if you tried to tell me you didn't enjoy it as much as I did."

"Oh, I enjoyed it very much," Sula retorted, flushing a darker blue at her impulsive response.

She could feel the heat intensify when Destin chuckled. Her lips pressed together at his slightly smug expression. That he could so easily cause her to lose her composure made a flash of irritation sweep through her.

"Where did you get the game?" he asked, nodding to the wooden toy.

"From a human nurse named Chelsea," Sula replied, picking up the pegs and inserting them into the wooden board. "When I was on your planet, I caught a horrible virus that made me miserable. I was afraid, because I was inoculated against all known diseases, but I guess it did not work for the cold virus. It had been a long time since I felt so poorly. I went to the healer on my assigned base for medical attention. Chelsea attended to me and became my friend. I hope to see her again when we arrive. I have a gift for her. She gave me this game and several files which I found to be very helpful."

"What kind of files?" Destin asked, curiously.

Sula's face darkened again and she looked down at the game again. "Files to help me understand humans better," she murmured, reluctant to explain exactly which ones.

"Documentaries?" Destin pressed as if sensing she was holding back from telling him everything.

"Yes. Well, some of them," she replied, biting her lower lip and peeking at him through her lashes. "Some were called romances. I wanted to know why she and her mate pressed their lips to each other. It did not look like it was done to help the other breathe, but as a sign of affection. I thought it important to gather as much information as I could about humans while I was assigned to your world. This was an area I did not think to research before I arrived."

"What other files were there? You said 'some of them'," Destin asked, sitting forward and pulling the game toward him.

"They were more detailed instructional files about human mating rituals," she stated with a shrug of her shoulders. "They were interesting, but I enjoyed the romance files better. I did give the other files to my brothers, who appear to be enjoying them from the number of requests I have received for more, now that they have discovered I am returning to your world. I swear I wouldn't be surprised if Sirius ends up appearing at my quarters. His questions are irritating."

"What type of questions?" Destin asked, pausing in the act of jumping over one of the pegs in her game.

Sula waved her hand in the air. "Sirius is an ignoramus. I have given up trying to understand his questions and usually delete them if they are not relevant to my assignment. You have to understand my brother; he is always trying to get me in trouble. I learned at a very young age to avoid his traps," she responded, frowning at the single peg remaining on the wooden game board. "How did you do that?!"

A devilish grin curved Destin's lips and he sat forward. "Come back to my living quarters and I'll show you," he suggested.

Sula's lips twitched in response. "Something tells me this might take a while to learn," she teased, suggestively stroking one of the pegs.

Destin's eyes narrowed and he laid his hand over hers. "You are dangerous," he murmured. "What's even more worrisome is that now you know it."

Sula twisted her hand under his and stroked his palm. "I do my research," she retorted, not backing down.

She pulled her hand free, taking the game with her. She quickly returned the items to the clear bag before sliding it into a larger one. Slipping out of her chair, she smiled at Destin. Her gaze ran over him and she could feel the heat rising again.

"Damn, Sula," Destin swore under his breath, standing up and adjusting his pants. "You keep looking at me like that and we might not make it back to my quarters."

The warrior sitting in the corner sat up and grinned at them. It was only then that she realized the other two couples already left. Besides Destin and her, there was only the warrior who she suspected had been awake since the moment Destin entered the room. She refused to be intimidated. Instead, she stepped closer to Destin, reaching up to brush a kiss across his lips even as her hand brushed across the front of his jeans.

"I wonder if the lift has a surveillance camera," she whispered, turning and walking toward the door.

Her chin lifted and she kept her focus forward when she heard Destin's muttered curse and soft threat. The smile she had been hiding grew when he quickly caught up to her and wrapped his arm around her. She would have plenty of time later to do the research her father assigned to her. For now, she was going to enjoy doing research of a different kind.

Chapter 10

Over the next several months, Destin and Sula's life fell into a daily routine that he found enjoyable. Since the first day aboard the *Star Raider*, there was an unspoken agreement between them: when they were not attending to their assigned duties, they spent their time together. Fortunately, Sula was able to modify her work schedule around his so they could be together more often.

Destin enjoyed the challenges of learning new things. Life aboard an alien spaceship gave him an appreciation for the complexities of running a self-sustaining habitat. On the trip to Rathon, he had been recovering from his injuries and spent most of his time in his cabin working on issues regarding Earth or in the training room working out.

This time, he was assigned a job which gave him a better understanding of what life on a spaceship was really like since he went to every section as part of his daily duties. He understood the difficulty of running a close-knit community from his own challenges on Earth, but this was a true Ecosphere. Each person was responsible for a specific task and held accountable because it meant the survival of everyone.

His assignment was minor, helping with the maintenance of the waste disposal units. He was pleasantly surprised when he discovered Sula in the Communications center. One of her specialties was frequencies and space noise, much like a radar technician on a submarine. She was responsible for monitoring the different frequencies to make sure there were no cosmic threats.

"I swear I have never seen a man grin as much as you do," Trig complained, rolling his head on his shoulders. "I will be glad when we arrive on your world tomorrow. I am almost sick of being on here. This is why I've always steered away from this division."

"And that makes four hundred eighty-one times you've said that," Destin remarked dryly, dumping the last of the trash into the incinerator before replacing the container.

Trig grinned. "I'm still under the five hundred mark you bet me," he retorted, leaning back against the wall, his smile fading. "Things are going to be different when we get to Earth, you know."

"How so? I'm not going to have you up my ass all the time?" Destin asked with a raised eyebrow.

"Actually, I'll be so far up it that you won't be able to take a shit without me knowing about it," Trig replied lightly.

Destin released a sigh and shook his head. "Where did you learn that phrase?" he asked with a raised eyebrow.

"Your current flame has been sharing some of her cultural verbiage with me – plus, I hang with Jordan regularly just to piss off my brother," Trig stated. "That means to irritate him, by the way."

"I know what being pissed off means," Destin replied dryly. "I swear if you start talking like a surfer, they'll never miss the fact you didn't make it down to the planet – and what did you mean my current flame? Have you been bothering Sula again?"

Trig shook his head. "She has assured me that I am not bothering her," he replied, straightening. "I meant what I said; things will be more difficult once we are down on the planet."

Destin frowned. "Everything has been quiet. I thought you said that there were no other reports on the Waxian or Drethulans," he commented, walking past Trig and pressing the controls to ignite the disposal unit.

"They found the man who attacked Razor's dwellings," Trig stated.

Destin frowned. "When did that happen? Why didn't you tell me?" he asked, pausing to stare at the other man.

Trig pressed his lips together and shrugged. "A couple of weeks ago. There was nothing to tell. The man was very resistant to talking. Of course, he was already dead, so that was a contributing factor. Unless you know how to survive in the forests of our world, you won't last long," he said with a wry grimace.

Destin shot Trig a disgusted glare before turning away. "Considering I was almost killed in the attack, I think I should have been told," he replied with a sarcastic bite to his voice. "What about the ship, or are you not allowed to share that with me either?"

Trig grunted and leaned against the console. "Razor said I might as well tell you, otherwise Kali would. I think he has given up on trying to keep Jordan from hacking into the system. He has finally hired her to keep everyone else out, but of course, she relays information to whoever she wants to, which usually includes Jesse, Taylor, and Kali," he said.

"That's great, and...," Destin snapped, throwing his hand up in the air with a twist to show he wanted Trig to get to the point.

"They were able to retrieve information from the transport that was on the beach," Trig said. "It came from Dises V, and there were communication logs linked between the transport and a Waxian named Prymorus Achler. From the little that Ajaska was able to relay to us, the bastard has a personal vendetta against Trivators, especially Razor and Hunter. Razor is trying to find out more, but we do know that the Waxian is the one who was behind Taylor's kidnapping."

Destin paused in what he was doing to study Trig. The familiar, blank mask had settled over the Trivator's face. The nagging feeling that something bigger was going on continued to eat at Destin to the point that he had already decided to part ways with the man once they were on Earth. He didn't need cryptic messages or uncertainty undermining his own men.

"I've had enough, Trig. If you and the others won't tell me honestly what the fuck is going on, leave me alone or I'll throw your ass in Chicago's worst jail. Trust works both ways. Either you trust me and share the information you know, or you stay the fuck away from me. I don't play games," Destin stated in a blunt, measured tone.

Trig's mouth tightened and for a second, Destin thought the other man would remain stubbornly silent. He didn't look away. This was the moment of truth. All the rules changed once they were off the ship.

"What I tell you will sound unbelievable," Trig warned, pausing again.

Destin's jaw tightened. "Do you really think I haven't dealt with some unbelievable shit in the last seven years?" he retorted.

Trig shook his head. "It isn't that Razor doesn't trust you, Destin," he replied in a quiet voice. "It's more like we are trying to figure out what is going on."

Confusion swept through Destin. He could see the flicker of indecision in the other man's eyes. Something told him this didn't happen often for Trig. He swallowed the caustic retort that had risen, instead waiting for Trig to continue.

"I'm listening," he finally said.

Trig nodded, glancing down at the console again and rested his arms on the top of it. "I'll try to make this as brief as possible, and if I'm lucky, without too much confusion. We don't know much about the Kassisans. They came into the Alliance a few years ago, but have been more observers than a participants. It was only recently that we, or I should say I, have found out much about their capabilities," he stated.

"You don't sound too happy about it," Destin observed.

"I'm not. I don't like any species who could potentially rival the Trivators. The close relationship between the Kassisans and the Elpidiosians makes them a superpower," Trig muttered with a shake of his head.

"Ajaska didn't give me the impression he was interested in going to war against the Trivators or the Alliance," Destin commented. "If anything, he appeared to want to help."

Trig nodded. "Yes," he said.

"So, what seems to be the issue? And… why all the melodrama?" Destin demanded with a wave of his hand. "If the threat with the Waxians and Drethulans turns out to be as bad as Razor and the others seem to think, then having a superpower on your side is a good thing. I know it would have made my fight on Earth a helluva lot easier if I'd had the Trivators on my side," he added bitterly before he broke off and pushed away from the console.

"Ajaska warned us that your life would be in danger and that it was of paramount importance that nothing happens to you. Razor assigned me to protect you."

Destin frowned and stared at Trig in disbelief. His life was in danger. Hell, when had it not been? Kali and he grew up on the streets, running them from the time they could walk until well after the Trivators announced their arrival and the Earth had dissolved into a fiery pit of hell and destruction. *Now,* the Trivators thought he needed a damn babysitter? Shaking his head, he crossed his arms and glared back at Trig.

"I hate to tell you this, but you are about twenty-four years too late on the babysitting job," he replied sarcastically. "I'll give my mom credit for the first two years of my life."

"Razor thought this was different," Trig replied with a shrug.

"Who am I supposed to be in danger from and what exactly did Ajaska say to make Razor think I might be in danger?" Destin asked with a skeptical expression.

"We don't know," Trig admitted, reaching up and running his hands through his hair in aggravation. "The damn Kassisan was pretty tight-lipped. The only thing he would say was that you were in danger and we needed to keep you alive for the future sake of your planet."

"For the future sake…." Destin shook his head.

"Yeah, well, we've been trying to anticipate how this or that factor might affect an outcome we don't even know the details of. All we know is you've got to live through what's coming," Trig said with a frustrated sigh.

Destin released a dry, rough chortle, and dropped his arms to his side. "News flash… My life was already in danger. I killed the man who was trying to kill me, and Chicago is being rebuilt. Ajaska missed the memo or forgot to send it out before reality hit. Plus, I already have a team in place to watch my back. I trust them – as much as I can trust anyone. I like you, Trig. I think you are a good man, but I've learned that even those you know aren't always what they appear to be. Go find someone else to piss off – that means to irritate in case you didn't know. I've got enough going on without tripping over your ass all the time."

"Tough shit."

Destin heard Trig's muttered reply, but ignored it. Once they were on the planet, he didn't answer to anyone, including the Trivator he had come to respect. He turned on his heel and strode out the door of the Disposal Unit. He could feel the tension growing inside him the closer they got to Earth. He was looking forward to returning home, but he was also feeling the stress of what it could mean for Sula and him.

He had been putting off discussing what her position on Earth would be, deciding they had plenty of time before they arrived to do that. It was hard to believe that they were almost out of time. He ran his hand over the back of his neck. A lot had changed over the last two years on Earth. Unfortunately, the feelings toward the aliens was not one of them. Many of the residents and those who had worked and fought with him did not believe that the Trivators were the good guys. They sure as hell were not going to open their arms to Sula – a Usoleum councilor who would remind them of Badrick.

Dropping his hand to his side, he veered in the opposite direction from his initial destination. He needed a quiet place to think. On a ship, that was not easy to find, even in the designated quiet rooms. Turning again, he stepped into one of the lifts.

"Level thirty-two," he murmured, leaning back against the wall.

A minute later, he was exiting onto Level Thirty-two. He nodded to several warriors when he passed them. Turning left, he paused long enough for the door to open. He drew in a deep breath and glanced around the training room. It was teeming with warriors. Some sparred while others worked out. While the room might be well occupied, there were still some places where he preferred to go that they could not.

Rolling his head on his shoulders, he loosened the muscles in his arms. He drew in several deep, calming breaths, mapping the room in his mind. Bench, mat, far bench, footrail, metal framing, ventilation ducts. The move formed in his mind and replayed over and over until he mentally closed everyone and everything else out.

He walked to a spot by the wall several feet from two long benches. A large sparring mat sat in the middle of the room. The farthest bench ended at the corner of the room. Taking off at a run, Destin jumped on the first bench, and ran across it before he did a flip off the end. He tumbled across the mat and jumped onto the second bench at top speed, one foot on the seat, then the back before he rotated in midair and grabbed the bottom of a footrail that was connected to an access ladder almost a foot above his head.

Destin pulled himself up, climbing to the top and stepping onto the large support beam that ran across the length of the training room. He ignored the chuckles and exclamations from under him. With a silent wave to the men below, he sprinted across it to the ventilation access. He pulled up on the metal rod holding it closed, opened the grating, and disappeared inside. Behind him, the metal door snapped closed.

The vent was narrow for about ten meters, so he had to stoop down. After that, it opened up and he was able to walk unimpeded. He paused, glancing at the walls. He had discovered this method of escaping Trig a week after they boarded. The Trivator was pretty good at keeping up with him. During one of the rare times when Sula worked an odd shift and Trig thought he was with her, Destin had decided to do some exploring. The training room had been packed, so he retreated to where he felt the most comfortable...Up.

He glanced at the wall again and turned. He had made notations on it. He had discovered an access tube that led to the deck where his living quarters were located. Following the symbols, he climbed the narrow access rungs leading from one level to the next.

* * *

Almost thirty minutes later, Destin could feel the burn in his arms and legs and knew he had a good workout. Walking along the edge of the access tunnel, he gazed down through the vents, occasionally catching sight of people moving about the ship. He reached the ladder to the last level and climbed up. At the end of the next vent, there was a larger service access where he could exit and drop down into the corridor.

Destin bent down, waiting for several people to pass by before he opened the access panel. He carefully lowered himself down and released the edge, dropping the remaining few feet to the floor. Reaching up, he grabbed the grate, jumped and released it in one motion so the magnetic latch would snap the grate closed. He strode down hall to his living quarters and entered.

Glancing at the time, he noted he had plenty of time to shower before Sula returned. He might even meet her when she got off and they could get an early dinner. He removed his clothes and placed them in the cleaning unit, then stepped into the shower. Closing his eyes, he stood under the heavy mist for almost a minute before he shook his head at his wandering thoughts.

Exiting the shower, he waited for the air dryer to dry him before he grabbed a towel and wrapped it around his waist. He reached for the comb and ran it through his hair. It was getting long again and he would need to get it cut. He preferred his hair short.

He turned when he heard the outer door open. A grin curved his lips. Sula was back early. Stepping toward the door, he paused when he heard her speaking to someone. Glancing down at the towel, he decided it would probably not be a good idea to walk out.

"I told you I would discover the information that was found pertaining to the missing women," Sula was saying.

"We need to make sure each of them is accounted for," a man's voice responded.

* * *

"Andric, the records I accessed showed that eighteen are still unaccounted for," Sula murmured, kicking off her shoes and wiggling her toes.

"What about the male you have befriended? Surely he can give you more information on the situation," Andric demanded. "Father wants the females found before it is too late."

"I am very much aware of what Father wants," Sula stated in an exasperated tone.

"You are lucky he gave you a second chance to gather the information," Andric said. "Have you accessed the human male's files yet?"

Sula wanted to make a face at her brother, but knew it wouldn't do anything but send him off on another tangent. She wanted to remind him that it was not her fault that the information was deleted off of Badrick's computers before she could access them.

Instead, she bit her lip to keep from aggravating him. He was also doing everything he could to search for the females – especially one in particular.

"No, I have not," Sula replied in what she hoped was a calm voice.

"Why not? What are you waiting for? Can't you break his access codes?" Andric demanded.

"If you want access to them so badly, why didn't you have Father send you to Earth? You are just as good at breaking into computers as I am," Sula snapped.

"Father thought that since you are a female it would work better. Both the Trivator and human males believe females to be less of a threat and would be less likely to suspect you. Why is it taking so long?" Andric pointed out.

Sula quickly hid her emotions. She would not let Andric know that his callous words hurt her. The oldest out of all of them, he was also the most blunt. Drawing in a deep breath, she glared at the screen in her hands wishing she had refused Andric's transmission. He had been tossing questions at her every step of the way to Destin's living quarters.

"I know what my assignment is, Andric. I do not answer to you, but to Father. I will discover any information I can about the missing humans and report it directly to him," she replied in a cool tone.

"Badrick's family is pressuring for retribution. They want the human male and Razor held accountable for his death," Andric warned.

"I am well aware of Councilor Badrick's family's petition and their desire to invoke the Law of Retribution. Father is also aware that the fact that Razor is a Trivator, a member of the Alliance, and the Chancellor, it would make it dangerous to allow any such action," Sula reminded her brother.

"But not for the human," Andric retorted. "Get the information, Sula. Father doesn't care how you do it. Seduce the bastard if you have to, but get it."

"I know what needs to be done, Andric," Sula whispered, seeing the flash of grief on his face. "I also know why you are so desperate. As soon as I find out the locations of the missing humans, I will let you know. Be careful, brother. There are strange things happening in the galaxy."

"Same to you, Sula," Andric said with an expression of regret in his eyes. "I didn't mean the last part."

"I know," Sula replied with a tender smile. "But, it isn't a bad idea," she added with a mischievous grin before she ended the transmission.

Her heart hurt for her brother. While she loved to pick on him, she also knew the heavy burden he faced. Their father was ill. Sula did not miss noticing the tiredness in her father's voice or the concern in her mother's eyes. Nor did she miss the frequent visits from a long line of healers the last time she was home. She suspected that was one reason she was sent to the Trivator home world, then to Earth. Her father wanted to right the wrong that had been done and he knew that she was not only very skilled in research, be she could also be trusted to help find the women. He had her other brothers doing the same. While she did not want to come at first, wishing Sirius was assigned instead after her last disastrous encounter with the Trivators and Destin, she was now very thankful.

"Sounds like your brother is pretty determined that you to ask me something," Destin commented.

Sula jumped and clutched the tablet to her chest. Her face flushed and she stared at Destin with wide, startled eyes. A shiver ran through her when she saw the icy reserve in his eyes. Automatically, her gaze swept over his damp hair, bare shoulders, broad chest, and down to the towel that hung low around his hips. He leaned against the door frame and crossed his arms.

"I… Yes, Andric…," Sula started to say before she bit her lip and looked down. "I've been meaning to talk to you. It is just when we are together…" Her lips curved into a rueful smile. "I have trouble thinking of anything else."

"I think you should talk to me now," Destin said, straightening and walking over to pull out some clean clothes.

Sula watched his stiff movements. "Destin," she whispered, placing the tablet on the table near the bed and walking over to him. Her hand ran down along his back. "It is not what you might think."

She could feel him stiffen at her touch. Her mind played back the conversation she just had with her brother, seeing it from Destin's point-of-view. If she had heard a conversation in reference to what was said as he had, she too would have felt betrayed and suspicious as well.

Destin turned toward her. "What should I think?" he asked, his jaw tight when she slid her hand up over his bare chest and tangled her fingers in his dark chest hair.

"That my father is mortified and devastated by Badrick's betrayal. The Usoleum value family, and despite my desire to torture my brothers, I love them very much and they love me. What Badrick did was not only unthinkable to my people but harmful to our relationship with the Trivators and the Alliance. We depend on them for protection," she explained in a soft, hesitant voice, staring up into his eyes. "We are a peaceful people, Destin. Others know that and would take advantage. Our strength is our logic and tactics, which makes us a valuable ally, but left to fare on our own, we would crumble against the brute force of our enemies."

"Do you honestly expect me to believe your brother is desperate enough to want you to seduce me in order to save a bunch of women – alien women – who he doesn't even know in order to keep the peace with the Trivators?" Destin demanded with a cynical expression.

Sula lifted her chin at his tone and her eyes flashed with determination. Without realizing it, she tugged at the hairs on his chest before pushing him backwards a step. Her lips were tight.

"I am Princess Jersula Ikera, only daughter of the Royal House of Usoleum, Councilor Select for the Alliance representative to the Earth, Destin Parks. One of those women sent out a message – a message that was intercepted by my older brother. He has become fixated on finding her. Her plea...." Sula's eyes filled with tears and she swallowed. "Destin, please, my father is very ill and the weight of what Badrick did weighs heavily on his conscience. He wishes to find and return those women to their families. It is more than shame or pride; it is a matter of responsibility and honor. He is the one who assigned Badrick to your world. He cannot bring back those that died because of Badrick's deception, but he can right this terrible wrong."

Sula's throat tightened on her admission. A low sob escaped her and she pulled her hands away from Destin to brush at the tears that had escaped. Drawing in a ragged breath, she started to turn away from him. She was an ugly crier. Her face always grew puffy, her nose would leak, and her eyes would turn almost black, making her look like a dead, bloated sea mammal that had washed up on shore.

A hiccup escaped her and she started crying harder when she felt his arms encircle her, drawing her against his chest. Now she was going to end up smearing her disgusting mucus all over him. Just the idea of it made her start to cry even harder which made her mad – at herself. All she wanted to do was escape into the 'bathroom', as she had started calling it now, and lock the door.

"Why didn't you tell me earlier?" Destin asked quietly, stroking her back.

"Because… because… I keep forgetting when I am with you," she wailed, frustrated at her uncharacteristic emotion. "I hate crying! I don't… I don't… cry."

"That makes me feel even worse," Destin teased with a sigh. "It sounded pretty bad and I'm a suspicious person by nature."

"I… know," Sula mumbled against his chest. "I had to deal with you once before when you weren't very ni… nice to me, remember? I need to borrow your cover."

Sula could feel her nose starting to drip. Reaching down, she pulled the towel from around Destin's waist and stepped back out of his arms. She blew her nose into it, then glanced at Destin. The thought of him seeing her like this sent another wave of tears to her eyes.

"What is it? I'm not upset anymore," Destin said, lifting a hand out to her.

"I don't cry pretty," Sula wailed again and turned on her heel to hurry into the bathroom.

She slammed her hand against the panel, closing the door behind her. Stepping over to the sink, she looked at her reflection. It was worse than she expected. Her nose looked like a big, blue blob. A long, uneven wail rose up in her throat and she buried her head in the towel.

"Sula...," Destin said from the other side of the door. "Open the door.... Sweetheart, please, open the door. I believe you."

"Go... go away!" Sula cried out, turning away from the mirror to sit on the toilet. "I'm not coming out until... until... I'm through making a fool of myself."

"That could take a while," Destin's muttered words filtered through the thin metal.

Sula glared at the door before rising off the seat and taking three steps to it. Palming the door open, she blinked and jerked her head back when she saw Destin standing so close to it. With a toss of her head and a loud sniff, she gave him her dirtiest look.

"I heard that," Sula informed him. Her bottom lip trembled when his expression softened. Afraid she was going to burst out crying again, she shook her head vehemently at him and closed the door again. She leaned her head against it and wrapped her arms around her waist. "Leave me alone, Destin."

"I didn't mean it that way, Sula," Destin's muffled voice swore through the closed door.

"I... I... I... Oh, go away!" Sula demanded before a loud, hiccupping sob escaped her and she turned her back to the door, buried her head in the towel again, and slid down to the floor to have a good, old-fashion cry as Chelsea would say.

Chapter 11

It seemed to take forever before she stopped crying. At one point, she got so quiet that he was concerned that she fainted or became ill. He was about to call maintenance to force the door open when the sound of the shower turning on assured him that she was okay.

After dressing in a pair of black jogging pants, he called Trig to see if he would mind bringing down some food for them. Trig gave him a questioning look, but didn't say anything. A short time later, Trig delivered a tray complete with a thick soup, bread, drinks, and dessert.

Twenty minutes after that, a very subdued and drained Sula exited the bathroom. She wore a thick towel wrapped around her pale figure, her long, white hair hanging in a limp, tangled mess around her. She gazed at him, her lower lip trembling, and he melted into a warm pile of mush in her hands.

"Let me," he gently murmured, taking the brush from her loose fingers.

"I'm sorry," she whispered in a soft, hoarse voice. "I don't normally cry."

"That's okay. I'm kinda used to it, having lived with my mom and Kali for so long," Destin teased. "Sit on the bed and let me brush your hair. That used to work for Kali when she would get her feelings hurt or when she wasn't feeling good."

"Are your parents still alive?" Sula asked, sinking down onto the bed and picking up a pillow to hug against her.

"No," Destin murmured, starting at the bottom of her hair and carefully working on the tangles. "We never knew our dad. He was in and out and finally gone by the time our mom had Kali. Our mom was a free spirit. She saw the good in everyone."

"You... The males of your species do not stay with the female?" she asked, puzzled because she was sure that Chelsea said that Thomas helped care for their young.

"Some do, some don't," Destin replied with a slight shrug. "Some guys are better off not having any kids and the kids are better off without them. Our dad wasn't made to be a dad. He liked to hit our mom. We were happier without him."

"How... old were you?" Sula asked, glancing over her shoulder at him in disbelief.

"I was close to four the last time I saw him. Some things you don't forget," Destin said, nodding for her to face the other direction again. "We had a good life until Mom was murdered by a couple of guys in the neighborhood. They got hooked up with the wrong crowd."

"What happened?" Sula whispered, her eyes burning again with tears at the thought of what life must have been like for Destin and Kali.

"Part of the initiation to join the gang was to rob a few stores," Destin murmured. "Our mom worked two, sometimes three jobs just to make ends meet. She never complained. She said working so many different places allowed her to meet all kinds of people. She was working down at the local convenience store when two kids walked in, pointed a gun at her, and demanded the money in the register. Mom didn't give a damn about the money but she did about the two boys. She knew them. Hell, we knew them. Someone came in while they were pointing the gun at her and it startled them. It went off. She was killed instantly." Destin paused as he ran the brush through her hair. "Kali was seventeen. I was taking classes down at the local college. I wanted to be a mechanical engineer and build things. Most of all, I wanted to get Mom and Kali out of that neighborhood before something like that happened."

Sula could hear the distance in his voice, as if he were deep in thought – or memories, in this case. Her heart ached for him because of the pain she could hear in his words. Her fingers twisted together as she resisted turning around. Something told her that he needed – wanted – to tell her this, but he couldn't do it while she was looking at him. The memories were too painful for him to share while he could see the sympathy in her eyes.

"What happened after that?" she asked in an emotion-laden voice.

Destin began brushing her hair in long, steady strokes. She could feel the precise movements, as if he were using the soothing rhythm to regain control of his emotions. She patiently waited for him to speak again.

"The aliens came," he finally said, leaning over to place the brush on the side table. He wrapped his arms around her and pulled her back against him. "And the humans opened the gates to hell."

* * *

Hours later, a message came in and Destin's arms briefly tightened around Sula. He reluctantly released her to roll onto his side. Leaning up on his elbow, he pulled the communicator around and read the message. He murmured a response in a quiet voice.

"What is it?" Sula asked, sliding an arm around his waist.

"We've reached Earth," he murmured, replacing the communicator back onto the side table.

A smile curved Destin's lips as he laid his hand over hers and rolled onto his back. Her face was still a little puffy from crying. Lifting his hand, he traced the outline of her cheek.

She turned her head to brush her lips against the palm of his hand. A teasing smile crossed his face and he suddenly rolled on top of her. Her startled giggle sent the now familiar wave of warmth through him. The lightheartedness of the moment faded and he gazed down at her with a serious expression.

"What is it?" Sula asked, tilting her head sideways on the pillow and giving him a questioning look.

"Things are going to be different on Earth," he said.

A flash of uncertainty swept across her face and she licked her bottom lip. Drawing in a deep breath, he turned his head and pressed his lips against her wrist when she threaded her fingers through his hair. He felt her slight tremble at the intimate gesture.

"We will work together this time," she promised, gazing at him. "There has to be information somewhere on where Badrick sent those women. I will find it. I will also work beside you to help with the rebuilding. As an Alliance representative, I can fight for any funding that is necessary and work with the other Councilors to ensure you receive the support you need. I know you will be busy helping your people, Destin. I will, also."

Destin leaned forward and rested his forehead against hers. He didn't have as much faith in finding the women as Sula did. Razor assigned two Trivators almost two years ago to locate the women. They found and returned over half of them before they were recalled.

Destin seriously doubted the Trivators would be able to find the rest of the women after all this time. Razor promised he would reassign the men, but Destin was skeptical of his brother-in-law's promise considering the new threats to the Alliance. From the little that he overheard, there was more at stake in the universe than the lives of a group of human women.

Destin bent and brushed a kiss across her lips. "I know you will," he murmured before he pulled back and grimaced when the communicator buzzed again.

"We'd better get a move on or Trig will be having puppies."

Sula's brow furrowed at the comment. "I do not think Trivator males can have puppies. They may obtain them, but the canine species are not found in their world," she said, following him when he slid out of bed.

Destin's eyes twinkled with amusement when she stood up and straightened the oversized Chicago Cubs T-shirt she confiscated from him. Sometimes Sula took his statements very literally, leading to some interesting – and often amusing – discussions. He shook his head and wrapped his arm around her. If it wasn't for the fact that Trig was getting impatient to get off the ship and wouldn't leave them alone, he would postpone going down to the planet for as long as possible. The communicator chimed again, almost as if Trig sensed his procrastination.

"For crying out loud," Destin muttered, glancing at the message on the communicator. "He is worse than a kid at Christmas!"

"What does it say?" Sula asked.

"'*Are you ready yet?*'" Destin replied with a slight growl in his voice. It pinged again. "'*How about now?*' I'm going to shove this damn thing down his throat."

"Wouldn't it just be easier to remove his ability to communicate with you?" Sula asked.

"Yes, but not near as much fun," Destin muttered, sliding his hand over Sula's hip and pressing a kiss to her shoulder. "I'm going to have Cutter assign him to latrine duty at the Army National Guard building if he doesn't stop driving me crazy."

Sula chuckled. "I think we better go," she murmured, kissing the corner of his mouth.

There was a bang on the outer door. Destin watched Sula quickly gather some clothing and step into the bathroom. Grabbing a pair of jogging pants, he quickly pulled them on before he strode the short distance to the door and opened it. He glared at Trig.

"I got your message," Destin replied dryly. "All of them."

Trig looked Destin up and down with a dark, impatient frown. Destin watched Trig shift from one foot to the other and glance over Destin's shoulder into the cabin behind him before scowling at him again. Destin raised an amused eyebrow at Trig and ignored the alien male's impatient glare.

"We're here," Trig stated.

"I know. You already told me that," Destin pointed out.

"Why aren't you ready?" Trig demanded. "I'm ready to get off this ship."

Destin casually leaned against the door frame. Amusement swept through him when Trig's expression darkened at his lack of motivation.

"I can kinda tell you are ready to get off the ship. Did your parents ever tell you that you are very annoying?" Destin asked before he shook his head. "The answer to your question is no, we are not ready. We were asleep until a few minutes ago. It should only take us about fifteen minutes if you stop interrupting us."

Trig's lips twitched and his eyes glittered with a rueful expression. "You don't want to ask my parents that question. It would take years to hear about how annoying I can be," he retorted, glancing over Destin's shoulder again. "Good morning, Councilor Ikera."

"Sula," Sula responded automatically, wrapping a tie around the end of her long braid. "Good morning to you as well, Trig. I understand that we have arrived. I have already submitted my request for delivery of my belongings to my new living quarters."

"At least one of you is organized," Trig replied with a satisfied nod before he stepped back and started to turn away. "I'll meet you in the shuttle bay in ten minutes."

"Fifteen," Destin called out behind the Trivator.

"Shuttle leaves in twenty," Trig retorted, not turning around.

Destin chuckled and straightened. Turning, he closed the door to his living quarters. His gaze swept over Sula. She looked beautiful, exotic, and definitely alien in the dark red, form fitting top, leggings, and silver transparent cover. Her hair was braided to the side and hung down over her shoulder. Thin ribbons of red and silver ran through it.

"You look beautiful," Destin murmured, stepping toward her.

He raised his hand and brushed the back of his knuckles down her cheek before turning his hand to trace the line along her throat. His fingers grazed the long scar on her neck. Bending, he brushed his lips against hers before releasing an annoyed grunt when his communicator chimed.

"I'll kill him while you go get ready," she laughed, lifting her hand to brush it across the rough skin of his jaw.

"Sounds good to me," he grunted out, reluctantly turning away from her. "I'll be out in a couple of minutes."

"Take your time. I'll need it to hide the body," she teased.

"Number Three in the Disposal Unit incinerates really well," he suggested, turning and retrieving some clothes before disappearing into the bathroom.

His amusement vanished and once again he felt the tightness grow in his chest at the thought that they were finally back on Earth. Reality was a brutal companion and it was tapping him on the shoulder at the moment, reminding him of his responsibilities. He stepped into the shower and quickly washed. Within minutes, he was dressed and stepping out of the bathroom.

Sula was gone. She had probably already headed down to the shuttle bay. It didn't take him long to gather the few articles of clothing and his other personal belongings. He wouldn't need anyone to transport them since they all fit into the duffel bag he pulled out from under his bed.

Glancing around one last time, he shouldered the large green bag and stepped out of the room. He nodded to several warriors he passed. He was beginning to disconnect himself from the ship, this strange, alien world. His mind was already focusing on going home.

The trip down to the shuttle bay took a lot less time than he anticipated. His gaze narrowed on Trig where he was talking quietly with Jag, the commander of the *Star Raider*. Jag glanced his way, nodded, and returned his attention to Trig. Both men's faces held an intense, grim expression.

"What is it?" Destin asked, glancing back and forth between the two men.

"A Waxian starship was intercepted while entering this part of the galaxy," Jag stated.

"When?" Destin demanded.

"A few hours ago. There was a brief battle before it was destroyed," Jag replied. "They are no match for our defenses."

"It only takes one ship to get through to discover an area of weakness," Destin said, glancing around the shuttle bay. "How many Waxian ships were there?"

"Just one," Jag replied. "It is not uncommon for them to travel alone and recklessly, but something feels wrong. There was very little resistance."

"It proves they are a threat, though," Trig added.

Destin nodded. "Where's Sula?" he asked, glancing around again.

"She has already boarded the shuttle to go down," Trig replied, turning to nod at the shuttle behind him. "Are you ready?"

"Yes," Destin said, noticing that Jag's attention was already redirected to another issue. "So, what happened with the Waxians?"

"A Waxian starship appeared near the planet you call Uranus. One of our patrols intercepted the ship when it came out of trans-galaxy acceleration. All our warnings to stand down for boarding were ignored. The Waxians on the ship opened fire on the patrol cruiser," Trig stated.

"And there were no other ships?" Destin asked.

"No, and that is what worries me," Trig replied, stepping up onto the platform."

Destin watched Trig for a moment, his eyes narrowing on the stiff shoulders of the Trivator. Trig had told him about what happened to Dagger. He also knew what Taylor had gone through. There were a lot of things that he still didn't know, but both events had deeply affected the man.

Sympathy for Trig swept through him. He remembered the feelings of helplessness when Kali was captured and almost killed. Fortunately, his sister was not subjected to years of torture the way Dagger was. It amazed him that the other man was even remotely functional.

It was obvious from the little he had seen of Dagger that the man suffered from some form of Post-Traumatic Stress Disorder. Destin had seen it over and over among members of his team while fighting against Colbert. Hell, he knew he suffered from PTSD himself. He quickly learned that each person handled the disorder differently. Only the person going through it knew how to handle the stress and the flashbacks. They needed to do it in their own way and at their own pace – without judgment or criticism.

He climbed the platform, stepping to the side to allow a few warriors carrying additional cargo to pass him before he headed through the narrow corridor toward the front. He paused at the entrance to the next section. Almost a dozen warriors were strapped into the rows of seats lining each side. His gaze narrowed on Sula.

She stood out like a glowing beacon among all the black clad warriors in her vivid dark red bodysuit and silver cover. Her feet were clad in a pair of red, knee high boots. A smile curved his lips when she absently tucked her feet under the seat when two large males passed by her. She was totally engrossed in whatever she was reading and did not see him yet.

"Is this seat taken?" Destin asked, grasping the handrail running above the seats and leaning on it.

Sula looked up at him and raised an eyebrow. "Yes, I was saving it for a very special human," she quipped.

Destin glanced around the cabin before turning his gaze back to her. "Looks like you'll have to settle for me," he said, turning and sitting down.

"Any time," she murmured, leaning toward him.

"You two need to get a room," Trig muttered when he walked past Sula and sat down on the seat next to her.

"I should have incinerated him like you suggested," Sula retorted under her breath, sitting back and shooting Trig a cool glance.

"There's still time… or maybe not," Destin briefly chuckled before the shuttle began to vibrate. He quickly pulled the straps over his shoulders and connected the ends. He groaned softly and grabbed her hand before closing his eyes. "God, I hate space ships."

Chapter 12

Almost three hours later, Destin gazed out of the window of the transport as it flew over the area now known as New Chicago. His breath caught when he saw all of the work that had been completed during his absence. Pride swelled through him at seeing the new buildings already completed and the ones still under construction.

The wall that had divided the city was completely gone. The scar from the wall was still present, but he was seeing progress spreading from the middle of the mark dividing the city outward, both east and west. The few historic buildings that were not destroyed in the fighting over the years and were salvageable stood out against the new construction. Cargo transports, assembly drones, and construction bots littered the city.

A soft whistle drew his attention. He looked over at Trig. The other man was staring down at all the destruction.

"I'm taking a guess that this is not the way your city looked before our arrival. Why would you humans destroy your own world?" Trig murmured with a shake of his head.

Destin could see the slight disgust in the other man's expression. He gazed down at the city, seeing it from Trig's point-of-view. His jaw tightened when they passed over the remains of the Harrison Hotel

Electric Garage. Completed in 1930, the building was one of the tallest left standing in the Chicago area after the first year of fighting. It had been Kali's favorite place to retreat and it was where she saved Razor's life.

At the moment, it was surrounded by construction platforms. There was a lot that the Trivators could do with new technology when it came to rebuilding the city, but reconstruction of the historical buildings was left to the humans. The preservation of as many historical sites as possible were paramount to Destin. He wanted future generations to have some visual examples of their history and heritage to show them what life was like before Earth received their first contact.

"What is it?" Sula asked, reaching over to grasp his hand.

"It's good to be home," Destin murmured, staring down at the city.

"It has changed for the better since I was last here. I now see hope for a better future." she said.

"So do I," Destin murmured, his lips curving up at the corners.

Destin felt Sula squeeze his hand. His throat tightened with emotion when the transport made a wide circle over the city. He knew that Trig requested the pilot to do a tour so he could see all the progress that was made since he was off planet.

He looked across the lake. A large skyscraper that looked like it was straight out of a science fiction movie rose up in front of them. It had been under construction when he left, but it looked like it was complete now. He shook his head in disbelief. Something that should have taken years to build was completed in less than one. The same went for many of the other buildings that were standing like sentinels dotted across the horizon. This one would be the headquarters for New Chicago as well as apartments for him and many of the others who had fought beside him. The other buildings were housing for the residents of the city. It had been one of his first goals: shelter from the biting winds and horrific winters for everyone.

"Prepare for landing," the pilot instructed.

Destin sat back and looked out the front windshield. The transport swept in a wide arc before aligning with the opening in the center of the building. He released a deep breath when the vehicle they were traveling in passed through easily. The craft rotated while hovering in the opening. It turned in midair before gently setting down on the landing platform. Even as they undid the straps holding them in, Destin could feel the platform moving the transport out of the landing area and back into the protected area of the building.

He bent and grabbed his duffel bag when the door opened. Trig jumped out and turned to help Sula down. Destin walked to the open door and stared out. A grin lit his face when he saw Tim and Mason standing off to the side near a door. He jumped down out of the transport and shouldered his bag.

He strode across the docking area to his two friends where they stood waiting. They both walked forward, grins on their faces. Tim reached him first and slapped him on the shoulder.

"Good to have you back, Destin," Tim said with a broad grin.

"Ain't that the damn truth," Mason added, his face creasing into a crooked smile.

"This place... The city... They both look incredible," Destin said, waving his hand at the opening behind him. "And this...." He paused, turning in a slow circle as he looked around. "I can't believe it's done."

"Yeah, well, while you were off playing, we've been working our asses off," Mason chuckled. "I tell you what, when those aliens decide they want to build something, they don't do it half-assed."

"It's good to be back and to see what was done while I was away," Destin admitted.

"How's Kali? Is she—," Tim started to say before his smile faded and his lips became taut. "What is she doing here?"

Destin stiffened and turned. Sula and Trig had walked up and were standing behind them. His gaze flickered to Tim and Mason's faces. Both men's expressions held a barely suppressed sneer of contempt.

"This is Councilor Jersula Ikera. She is the Usoleum representative who was assigned to act as a liaison between the Alliance Council and the rebuilding of New Chicago. She is also with me,"

Destin added in a warning tone. "Sula, I'd like to introduce Tim Daniels, my right-hand man, and Mason Cruz, the best damn builder on the planet."

"It is a pleasure to meet both of you again," Sula replied, extending her hand in the Earth greeting.

"Yeah, I'm sure," Tim replied, not taking her outstretched hand. "What do you mean she is with you?"

Destin didn't miss that Mason hadn't said a word, nor the fact that Tim had ignored Sula's outstretched hand. His eyes narrowed at their rudeness and his lips tightened when he saw the flash of uncertainty cross Sula's face. She lowered her hand back to her side. Taking a step closer to her, he wrapped his arm around her waist in a protective, and obviously possessive, statement.

"As in 'she is with me'," Destin repeated with a slight bite to his voice. "Any disrespect toward her is disrespect toward me."

"Destin…," Tim muttered, glancing at Sula then back at Destin.

Destin shook his head grimly. "I want to drop my stuff off at my apartment and give Sula time to settle in. Her belongings are being transferred here. When they arrive, have them delivered to my quarters. I'll meet with the team in one hour to get a briefing on everything that has happened since I left and to discuss any new developments that need to be seen to," he ordered.

"I'll show you to your apartment," Tim muttered, glancing over Destin's shoulder to Trig. "What about that one?"

"Trig will need accommodations, as well," Destin replied.

"I'll show the alien where he can stay and inform the others about Destin's return," Mason muttered with a jerk of his head. "Come on."

Destin didn't miss the tight, assessing look in Trig's gaze at Mason's attitude. He knew that getting his people to accept the aliens wasn't going to be easy. He had hoped that working with them side by side for the past year would have made a difference. True, the alien species doing the rebuilding were smaller and less threatening than the Trivators, but still… Tim and Mason both knew and respected Cutter and some of the other Trivators who had worked with them over the past two years since Colbert's death and the end of the war.

"What floor are we on?" Destin asked, following Tim when he turned toward the lifts set into the wall behind them.

"Nothing but the best for the leader of New Chicago. You get the penthouse," Tim replied in a cool, distant tone. "Most of it isn't furnished. There is still some work that needs to be done on the interior. The kitchen, one of the bathrooms, and the rest of the furnishings should be completed within the next couple of weeks. Still, you'll be able to live in it while the work is being done."

"I'm sure," Destin murmured, holding Sula's hand as the lift rose. "Thanks. What safety precautions have been installed to make sure that the top residents are not cut off in the event of a transport or shuttle accident?" Destin asked, holding Sula's hand when the lift rose.

Tim gazed at him as they entered the lift. "Each unit has an external room with an escape pod capable of holding up to ten people. The pod will automatically eject once life forms are detected inside if there is a structural failure. It is capable of flying up to twenty miles before landing, but is programmed to identify and land in the nearest green area. The Trivators are huge on green areas in their designs. The city will be larger than before, but contain half the number of buildings, if you remember," Tim explained.

"I remembered discussing it in the planning sessions, but wasn't sure it was a possibility," Destin replied with a pleased nod. "In the original designs, there were only two such pods per floor."

"Yeah, one of the alien engineers working on the building thought it might overtax the pods if there were additional people attending a function. She was also concerned that residents could become trapped and unable to reach a pod in the designated area. The change in design is the primary reason the apartments aren't completely finished," Tim explained, stepping out of the elevator on the one hundred and twenty-fifth floor.

"It seems strange being in such a fancy place after so many years living in the rubbles of the city," Destin remarked. He paused when Tim stopped in front of a door across from the lift.

"I know what you mean," Tim stated, pressing his palm to the door panel and waiting for it to open before he stepped back and motioned for Destin and Sula to enter first. "Welcome home, Destin. I'll show you how to program the door."

"Thank you. I appreciate everything you've done while I was gone, Tim. I look forward to finding out what else was accomplished." Destin responded, releasing Sula's hand when she tugged at it so that she could walk over to the large expanse of windows and look down at the city.

"Yeah, well... I'd like to know what in the hell happened to you, too; and, how you ended up with a Usoleum bit... broad on your arm." Tim muttered under his breath. His gaze was fixed on Sula's slender back.

Destin's jaw tightened into a stiff line and he could feel a hard, steely mask settle over his features. An air of displeasure and warning settled between him and his best friend, who was also his second-in-command. The only reason he didn't physically strike out at Tim was because he knew Tim had a right to be distrustful of the Usoleums, namely because of Badrick.

"She isn't like him," Destin stated.

"She looks a helluva a lot like him to me. Same color hair, same color skin, same build," Tim gritted out with a glare of distrust at Sula.

"Tim...," Destin waited until his friend turned his eyes back toward him. "She isn't like Badrick."

"How do you know... for sure?" Tim demanded.

"I know," Destin replied, not clarifying anything.

Tim returned Destin's look with one of his own before he turned back to the door. "I'll go help Mason get the group together," he said.

Destin watched Tim leave. It wasn't until after the door shut that he realized that neither one of them remembered that Tim needed to show him how to reset the control panel. He would have to get Tim to show him when he saw him again.

He turned, feeling the silence descend in the room. His gaze swept over toward Sula where she was silhouetted by the brilliant blue sky and fluffy white clouds. From his vantage point in the room, all he could see was the sky. He walked silently across the thick carpet. He couldn't see the scarred surface of the city until he was almost in front of the window.

"For the first time, I can honestly see a brighter future for my people," Destin said in a quiet voice, staring down at the buildings still under construction. "It is just like Kali and I used to talk and dream about."

He turned his head when Sula didn't answer him. It was only then that he saw the single tear glistening on her cheek. Her arms were wrapped protectively around her waist.

"Sula...," Destin murmured, turning her to face him.

She shook her head and lifted a trembling hand to wipe the tear from her cheek. A soft, uneven laugh escaped her and she blinked. He reached up and grasped her hand before she could return it to her waist.

"I assumed I would not be very welcomed due to the previous events," she said.

"I'll have another talk with them, this time with all of them," Destin promised. "Most of them lost family and friends in the fighting. Badrick was instrumental in supplying weapons to Colbert and his followers. Some of them were separated from their families when Colbert took over. Tim was one of them. His younger sister, Lina, is one of the missing women. A few people who knew Lina said she was rounded up with a group of women and then taken way."

Sula glanced down at their joined hands. Destin could feel her hands tremble as he spoke. It wasn't just that, and he knew it. There were a lot of unhealed scars left over from not only the fight with Colbert but also because of their resentment toward the aliens for making first contact which had set off a horrendous chain of events on Earth.

"I will do everything I can to help locate her. If… If you have any images of the missing women, that will help. I promise, Destin. I promise to do everything I can to locate the rest of the missing women," Sula whispered, gazing at him.

Destin's lips curved into a tender smile and brushed his thumb across her damp cheek. "I know you will. If there is one thing that I have learned about you over the last several months, it is that you are one helluva a tenacious woman when you set your mind to something," he murmured.

"I hate crying," she sniffed with a rueful shake of her head. "I never cried until I met you – well, almost never."

"I know," Destin replied, brushing a tender kiss across her lips. "But, you are a beautiful crier to me."

Sula chuckled and lifted her arms to wrap them around his neck. He could feel her warm breath against his skin and, he moaned softly when his body responded to her as she pressed up against him. His lips moved along her temple and his arms tightened around her waist.

"I wish to hell we were still on the spaceship. I want to make love to you, but I need to go meet with my team," Destin breathed, bending his head to kiss the long column of her neck.

"I could pleasure you before you go," Sula suggested, sliding a hand down his chest and across his flat stomach before she moved it lower. "You would have time for that."

Destin reached down and gripped her wrist. His eyes glittered with desire. His thumb brushed over her wrist, feeling her pulse quicken at his caress.

"It wouldn't be fair to you," he muttered in a terse voice. "Your pleasure comes first."

Sula's bottom lip pouted, and she gave him one of her wide-eyed, sad looks. A giggle escaped her when he groaned and captured her lips, crushing them in a deep, passionate kiss that quickly spiraled out of control. His body throbbed with the desire to take her now.

Releasing her lips, he turned her until she faced away from him. Pressing a series of hot, open-mouth kisses along her neck, he positioned her until she was facing the large expanse of tinted windows that looked out over the city. She gasped softly when he slid his hands down her arms before gripping her hands and placing them on the glass.

"Stay like that," he ordered in a thick voice filled with need.

"Destin," Sula moaned when he lifted the silky, almost transparent silver cover up around her waist and pulled her leggings down to her thighs. "What...?"

"I want you, but I said your pleasure first. We'll come together," he gritted out, unzipping his jeans and pushing them down part way before he wrapped an arm around her waist and aligned his cock with her entrance. "I need to play with you."

"My breasts," she moaned, staring at his reflection in the window. "They... They are so sensitive... Yes!"

Her loud cry echoed through the room when he slid both of his hands up under her top and grasped the pebbled tips between his forefinger and thumb. Her ass moved back against his stomach and her small, firm breasts filled his hands. The sudden touch of liquid on the bulbous tip of his cock told him that Sula's body was already opening for him.

"That's it, Sula, open more for me," Destin murmured, pinching her swelling nipples between his fingers. "Open...."

A shudder ripped through him when he felt his cock start to slide into her. The head of it swelled, filling with blood as he became more aroused. He could feel the four nubs along the inside of her vagina when he slid past them. The moment the head of his cock sank all the way in, he could feel the muscles lining her vaginal channel begin to pulse.

"Sweet heaven," Destin groaned when she tilted her hips so he could sink deeper.

"I... like... this," Sula whispered, trying to keep her head up so she could watch the expressions flashing across his face reflected in the window. "I want more...."

"Oh, you'll get it," Destin promised. "Like this...."

His fingers tightened on the soft flesh of her hips and he thrust forward, burying his cock as far as he could go. Sula's guttural moans echoed through the room and her head fell forward while her fingers curled against the glass.

"You are mine, Sula," Destin muttered, pulling his cock back against the muscles trying to keep him inside before thrusting forward again with hard, deliberate strokes. "Say it. Say you are mine."

Sula's head slowly rose and she gazed back at him with an expression filled with desire. Instead of answering him, she closed her eyes and smiled. For a second, Destin thought she was going to ignore him before he caught her softly whispered words.

"I am yours, Destin, but you are mine as well," she murmured before she opened her eyes to look directly into his. "How does this feel?"

"How does…. What the…?" Destin's strained tone hissed through the air.

"It is a talent Usoleum females have for pleasing her male. I've been practicing it," Sula whispered.

Destin was speechless. A shock ran through his cock, stimulating it until he felt like he was literally going to burst if he didn't come. His body jerked when it happened again, this time a little stronger than before. His hips took on a life of their own, matching the rhythm of the pulses surging around him. The head of his cock was squeezed and released. Every inch of it was caressed, stroked, and squeezed. A shudder ran through him when he felt his body surging toward a powerful orgasm. Sula's body responded, gripping him as if begging for more.

Bending forward, he slid his hand under her shirt again and desperately grabbed for her nipples. His body was draped across her back, his legs together while hers were spread open for him. With a grunt, he pinched her swollen nipples hard, increasing the pressure until she cried out, her body overstimulated and her orgasm coaxing his cock to the edge of his control. Destin's grip tightened when he felt her channel close around him, pulsing and sending miniature shocks along his length.

Another loud cry filled the room, this time a masculine one when Destin's control snapped and he came hard, filling her womb with his hot semen. His arms pulled her up against him and he straightened his legs until she was caught completely in his grasp. She was his captive, their bodies locked together.

"I am yours, Sula," Destin muttered, locking his legs so that he didn't sink down to the floor as the last of his semen drained from him into her.

"I know," Sula whispered in a shaky, relaxed voice.

Destin chuckled and slowly lowered her feet back to the floor. It would be a few minutes before he could safely pull free. Until then, he rubbed his hands up and down her side and stared out over the city.

"You've been holding back on me. I think we'll need to do a little more exploring to discover what else you can do." he murmured.

Sula groaned when she felt his cock begin to slide from her over-sensitive channel. Destin had to bite the inside of his cheek to keep from echoing her groan when she tightened briefly as the flange around the head of his cock caught before sliding free. His hand ran down over the curve of her ass and without thinking, he slapped it lightly.

"Oh!" Sula reacted with surprise, straightening and glancing over her shoulder with wide eyes. "Why did you do that?"

Destin reached out and rubbed where he had gently slapped her. "For almost making me come first, and because I wanted to," he replied with a grin before he remembered he was supposed to meet with Tim and the others. "I have to go. Your belongings should be delivered at any time. Stay here, if you don't mind, until I return."

Sula nodded, pulling up her leggings and smoothing her cover over her hips before she turned to face him. He cleared his expression so she couldn't see that he was concerned for her safety. Tim and Mason's barely veiled hostility towards her worried him. He pulled his jeans up and tucked his shirt in. Thank goodness he did not remember to put his belt on this morning, or he might have ended up coming in his shorts.

"I will. It will give me a chance to explore and complete some work that I haven't finished." Sula promised, glancing around the sparsely decorated living room. Destin leaned forward, brushing a lingering kiss on her lips. Once again, he wished he could just say to hell with all the responsibility he had taken on. He would much rather spend the rest of the day exploring Sula – exploring *with* Sula, he corrected in his horny mind with a sense of exasperation.

"You are addictive," he muttered, reluctantly pulling away and turning. "I'll see you in a few hours."

"I'll be here," Sula said, following him to the door and opening it. "Destin...."

Destin turned to look at her. "Yes...."

Sula opened her mouth and closed it before she opened it again. "Be safe," she said.

"Always," he promised, grimacing when the lift opened and Trig stood in the middle of it. "Surprised to see you here, Trig."

"I thought I'd give you two time to settle in," Trig quipped, his assessing gaze taking in their flushed and tousled appearances with a grin. "Looks like I was right."

"Shut up, Trig," Destin muttered, walking over and stepping into the lift.

Thankfully, the lift doors closed and cut off Trig's laughter. Destin did not want Sula to be embarrassed. He leaned back and shook his head.

"I can always order you thrown in jail," Destin muttered when the lift began to descend.

"It wouldn't help you. I'd just escape," Trig replied, leaning back against the railing.

Chapter 13

Prymorus studied the surrounding area. The ruins of buildings rose up all around him. The men with him were gathering an array of weapons. It was seldom that a Waxian would wage full out war with another species. Their preference was strike from within, cutting the artery of their prey and watching them bleed to death. Prymorus would leave the direct attacks to his Drethulan counterparts.

"What have you found?" Prymorus asked, not turning to look at the other man, but continuing to scan the area.

"The surrounding buildings are clear. They appear to be abandoned," the man stated.

"Search them again and set up guards. I want to make sure the perimeter is secure. I do not want the Trivators to be alerted to our presence yet. We will set up a command center in the abandoned building to the left. Cover the freighter; I don't want it found," Prymorus ordered.

"Yes, sir," the other Waxian male said with a bow of his head before he backed away and turned.

"Retris...," Prymorus said.

"Yes, sir," Retris replied, turning to face Prymorus again.

"I notified the Jawtaw, Omini, that we are here. He is sending a Raftian as a liaison for me; search him thoroughly before bringing him here," Prymorus ordered.

"I will supervise the search myself," Retris promised, placing his hand on the pistol at his side.

"I will hold you personally responsible if anything should happen," Prymorus responded before dismissing the other man.

He walked over to one of the buildings he chose for his headquarters. It was a far cry from his accommodations on Dises V or the other dozens of places he controlled for the Waxian regime on different worlds. While he had no need for a permanent residence, Prymorus learned to appreciate the luxuries his authority afforded him.

Stepping through the crumbling door of the building, he glanced around the dim interior. His top lip pulled upward in distaste when he saw the condition of the ruined foyer. A long counter divided a section on the left side of the room. The top of the counter was covered in dust. One of the paintings hung at an odd angle. The painting that had once hung next to the first now lay broken behind the counter.

The bottom floor of the building opened into a spacious area where numerous chairs, low tables, and long couches resided, eerie reminders of the once magnificent building where humans came to gather and rest. Large and small fake plants lay on their sides and were covered in dust. On the far right side, it appeared to have been some form of dining section.

Prymorus walked over to the desk area. His sharp gaze settled on a door that separated the large open area from the section behind the counter. He tested the handle and discovered it was locked. He took a step back and kicked just above the handle. The loud sound of the door breaking echoed through the interior. He watched dispassionately as the door swung inward.

He pushed it out of the way and walked behind the desk, noting the different items on the counter behind it. It reminded him of a resting facility on several of the Spaceports he had visited. Stepping over the debris, he walked around the back of the partition. Satisfaction coursed through him when he discovered a large room. It would work well as a temporary base.

He turned when he heard footsteps in the other area. Drawing his laser pistol, he walked over and peered around the wall. Several men were bringing in equipment.

"Install the communication systems in here," Prymorus ordered.

"Yes, sir," the men replied, slightly out of breath.

Prymorus watched the men unload several of the crates of equipment onto the counter. It would take them approximately an hour to clear the back area and set everything up. In the meantime, he would return to the freighter they had stolen and work from there.

"General Achler, the Raftian has notified us that he can leave without being noticed," Retris said, falling into step next to Prymorus as he strode across the road.

"Make sure he comes alone and unarmed," Prymorus instructed.

"Yes, sir," Retris replied.

Prymorus' lips tightened. "When he arrives, bring him to me," he ordered.

"Immediately, General," Retris replied. He paused and turned to bark out a command to a warrior waiting for his instructions. "Tell the Raftian to meet at the chosen rendezvous point. I will bring him in from there."

Prymorus continued to the freighter. It was covered with a reflective fabric, making it virtually invisible from above. Bowing his head, he stepped under the cover and strode up the platform. Within minutes, he was settled in the small room he had appropriated to use for an office.

He quickly accessed his console, bringing up the vidcom and the image feeds from his team leaders. He wanted confirmation of the deaths of the women and children at the Trivators' residences, and then he wanted to broadcast the vidcoms to Razor, Hunter, and the Alliance Council. It would be a definitive message to the rest of the Council of what was to come.

A cold fury pooled in his veins when he watched his men die instead of the helpless women and children they were sent to kill. He could not care less about the men; they were expendable. No, the fury came from the knowledge that not only did the men fail their mission, an act that would have gotten each one of them executed anyway, but Razor and Hunter had been on the Rathon when they should have been detained on Dises V. He wanted to know how they managed to escape.

He zoomed in on each face, focusing first on the team attacking Lord Hunter's residence. He paused, staring at the blazing eyes of the man with a long scar across one cheek – Lord Ajaska Ja Kel Coradon, the Kassisan Ambassador to the Alliance. The suspicion that Dakar, the Kassisan he dealt with on Dises V, was a traitor among the Drethulan ranks solidified into fact. Dakar must have helped them escape. He knew the inner workings of the transport systems on Dises V.

Prymorus' hand clenched in an effort to keep from putting his fist through the image on the screen. Releasing a long, deep breath, he continued the video and paused on the next useful image. Facial recognition stated this was Scout, the father of Razor and Hunter. Prymorus studied the older man's face. With a swipe of his finger, he added the him to the file for termination. Before this was over, he would eliminate the families of each member of the Alliance Council, starting with the Trivators. They *would* fear him. They would damn well quake in their boots wondering what he would do next.

The next image showed two additional Trivators. He immediately recognized both men – Hunter and Dagger. Dagger should have died in the fight rings. Cordus Kelman had used the Trivator for his own personal financial gain for years. It had been audacious, Prymorus would give him that, but in the end it had clearly been a mistake, one that resulted in Kelman's death.

He quickly ran through the man's history. A sneer curled his lip when he discovered that the man was mated to a human female named Jordan. What infuriated him even more was the fact that Jordan was the sibling of Taylor, the young human female that escaped captivity on Dises V.

"I will strike at your heart and rip it out, female, making sure that you feel the pain as I do it," Prymorus murmured, sliding his fingers across an image of Jesse, Jordan, and Taylor Sampson. "Now, to find the weakness of Razor's mate."

Prymorus brought up the next file. His lips tightened when he saw Razor's cold face. He followed each move in slow motion, pausing when he saw the blurred image of another man come into view. Zooming in on the screen, he captured the image and tapped to process the facial recognition. Frustration burned through him when it came up negative. Continuing the feed, he paused it again when the familiar coloring of an Usoleum moved into view.

"Well, well, well, another member of the Council has joined the fight," Prymorus murmured, studying the female's face. The facial recognition immediately identified her. "Princess Jersula Ikera, a member of the royal house and Councilor Select for Earth."

"General Achler," Retris' voice murmured behind him. "The Raftian has arrived."

Prymorus started to close the image on his screen, then paused. The Raftian might know where Princess Ikera was at the moment. Rising out of his seat, he nodded to Retris. He folded his hands behind his back, pulling the sharp blade from the sheath he had attached at his waist.

The Raftian entered and warily stood near the entrance. The small reptilian creature's tongue swept out and nervously ran over his lips. The male was dressed in a long dark green tunic, baggy black trousers and short black boots. His clothing was covered with building dust. Pinned to his chest was a badge showing he was a maintenance worker.

"Identify yourself," Prymorus demanded.

"I am called Cartis. I do maintenance, and work as a Level Three builder." the male replied in a deep, rough voice.

"Did the Jawtaw tell you who I am?" Prymorus asked, gazing at the other alien male.

"Yes," Cartis replied with a bow of his head in acknowledgement before falling silent.

Prymorus walked around his desk and over to the other male. Lifting his hand, he used the tip of his knife to tilt the Raftian's head back. He glanced under Cartis' chin. A small, intricate tattoo was visible in the dim lighting of the cabin.

Prymorus pulled the knife away, drawing a thin cut under the reptilian's chin. The tattoo was a mark showing the Raftian had spent time in a Tartarus prison colony.

"How did you escape the prison colony?" Prymorus asked suspiciously.

"There was a prison break ten revolutions of Tartarus sun ago. You'll find it documented in file E48231. I was in Cell Level 59. A Drethulan named Drex was in the cell next to me. After we escaped, he hired me to kidnap fighters for his fight rings. We both eventually ended up on Bruttus, a spaceport located in the Tressalon galaxy, and he took over a fight arena called *The Hole* after killing the previous owner," Cartis replied.

"What happened to Drex?" Prymorus asked dispassionately.

"He was killed by the Trivators. Drex risked everything to host one of Cordus Kelman's fighters, a Trivator, then capture Chancellor Razor. The fight ring was shut down and Bruttus is now under the control of the Alliance Council," Cartis replied, pulling a dirty cloth out of his pocket and holding it under his chin to stop the bleeding.

"How did you get here?" Prymorus inquired.

"Bruttus was crawling with Trivators after that, but before I left, I saw an unusual female, a human, one that I didn't have a chance in hell of taking with me, but I knew there'd be a high demand to own one. I bartered for transportation off the spaceport. I eventually ran into Omini. He knew of a group running a slave ring that had purchased a large group of human females. We went to find out where they came from, but arrived too late. The females were delivered to an Armatrux trading asteroid to house until they could be sold. Two Trivators discovered the females, killed the guards, and returned them here. There are big credits to be had.... Omini said he ran weapons with you when he was younger and that you might overthrow the Armatrux."

"My interest is larger than the trafficking of a few human females," Prymorus stated with a wave of his hand. "If you are shipping slaves off the planet, you must have some knowledge of the Trivator security and personnel."

"I know there are not as many as there were. A Trivator named Cutter has taken command of the forces here. I was told Chancellor Razor eliminated the last of the large scale human resistance. While small pockets still exist, the Trivators are monitoring them and are working with the human leaders to contain it," Cartis said, with a wary expression.

"I am aware of the events you speak of. I want specific information about the security of their base camps, and what is happening within them," Prymorus demanded, twirling the knife he was holding between his fingers.

Cartis eyed the knife before jerking his gaze back to Prymorus' face. "I saw an arrival today at the city's main headquarters. I heard their leader had returned from the Trivator home world. I can gather the other information you are requesting. One of my assignments is in the Trivator base, down near the lake," Cartis muttered, nervously licking his lips again. "I also overheard that a Waxian ship was destroyed near one of the outer planets."

"I am aware of the Waxian warship's destruction. What can you tell me about the human leader?" Prymorus demanded with a wave of his hand.

"I heard his name is Destin Parks and that his sibling is the mate of Chancellor Razor. He arrived with the new Usoleum Councilor and another Trivator a few hours ago," Cartis informed, blinking nervously.

Prymorus took a step closer to the Raftian. He assessed the male for several long seconds. The male could prove useful – as would the Jawtaw. The Waxians and Armatrux had a tense working arrangement. He would not contact them until he was ready to make a move. "You will work for me now. I want information on the Trivators movements. I also want information on Destin Parks and the Usoleum Council woman," he instructed briskly.

"I...," Cartis started to argue before reluctantly nodding his head. "I will find out whatever information you request."

"Make sure you do, Raftian. Keep our meetings private if you value your life," Prymorus warned.

"What about Omini? Will he be informed about what is going on?" Cartis asked.

"I will deal with the Jawtaw. You will bring a detailed report to me of the Trivator movements in this area, but more importantly, I want the location and movements of Destin Parks."

"It will take me a few days to do it without raising suspicion," Cartis warned. "The last thing I want is for the Trivators to discover the shipment of females scheduled for departure at the end of the month. Omini wouldn't like it if we lost that many credits."

"I will give you three revolutions of the planet to get me the information. If you do not have it, I will find someone who can," Prymorus stated in a cold tone that left no doubt in Cartis' mind as to what would happen to him if he failed. "Go and report back in three Earth days."

"Yes, sir," Cartis replied, backing out of the room before turning and hurrying through the freighter.

Prymorus stood still, deep in thought. The Armatrux could be a problem, but they would scatter the moment the Drethulans arrived. The Armatrux could fight, but their numbers were decimated centuries before when they tried to take over the Drethulan home world, unaware of what lay beneath the sands. Still, they may prove to be a good distraction when the Drethulans arrived. Until then, he would begin preparations for an internal attack.

"Slice through the artery and watch them bleed before removing their head," Prymorus murmured, returning to his seat and the neglected vidcom screen. He sat back in the chair, gazing thoughtfully at the image. "Councilor Ikera and Destin Parks will be a good beginning."

Chapter 14

Destin leaned back against the lift and ignored Trig. He had not felt this relaxed – ever. His body was still humming from the experience a short time ago and he could not quite hide the pleased smile that curved his lips.

It had been a long time since he completely let go of the strict control he kept over his mind and body. He wasn't exactly sure what the hell just happened upstairs between him and Sula, but whatever it was, he wanted more. He felt a connection to her that went beyond what they shared on board the *Star Raider*. The wild abandon, with an almost primitive explosion of need, had excited him with a vision of what the future could hold.

"You smell like you had a good time," Trig muttered with a sigh.

"Keep your damn nose out of my business," Destin retorted dryly.

"That's a little hard to do when you have a sense of smell like we do," Trig replied, glancing at Destin with a pained expression. "We are also in an enclosed space and I have to tell you it has been a long time since I've been with a female, so you 'rubbing it in my face', as Jordan would say, isn't helping matters."

"Breathe through your mouth," Destin suggested, straightening when the lift slowed to a stop.

"Great, then I get to taste it as well as smell it," Trig muttered under his breath. "That doesn't help, Destin."

If he wasn't feeling so good, he might have been annoyed. At the moment, though, he was feeling good and he wasn't going to allow some sex-deprived Trivator to get under his skin. In fact, the more he thought about it, the more the image of the fierce alien having a set of blue-balls, if they had them, amused him.

"You don't know what you are missing, Trig," Destin replied with a deep, satisfied sigh.

"Something tells me you are going to enjoy rubbing in that fact," Trig muttered, following Destin when he pushed open the door to the office three floors below his apartment.

"If it drives you nuts – yep!" Destin chuckled before he grew serious when he saw the group waiting for them.

"They don't look too happy to see you," Trig murmured under his breath.

"I'm sure you being here isn't helping," Destin replied before stepping forward with a serious expression. "Let's go to the conference room – assuming there is one – and deal with your concerns."

"Is the alien coming, too?" Jason asked with a hint of a sneer in his voice.

"What's with the alien glued to your ass, Destin? Since when have they been privy to our meetings?" Richard asked with a frown.

"Yeah, you never let that other one interfere with what we were doing," Troy added, shifting uncomfortably when he glanced between Destin and Trig.

Destin studied each face intently, trying to determine which one of them might support him. Out of the seven men standing in front of him, none of them looked like they were on the fence about this particular issue.

"Come on, guys. Get your panties out of the crack of your ass. I thought only women wore them that way. It's good to see you back, Destin," a cheerful voice commented from behind Tim. "Move your ass, Tim, before I put my foot up it as well."

"You'd better watch your mouth, Beth, or I'll be telling Mary on you," Mike warned, half-serious, half-joking.

"If you do, you'd better plan to never sleep again, Mikey," Beth laughed, squeezing past Tim and walking up to Destin. She stared at him for a moment before she threw her arms around his neck and hugged him. "Grandma said to give you a hug when you got back," she whispered near his ear before releasing him and stepping back. "How's Kali doing?"

Destin smiled at Beth Clark's glowing face. She had filled out over the last few months. He had known Beth since she came home from the hospital twenty years ago. She was the granddaughter of Mary, one of his most staunch supporters. Mary and Beth had lived in the apartment beneath them. A few months after the Trivators appeared they came out of hiding and found him and Kali.

"She's doing great. She wanted me to tell you and Mary hello. I'll show you some pictures of her and Ami later," Destin replied.

Beth shoved her hands into the back pockets of her faded jeans. The movement pulled her pink T-shirt tight across her breasts. She gazed with amusement at the alien standing next to Destin when he smothered what sounded like a muted grunt or groan. Tilting her head to the side, her dark brown eyes twinkling with mischief. The long rows of tiny black braids fell to the side.

"Hi, I'm Bethany Clark, but everyone calls me Beth," Beth said, sticking her hand out.

"No, we all call you Pain-in-the-Ass," Justin snorted under his breath loud enough to be heard.

Beth glanced over her shoulder and glared at Justin. "You're just jealous because I can make it through the patrol without getting winded, old man," she said, tossing her mane of dark braids over her shoulder and looking back at Trig. "Ignore the sour pusses, most of them are just mad that Destin took some time off and didn't bring Kali back."

Destin watched Trig's reaction to Beth with a raised eyebrow. Trig looked like she had thrown a right hook instead of trying to shake his hand. The Trivator's gaze was frozen on Beth's warm, dark brown face. Beth used to tease Kali and him when she was little, saying she was the chocolate filling between two vanilla cookies. In other words, the delicious part. Right now, Trig looked like he would love to be the one eating Beth up.

"Uh, I think it is time we moved into the conference room. There is a lot going on and some possible new threats that I would like to discuss with everyone. I'd also like to know what has been happening since I've been gone," Destin said, turning to look pointedly at Tim. "Tim, you can start the briefing."

The group slowly turned and filed through the door behind them. They continued down the hall and into a large room. In the center was a table with a few modern features. It reminded Destin of the conference rooms he had been in on the *Star Raider*.

"This is totally cool, Destin. I asked the ladies who installed it to show me how it works," Beth said, sliding down to sit near the head of the table. "We each have a control station. Destin, your console has the ability to lock any of us out."

Destin listened to Beth explain the operation of the console before turning the meeting over to Tim. His second-in-command started off hesitantly at first, his gaze moving to Trig when he started explaining some of the resistance they were still facing and some issues with rolling out the housing for the residents by sections, trying to focus on families first. Soon, the intense discussion and the need to be proactive in rebuilding the city relaxed the group, and they grew more comfortable in discussing each project they were currently working on.

"What about you, Destin? You said you had a possible situation that we needed to be aware of," Tim said when the last of the current agenda was discussed.

Destin glanced at Trig, then looked at the men and Beth sitting around the table. He had fought alongside each of them for almost ten years now. They had patched each other up, listened to each other when the grief or stress became too much, and watched each other's backs so they could grab a few hours sleep without fear of getting their throats slit.

"There was a situation on Rathon, the Trivator home world," Destin said, leaning forward and resting his elbows on the table in front of him.

"What kind of situation?" Mason asked.

"A group of aliens known as the Waxians tried to assassinate Razor and Hunter's families, including Kali and Ami," Destin replied with a heavy sigh.

"Well, if they have so many fucking problems on their own world, why did they come screw ours up? Wouldn't it have made sense to just keep your trash to yourself?" Jason asked in a bitter voice.

"Watch your language, Jason. Mikey might tell Grandma on you," Beth murmured.

Jason picked up a pen on the table and threw it at Beth. Destin was not sure exactly what happened next. One second Trig was sitting slightly off to the side, the next, Jason was on his back on the conference room table with Trig snarling down at him, his hand wrapped around Jason's throat.

Destin pushed his chair back and stood up. The other men did the same and aimed their guns at Trig. Only Beth seemed to have her head in the game. She had launched onto the table and knelt between them, her hand pressed against Trig's shoulder.

"Down, big guy," Beth whispered in a soft voice. "You don't strike me as the temperamental sort. What triggered you?"

"Beth, get away from him," Mike muttered, thumbing the safety off his gun.

"You boys are always playing rough," Beth replied, not raising her voice. "He was just playing, Trig."

"He threw something at you," Trig gritted out.

Beth chuckled. "Where were you when I was ten and the local gang was throwing rocks at me and Grandma? Jason didn't mean nothing. He's just sore over losing Kali. Let him go," she whispered, sliding her hand down his arm to his wrist and wrapping her fingers around it. "Let him go, big guy. He didn't mean no harm."

Beth's loud gasp filled the room when Trig suddenly released Jason and wrapped his arm around her, pulling her off the table and into his arms. Loud curses echoed over the sound of Jason's coughing. Destin ignored them all. He had seen this aggressive, protective behavior before – in Razor. His gaze moved to Beth's face. Instead of being scared, she looked confused... and amused as hell.

"Beth, why don't you take Trig for a cup of coffee?" Destin suggested with a pointed look.

"Coffee? Hell, I'm thinking a keg of beer," she muttered. "Do I walk or do I get carried?"

"I think carried for the moment," Destin said with a nod of his head. "You can work on the walking once he calms down."

Beth looked at Destin with a cheeky grin. "Has he had his rabies shots?" she asked with a raised eyebrow.

"I don't know. You'll have to ask him that," Destin replied, running a tired hand down his face.

"Destin...," Trig muttered, looking conflicted and a bit dazed.

"I've got seven men with enough firepower to stop a tank, I think I'll be safe," Destin interrupted, dropping his hand back down to his side. "Go on. Get a drink, calm down, and avoid Mary at the moment if you value your life."

"Who is Mary?" Trig asked.

"I'll explain," Beth promised, seeing the expression of exasperation on Destin's face. "That way, big guy. To the fancy coffee machine."

Destin watched Trig carry Beth out of the conference room. He shook his head and glanced around the room. With a wave of his hand, he indicated to the men to put their weapons away and return to their seats.

"What about Beth?" Mike asked, staring at the door with a look of indecision.

"Trust me, Trig is in more danger at the moment than Beth is," Destin replied, sitting down in his chair. "Now, where was I...?"

Chapter 15

Sula shook her head and groaned. Closing her eyes, she drew in a series of deep, calming breaths before she opened her eyes and gazed out of the window. She was having trouble focusing on the report in front of her. All she could think about was Destin.

"Open file Earth - 21589," Sula requested, rising to step closer to the window so she could look down over the city.

"Authorization," the computer responded.

"JSula voice authorization," she replied.

"Authorization for JSula granted. File Earth - 21589 accessed," the computer responded.

"List contacts of Badrick on Earth," Sula requested.

"Documented contacts include the following individuals: Destin Parks – adversary. Recorded encounter available; Colbert Allen – allied. Recorded encounter available…." the computer began listing in a soft, feminine voice.

"Display recorded encounter with Destin Parks," Sula murmured, turning to look down at the tablet she had placed on the long table in front of the couch.

The holographic image of a dimly lit room appeared. The image wavered slightly. Badrick must have been wearing it on his outer clothing. Sula had recently discovered a cache of the vidcoms hidden among the files Badrick had uploaded to a personal account file on Usoleum.

She wasn't quite sure why he decided to keep a record of his encounters. The only thing she could deduce was he wanted to use them for blackmail, or perhaps as protection. She had finally broken through the encrypted passwords he used, which had been a very delicate process because many were programed to auto-erase if too many unsuccessful attempts were made. As it was, Sula had lost close to a dozen of the files before she discovered a backdoor.

Her breath caught when Badrick walked down a long hallway. People lined the wide corridor. There were women with small children, more men and women cleaning weapons or working a variety of projects, and still others with bandages or sleeping on pallets on the floor. Each one stopped and stared at Badrick, their eyes filled with fear and distrust. There were a few times when Badrick paused and turned to face a human. Sula quickly discovered he only did it when he passed certain young females.

Sula's heart broke at the exhaustion on some of the their faces. Badrick turned back to face the long stretch of hallway. Her eyes widened when she saw Kali walking down the hall with long, confident strides. This was a woman far different from the one she met at the wedding. Kali was dressed all in black, her hair was short and she had a weapon strapped to each thigh. Her face was a cool, expressionless mask.

"What is your purpose here, alien?" Kali demanded, stopping in front of Badrick.

Sula could almost feel Badrick's gaze moving over Kali. She could see a faint flicker of disgust in Kali's eyes before it disappeared. Sula lifted her arms and rubbed her hands up and down them when a shiver ran through her body. Kali's hands now rested on the weapons at her side.

"I came to speak with the – leader – Destin Parks," Badrick stated with a sniff of disdain.

"What is your business with him?" Kali asked, not moving out of his way.

"Maybe he wants to surrender, Kali," a man standing behind Kali muttered.

"Hardly," Badrick replied. "I came to negotiate assistance in the fight over this region."

"What kind of assistance?" Kali demanded, her gaze narrowing on Badrick's face.

"In defeating Colbert Allen," Badrick responded. "I believe that is what this human rebel wishes to accomplish."

Sula watched Kali's face tighten when Badrick mentioned Allen's name. She made a mental note to research everything she could about the human male. The two men standing behind Kali stepped forward in unison.

"You will wait here," Kali ordered. "If Destin agrees to see you, your guards will not be allowed to enter the room."

"I do not take orders from a female," Badrick retorted.

Kali took a step closer to Badrick. Sula drew in a deep breath when she saw the intense expression in

Kali's eyes. Her hand moved to her throat and she waited for Kali's reply.

"You do while you are here or you and your guards are dead," Kali stated.

The image moved around the corridor when Badrick turned to glance around him. The two guards he brought with him were standing frozen behind him, guns pressed against their temples. Sula counted at least a dozen or more weapons aimed at the former Usoleum Councilor. Swallowing, she waited for Badrick's response.

"My guards will remain here. I will let Parks decide if you remain in the room," Badrick replied.

Kali stepped back several steps before she turned on her heel and strode down the hallway. Sula waited in tense silence, fascinated by the scene in front of her. The corridor that had been teaming with activity minutes earlier was now absent of anyone not pointing a weapon at their alien visitors. Sula could hear Badrick's heavy breathing.

Sula frowned when a man came down the corridor instead of Kali. The man stopped in front of Badrick, looked him up and down, then motioned for Badrick to follow him. Everywhere Sula saw a face, she saw the same look of hatred and distrust. She had never been on a newly acquired world before, so this was a new experience for her.

"Badrick," a deep voice greeted.

A wave of recognition swept through Sula and she crossed over to sit on the couch. Her gaze was glued to Destin's face. Reaching out, her fingers paused just a breath away from his image. She ached to touch his face.

"I am pleased that you ordered the female to allow us to speak in private," Badrick murmured in approval.

"What do you want, alien?" Destin demanded, keeping the desk between him and Badrick.

Sula could just imagine Badrick's expression, or at least the one he would like to give Destin. She had faced Destin when she first arrived and remembered how terrified she was at the icy hardness in his eyes and voice. Yet, even then she was attracted to him, which caused a great deal of confused and conflicted thoughts long after they parted.

"I have a... what is the word you humans use... a proposition for you," Badrick replied with a wave of his hand. Sula noticed a glimmer when he did it and paused the vidcom for a moment.

"Enlarge area around the hand," she ordered, waiting. "Enlarge. Capture image and run analysis with detailed graphics. Return to normal and continue playing."

"What kind of proposition?" Destin asked.

"If the fighting does not cease between you and the other human, I will not be able to protect this area any longer. The Trivators have already expressed a desire to end all conflict so rebuilding can occur. Their Chancellor, a Trivator named Razor, is already on his way," Badrick said in a calm, almost bored tone.

Sula caught a glimpse of Badrick's finger running along the edge of the desk in the vidcom. He turned his hand over and she saw the line of dust along the tip before he wiped his finger clean and his hand disappeared from view again. Her gaze returned to Destin's face.

"If he comes, we'll deal with him just like we have every other alien that has set foot on this side of Chicago," Destin replied in a clipped tone.

"I find you humans rather amusing. You say such things without realizing how… inadequate you really are against the powers of the Trivators," Badrick replied with a loud sigh.

"What's your point, alien?" Destin demanded, crossing his arms.

"Razor is the last resort. He will destroy the city, leaving nothing. The Destroyers will flatten it, scanning for any life form and eliminating it without mercy. The Trivator will annihilate all life-forms from this city – but, there is a way to prevent that," Badrick stated.

Sula's fists clenched at the smug tone in Badrick's voice. Oh, how she wanted to put her fist through his face. It was a good thing he was dead or she would've killed him.

"And this is where you tell me what your 'proposition' is, I take it," Destin remarked, dropping his arms to grip the back of the chair.

"Yes," Badrick replied. "I propose supplying you and your followers with alien weaponry and support. If you were to defeat Colbert Allen and regain control of the southern half of Chicago, I could convince Razor to ignore this… region. You would deal directly with me."

"And, what do you want in exchange for supplying us with this support?" Destin asked in a voice that chilled Sula's blood.

"Don't," she whispered, already knowing what Badrick was going to say. She shook her head. "Don't, Badrick."

"Human females – within a specific age range and healthy, of course. Those that are not within this range would be of little use to me. Females like the pne that greeted me would be sufficient. Though, that specific female would need to be retrained," Badrick said.

"Why?" Destin asked, staring at Badrick through narrowed eyes.

"The universe is about credits, Mr. Parks. Healthy human females would bring a large number of credits. Your world has a plentiful supply of them and this…." Once again, Badrick's hand waved into view. "Their lives would be no worse off than what they have here. There is a shortage of females in space. Business is about supply and demand. You supply me with what I need and in return, I give you Chicago. As I stated, I would start by taking a retainer of the dark-haired female that greeted me. In return, I'll have a shipment of weapons delivered to you by tonight."

Destin slowly walked around the desk. Pride flooded Sula when she saw Badrick take several steps back at Destin's approach. Unconsciously, she rubbed her left fist with her right hand.

"If you so much as set one foot back on the north side of Chicago, I will slit your throat. Every man, woman, and child are under my protection. In fact, if I find out you've touched one hair on the head of any human woman; I will hunt your ass down and stake it to the tallest building still standing and leave it to rot. Tim! Jason!"

"Yes, Destin," Tim said, appearing immediately in the doorway.

"Toss this piece of alien trash and his comrades over the wall and make sure none of them come back. If he tries anything, kill him. If he even looks at a woman, kill him. Do you understand?" Destin ordered.

"Oh, I understand, alright," Tim replied in a grim tone.

"You have made a vital mistake, Mr. Parks," Badrick hissed out, stumbling when Tim grabbed his arm and he jerked it free. "Chancellor Razor will level this city and everyone will die anyway."

"Get him out of here," Destin ordered again with a jerk of his head.

Sula watched as Badrick and his guards were roughly escorted away from the building. Whatever happened after they stepped outside was lost when he cut the recording. She sat back, her stomach churning with nausea.

The thought of what must have happened to the women that Colbert sold to Badrick was too much for her. Rising off the couch, Sula hurried to the bathroom. She barely made it to the toilet before she threw up. Her legs shook and she sank down to the cool tile, her hand braced on it to keep from falling over. She groan softly, gave up, and slid down until her forehead rested against the cool tile.

"Eighteen…," she whispered, blinking back the tears in her eyes. "Eighteen females are still missing."

She closed her eyes. Her mind swirled, replaying the vidcom over and over. There was something bugging her, something she couldn't quite put her finger on. Rolling onto her back, she pressed the palm of her right hand against her forehead.

"What am I missing?" she whispered, thinking about each part until her eyes snapped open. "The ring… I have to locate the ring!"

Sitting up, Sula grabbed the edge of the counter and pulled herself up. She quickly rinsed her mouth and cleaned her teeth. A shudder went through her when she saw that she was so pale, she looked almost as white as her hair. Wrinkling her nose, she shook her head and reached for the towel hanging on the bar next to the sink. She wiped her hands and mouth before pushing back her hair. Her color was slowly coming back.

"You have to pull yourself together, Sula," she firmly told her reflection. "You are Princess Jersula Ikera of Usoleum. You have a duty and a responsibility to your people and to the women who were under the protection of the Usoleum government to find and return those women to their world. You will not fail!"

Nodding her head, she gave herself one last, quick assessment. *Good enough*, she thought. She did not have time to be ill. Over the next few days if she felt ill again she would take a transport over to the medical unit on the Trivator's base and have the healer give her a booster to help prevent her from catching another horrible virus. Until then, she would have to be careful.

"Now, to see if the ring is what I think it is," Sula whispered, replacing the towel and walking back to the living room.

Within minutes, she was gazing at the three-dimensional image the computer recreated. She scanned all the documentation pertaining to Badrick's remains. No ring was mentioned in the inventory of his personal belongs. She opened an image of his body laid out on a long metal table, and turned it, trying to focus on his hands, not the puncture wounds that riddled his body. She had to close her eyes and focus on her breathing to keep the nausea from overwhelming her again before she could continue. Opening her eyes, she carefully examined his hands. They were bare.

She finally closed all the files, accessed the communications array set up around the planet, and sent a message to her brother. It would take hours, if not days for him to receive it, but she wanted him – and her parents – to know that she was making progress.

Once she was finished, she quickly returned to the bathroom to refresh herself before gathering her tablet and her baton. She needed to find Destin and inform him of what she suspected. It was imperative that she return to the quarters that were assigned to her at the former US Army National Guard building – the quarters that once belonged to Badrick.

Chapter 16

Destin stood with his back to the other men in the room. Over the past three hours, they explained the changes that occurred while he was gone. Most of them were in alignment with what he set in motion before he left. Some, though, were not.

"How many are missing?" he asked in a low, somber tone.

"Ten – that we know of – who knows how many more that we don't. We still don't have an accurate count from the south side of the city. Colbert scared most of the decent residents into every nook and cranny they could find. At times, it's like rats pouring out of the sewers when we go searching for them. Mason has about three-quarters of the underground system – both subway and sewer – cleared," Tim said.

Destin turned to see their grim faces. There was no proof that the missing women Tim just told him about were victims of a crime, but he wanted to make sure.

"What do we know? I want facts only, no speculation – yet," Destin said.

"They were working in different parts of the city under construction. Six were working with the rebuilding. They were near the old downtown area. Three more worked in Food Services and Clerical Support, so they commuted every day to the Trivator base," Tim said, nodding at the map showing the last known location of the women.

"What about the last one?" Destin asked, walking closer to the map to study it.

"Her name is Alissa Garcia. She's a thirty-eight year old Hispanic female with about ten years under her belt with the Chicago Police Department before the world went to hell. I worked with her on several cases when I was with the force. As you know, over the last year, I've been able to recruit those in the force that haven't fled or died. We've got about one hundred and fifty of our old force back together and about two hundred new recruits that we're training. I hate to admit it, but Cutter was a huge help in that. He sent men to help train us on the new transports and other equipment. Alissa was working closely with the Trivators to train the recruits. She disappeared a couple of days ago. No one has seen or heard from her since."

"Who was the last person to see her?" Destin asked.

Richard hesitated and glanced around the table at the other men. His lips tightened for a moment before he released a deep sigh and glanced down at the table.

"Cutter," Richard finally admitted with a grimace. "She was last seen with the Trivator."

"I knew it! None of them can be trusted," Jason exclaimed, slamming his hand down on the dark table. "They give us all of this while kidnapping women from right under our noses."

"We don't know if he had anything to do with Alissa's disappearance. Cutter was a huge supporter of the rebuilding of Chicago and our law enforcement," Richard protested, turning to glare at Jason.

"Each of those areas is littered with aliens," Mike pointed out.

"Yeah, and there are a lot of humans working there, too. We could be dealing with a serial killer for all we know," Richard argued.

"Why are you defending them, Richard? You know what they did over on Colbert's side. The women were shipped off world as fast as they could grab them," Troy pointed out.

"And we have found more than half of the missing women and returned them," a steely voice from the door stated. "Destin."

Destin drew up to his full five foot eleven inches. While he wasn't as tall as the Trivators, years of hard work made him almost as broad. One thing he learned during his trip across the galaxy and back: he could hold his own against most of them.

"Cutter," Destin greeted.

All of the men stood and turned to face Cutter. The man glanced around the room, his face a calm mask. Destin had no doubt that Cutter heard what they were discussing. A Trivator's senses were more sensitive than a human's – something that Trig unhappily pointed out several hours ago.

"Where's Trig?" Cutter inquired, glancing around.

"I'm here," Trig said, stepping into the room.

"Where's Beth?" Mike asked, frowning when he didn't see her behind Trig.

"She is with Councilor Ikera," Trig replied. "The apartment upstairs didn't have any food."

"Shit, I forgot about that," Tim muttered, running his hand down over his face. "Sorry about that, Destin."

"I should have checked it. It isn't your fault, Tim," Destin reassured the other man with a grimace. "Cutter, what are you doing here?"

"Councilor Ikera requested transport to the base. I was in the area. I wanted to discuss several things with you, now that you've returned," Cutter explained in a quiet voice. "It would appear that I came in at the appropriate time."

"I would like to take a ten minute break first. We'll meet back here," Destin replied.

"Who is Councilor Ikera?" Justin asked under his breath.

"A blue bitch like the Usoleum bastard Badrick," Mason replied.

Destin reacted without thinking. He moved around the table, invading the large, older man's space. His face was tight with anger and he didn't bother to hide it. His fist wrapped in the front of Mason's shirt and he stared the man down.

"That 'blue bitch' is my woman," Destin warned in a voice devoid of all civility. "You will address her with respect. Her name is Princess Jersula Ikera." He released the front of Mason's shirt, slightly pushing the man before he stepped back and slowly turned to make sure each man in the room knew he was pissed. "If you can't be civil to her, stay the hell away from her. You insult Sula, you insult me. I'll meet you back here in ten fucking minutes. Don't be late."

Destin didn't say anything else. He was afraid if he did, it would be with his fists. He strode out the door and headed down the hallway toward the break room. He didn't know how Beth would handle Sula being around.

Turning the corner, he slowed when he heard the soft sound of laughter and Beth's bubbly voice. Pausing outside of the break room, he leaned back against the wall and listened. It was hard to hear what they were saying above the sound of music playing in the background.

"So, you're a real live Princess, like in the movies?" Beth was asking in a voice filled with awe.

"What is a movie?" Sula asked.

"Movies are videos where you can relax, eat popcorn, drink soda, and lose yourself in people acting out things on a large screen. My grandma and I used to go to the dollar matinee on Wednesdays during the summer. My favorites were the classics. Don't you have movies where you come from?" Beth asked.

"Oh, yes. Entertainment plays," Sula laughed. "I enjoy them very much. Chelsea gave me quite a few of them the last time I was here."

Relief flooded Destin at the sound of Sula's warm laughter. Beth had the type of personality where no one was a stranger. Straightening, he stepped around the corner and into the break room.

"Thank you for helping out, Beth," Destin murmured with a nod.

"No problem. I'm good with wild animals and aliens," she teased, winking at Sula. "You're the alien. I'll classify Trig as the wild animal."

Sula laughed again, unable to resist the infectious personality of the other woman. Destin watched Beth rise gracefully out of her seat.

"I'll let Grandma know you're back. She and Mabel have been worried about you, and they wanted to know about Kali, too," Beth said, glancing back and forth between Destin and Sula with an amused smile.

Destin nodded. "Tell them that Sula and I will be by later to show them pictures of Kali and Ami," he added, stepping to the side so Beth could exit the room.

"I will. See you later, Sula. It was nice meeting you," Beth said with a smile.

"It was a pleasure meeting you, Beth," Sula responded.

Destin reached over and closed the door behind Beth.

"Cutter said you requested transport over to the base," Destin said in a quiet tone, walking over to sit down in the chair next to her.

Sula's gaze softened and she nodded. "Yes. I've been doing some research on the missing women," she murmured.

Destin's lips tightened. "I want to assign some security to you. I don't want you traveling alone," he said, reaching for her hand. "Even with all the new construction and rebuilding, there are a lot of people who aren't happy with the fact that aliens are still on the planet."

"They lost so much. I can hardly blame them, Destin," Sula murmured.

Destin gently squeezed her hand and released it. The confrontation with Mason and the others disturbed him, but he understood their feelings. Hell, he had felt the same way, but after spending so many months on the spaceships and then on Rathon, he had a better appreciation for just how naïve he was in his understanding of the universe he lived in.

Sitting back in his seat, he noted that she looked a little pale. He didn't have much time left before he was supposed to meet with the others. It would be nice if he could assign one of the men to Sula, but after the reaction he just saw from them, there was no way he would let them near her. That left only one person he could trust at the moment – Beth.

"I'll have Beth stay with you when I can't. She knows this city like the back of her hand and can fight," Destin said. "I've got to return to the meeting. I'll let her know."

"I'm not sure how long I will be gone. I'd like to see if Chelsea is still at the medical unit as well. I enjoyed her company the last time I was here," Sula said, stirring the spoon in the cup of soup in front of her.

"Make sure you have your communicator with you," he instructed, still leery about letting her out of his sight. "Sula...."

"Yes?" Sula responded.

"I...," Destin began before he released a frustrated sigh and stood up. "Be careful."

Destin bent and pressed a hard, possessive kiss to her upturned lips. For added measure, he teased them with his tongue. She immediately opened for him like a blossom seeking the sun. A soft moan escaped her and he lifted his hands to frame her jaw while he deepened the kiss. They were both breathing heavily when he reluctantly ended the kiss. His thumbs caressed her cheek, sliding over the smooth, silky skin.

"I'll see you later this evening," he murmured, straightening. "Cutter is here. He'll take you back to the base. I need to speak with him first, though. In the meantime, I'll have Beth meet you back here and let her know that she'll be assigned to you when I'm not available."

"Thank you," Sula said, watching him walk back to the closed door. "Destin.... Will my being here – with you – compromise you in any way among your men?"

Destin turned, his hand on the door.

"Why would you think that? Has anyone said or done anything?" Destin asked in a calm, controlled voice.

"No... It's just...." Her hand lifted and she played with the end of the braid lying over her shoulder. "I saw the way those two men looked at me when we arrived. I don't want to cause you any difficulty. If necessary, I can stay at the base."

"Is that want you want?" Destin asked, gazing back at her with an emotionless mask.

Sula's lips firmed and she shook her head. "No. I would prefer to kick their asses if they make your life difficult, but something tells me that wouldn't help my cause any," she admitted with a rueful smile.

Destin released an unexpected chuckle and his eyes glittered with amusement. He smiled back at her, his shoulders relaxing. This is what he loved about her, her ability to surprise him and make him proud.

"It might not, but I would prefer that over you staying at the base. Don't worry about my men. They know you are mine," Destin replied. "I'll see you later."

Destin pulled the door open and stepped out of the break room. He drew in a deep breath, his mind churning. He loved her. He loved Sula.

"So it is true," Cutter replied, straightening from where he was leaning against the wall outside of the break room.

Destin scowled, wondering how long the Trivator had been standing there – with Trig. Destin seriously contemplated a large roll of Duct tape for Trig's mouth.

"I didn't say a thing. You did that earlier in the other room," Trig stated as if reading Destin's mind.

Ignoring the statement, Destin turned his gaze back to Cutter. Over the last two years, the Trivator and he formed a tentative truce. He knew the man was here for more than a social visit. Something else was going on.

"Richard said that Alissa Garcia was last seen with you. What do you know about her?" Destin asked, continuing down the hallway when Cutter stepped beside him.

"It was when I stopped by to see how her new security forces trainees were doing. She asked to speak to me in private and explained that she was investigating the disappearance of several human females. The location made her suspect alien involvement. I assured her I would look into it and stepped up patrols in those areas," Cutter replied. "Razor contacted me to describe what happened on Rathon. The attack on his and Hunter's residence was disturbing."

"I agree. If Kali had been there alone with Ami, it could have had a completely different outcome," Destin replied. "Those were skilled assassins."

"Be thankful they weren't Drethulans," Cutter muttered, glancing over his shoulder at Trig who followed them in silence. "How is Dagger?"

"Dangerous," Trig answered in a clipped tone. "Jordan is the only thing that keeps him grounded."

Cutter nodded in satisfaction and turned to face forward again. "It is good he is alive," he said before he slowed to a stop outside of the conference room.

"What is it?" Destin asked with a frown when he saw the steely expression in Cutter's gaze.

"I've gone over the Waxian warship incident with Jag. We both felt something was wrong. Even outmatched, they should have put up more of a fight. Jag took the *Star Raider* to the location to investigate the wreckage. Until he files a report, we are on high alert. Razor believes there is a larger assault amassing against Earth. If it is true that the Drethulan and the Waxians are working together, we will have a battle on our hands," Cutter informed Destin in a terse tone.

Destin glanced through the door at his men sitting around the table. They had a right to know what was going on. If the Drethulan and Waxians did attack, they would be in the middle of it.

"How soon will you know?" he asked, glancing back at Cutter.

"A few days. There is a lot of space out there and a lot of debris to sift through," Cutter replied.

"Thank you for letting me know what is going on," Destin said.

Cutter gave him a brief nod. "I've informed the human leaders of Earth and put our ground troops and ships on alert...."

"But...," Destin inquired with a raised eyebrow.

"I received a message earlier," Cutter admitted, lifting a hand to rub his jaw, his gaze moving from the conference room back to Destin. "It flashed for a brief moment, then disappeared."

"What did it say? Who was it from?" Destin asked with a frown.

Cutter shook his head. "I don't know who it was from and could not trace it. It was as if it never existed. The message consisted of three words. If I didn't know any better, I would have thought I had imagined it," he admitted.

"What did it say?" Destin asked in exasperation.

Cutter dropped his hand and stared intently back at him. "It said protect Destin Parks," he replied.

* * *

Several hours later, Destin punched in the code to his living quarters that Tim gave him, then slid in a disk that would install a range extender and a new program for the sensors. With this he would be alerted when anyone approached the door, not just when they put their palm on the scanner or punched a wrong number into the keypad. Next he changed the code to one unique to him and Sula. It was the same one they used on board the *Star Raider*. He ejected the disk and pocketed it.

It had been a long but informative day. Destin walked across the gleaming tile. The apartment was dark, lit only by the soft glow of the moonlight shining through the windows. With a murmured command, a set of accent lights came on. Most of the city finally had some form of power restored to it. The only areas missing were those still too heavily damaged to safely activate it.

The power grids were different from before. This time, alien technology was employed. Destin was still trying to wrap his head around it, but each building, whether a home or a business, would have a self-contained energy source. The technology was a product of Trivator and Kassisan engineers working together to create something new.

In the early years when electricity was first used, most buildings and streets had to be retrofitted with power lines and cables to a substation which received power from one major power plant.

Destin understood the hazards of that. It meant miles and miles of cables that would need to be maintained and upgraded to handle the additional load as the country grew. It also meant an area of weakness. A devastating storm, a demand overload, extreme temperatures, or an attack on the power sources could all lead to critical failure and mean days, weeks, months, or in the case of what happened when the aliens appeared, years of disruptions. The aliens already discovered that was not a good idea.

"It is amazing that we made it as long as we did," Destin murmured, walking over to stare out at the city far below him.

Low, shielded lights illuminated the streets, but he was unable to see them from this far. The idea was to preserve the natural balance of light and dark. Once humans discovered artificial light, they wanted to light up their world. Often driven by fear, misconceptions, and excellent marketing, homes, streets, and businesses lit up the darkness, drowning the brilliance of the night sky. The most densely populated areas had not been hard to see from space, which helped the Trivators decide where to contact first.

In contrast, Destin remembered the first time he saw Rathon from space. It had been nighttime there and despite having two moons, the planet was devoid of light. He had wondered if it was even inhabited until the shuttle he was in landed on the base. Their lighting was designed to preserve their night vision. He knew deep down that it would take a generation or two before humans fully adapted to the concept, despite the fact that they had lived without electricity for thousands of years before that.

In the distance, he could see the continuing construction. That was another thing he and the others learned. Once Destin and his people agreed to work with Cutter on the rebuilding of the city, the Trivators did not waste any time. Large machines scooped up the debris, filtering, crushing, or incinerating it while transports and workers swarmed over one section of the city at a time.

He shrugged off his jacket, and threw it over the back of the couch before walking over to the large chair near the window. He turned it around so that it was facing the windows and sank onto it. Leaning forward, he saw the large green areas that were planted in perfect symmetry and the roads leading around them. Commuters could either step into one of the individual compartments of the slender ground public transport or the automated flying transports where they could enter in their destination, sit back, and enjoy the ride. All buildings were a mixture of homes and businesses. There would be no individual houses, at least not in the city. Chicago would be larger, but take up a quarter of its original size in buildings, thus freeing up land for forests and recreational preserves.

Sitting back in the chair, Destin could feel the fatigue pulling on his body. He toed his shoes off and kicked them to the side so he could stretch his legs out. Observing the construction going on in the distance, he wasn't consciously aware of his eyes growing heavier or his head falling back against the plush, dark brown leather of the chair.

Chapter 17

Sula ran a tired hand over her eyes. Beth didn't look much better than she did. A wry smile curved Sula's lips when she saw the other girl sprawled out on the long couch with her eyes partially closed.

"We have checked everywhere. He must have hidden the ring somewhere else or it was stolen," Sula finally said.

"What's so important about it anyway?" Beth asked, turning her head to look over at Sula where she was sunk down in a chair.

"I've seen a ring similar to it before, but I can't remember where. I've sent a copy of the ring to my brother to see if he might know. It is so frustrating," Sula muttered with a groan, leaning her head back and staring at the ceiling.

"How long will it take for him to get back to you?" Beth asked with a yawn.

Sula tilted her head to the side. The lights on the base were the old human kind. There was one overhead light with three round, frosted white glass globes over the light bulbs and a fan. One of the frosted globes had a shadow in it. Rising out of her seat, she stared at it.

"I'm not sure. Anywhere from hours to days," she murmured.

Beth must have heard the distraction in her tone of voice, because she opened her eyes and sat up. Beth rubbed her eyes and glanced up at the light with a frown. Focusing on her task, Sula bent and tugged the long table in front of the couch until it was centered under the light.

"What is it?" Beth asked, standing up.

"It may be nothing, but I see a shadow of something in the globe," Sula murmured.

"Let me turn off the light. The globe may be hot," Beth said, hurrying over to turn off the overhead light switch.

The room was now cast into shadows by the single lamp on the end table. Sula climbed up onto the coffee table and reached for the globe. She paused, checking to see if it was hot as Beth had warned, but found it was cool to the touch. Studying the construction of it, she saw three small screws holding it on.

"They must have changed all the lights with LED bulbs," Beth said, walking over to stand next to Sula.

Sula didn't know what an LED was, she was just grateful the fixture was not hot. She quickly loosened the screws and removed the glass covering. Glancing inside the globe, a frown of disappointment creased her brow. Her hope that it was the ring they were searching for quickly faded.

"What is it?" Beth asked, impatiently waiting.

"I'm not sure," Sula admitted, turning the globe so the item fell out into her hand. She paled when she realized what it was and closed her fist around it. "We have to get out of here!" she whispered, turning to gaze down at Beth with growing alarm.

"Why? Do you know what it is?" Beth asked, holding up a hand to help steady Sula when she started to climb off the table.

"Yes," Sula muttered, glancing around. Her eyes stopped on the bathroom door. Striding over to it, she dropped the small device into the toilet and flushed it. "Someone was listening to everything we have said. They know what we are looking for."

"You mean… a bug? Someone bugged the place?" Beth asked in confusion, glancing around. "Do you think it was left over from the guy who lived here before?"

Sula shook her head and hurried back into the living area to grab her weapon. "No, the fixtures and fan are clean. It was done recently. We have to go now," she replied in a soft urgent tone.

"Where? We're on a Trivator base. You'd think if we were going to be safe, it would be here," Beth replied, following Sula to the door.

"This building is set farther away from the others," Sula said.

"I noticed that, but figured from what I heard about the last guy that was here, it was because he was such an ass," Beth said, reaching out to touch Sula's arm. "Let me go first."

"No," Sula murmured, shaking her head. "I will not put you in danger."

Beth chuckled and reached for the handle. "If anything happens to you, Destin will skin my hide," she retorted, nodding to the lamp behind Sula. "Turn off the light."

Sula turned and hurried back to the lamp. Switching it off, she swiveled to return to the front entrance where Beth was waiting. Beth turned and started to open the door when it exploded inward. Sula watched in horror as Beth's body flew backwards. She automatically lifted her baton when she saw the weapon in the intruder's hands.

Sula released a stream of energy from the tip of the baton. The line swarmed out and encased the weapon, heating it until it glowed a brilliant red. The attacker cursed and released it.

The sound of a loud shot stunned Sula. She watched in shock when the attacker staggered backwards into the two males behind him. Glancing down in surprise, she saw Beth in a partial sitting position with a primitive weapon firmly clenched between her palms. She fired several more times.

"Run," Beth ordered, rising to her feet and backing up as she continued to fire.

Sula turned and ran for the bedroom. She swept through the door, turning when Beth followed her. Slamming it shut, she pointed the baton at the handle and melted the metal before doing the same to the three hinges. The door was essentially welded shut. It wouldn't stop the attackers for long, but it would help some.

Beth was also pushing a heavy piece of furniture in front of it. Sula grabbed the end and helped her align it in front of the door. A startled squeal escaped Beth when a blast from a laser burned through the door and barely missed her head.

"Holy shit!" Beth exclaimed, turning and aiming the weapon at the door before pulling the trigger. The weapon made a clicking noise instead of the loud sound from earlier. "Double shit!"

"The window," Sula urged swirling the baton in her hand and forming a shield against the blasts opening up holes in the door. "Hurry."

Beth ran to the window and unlocked it. Pushing it open, she looked through it to make sure there was no one waiting outside for them. Sula backed up, wincing when the shield lit up.

"It's clear," Beth called out, waving for Sula to hurry. "Come on before they figure out what we are doing."

Sula twisted, trying to keep the shield between her and the door as she slid out of the window. She released her control of the shield once she was outside. Beth was inserting a long clip in her weapon and pocketing the depleted one.

"This way," Beth murmured, holding her weapon up.

Behind them, Sula heard the screeching of the furniture. She followed Beth around the corner of the house. Together, they ran for the next building.

"Do you have your communicator with you?" Beth asked in a quiet voice when they reached a small storage building.

"Yes," Sula replied with disgust at not thinking of it sooner. She pulled it out and pressed the emergency number Trig programmed into the device when they arrived.

"State your emergency," a male voice responded.

"This is Councilor Ikera. Intruders have attacked my residence on the base," Sula whispered, wincing when Beth's weapon made another loud bang.

"Warriors have been dispatched," the voice replied.

Suddenly Beth cried out, jerking and dropping her weapon. Sula turned, the communicator lowering in her hand. One of the attackers had circled around and come up behind them from the opposite side of the shed. Either that, or there were more than the three they had first seen.

"Cut the transmission," the male demanded, pointing his pistol at Sula.

Sula cut the transmission and dropped the communicator on the ground. Behind her, she could hear Beth's smothered whimper of pain. Her hand tightened on the baton in her hand. She froze when she felt the end of another weapon pressed against the back of her head.

"She notified security," the first male said. "Kill the other female; we don't need her. Take the Councilor. General Achler wants her alive."

Fear unlike anything Sula had ever felt before swept through her. Her fingers moved along the baton. With a flick of her wrist, she tossed it behind her to land on the ground next to Beth. There was a slight delay before the shield engulfed the other woman. It wouldn't last for long and it only worked because Beth slid down along the back of the shed to the ground.

The second attacker turned to fire on Beth, but the shield absorbed the blasts. Sula took advantage of his distraction and the fact that he had moved his weapon from her head. With the fluid grace of years of training, she kicked the weapon the first attacker was pointing at her to the side. She bent forward when the other male turned to fire on her. The blast struck his comrade in the chest, knocking him back several feet before he collapsed.

Sula grabbed the male's wrist, forced his weapon upward, and hooked her leg behind his knee. Falling backwards, she used her weight, surprise, and her grip to pull the heavy male with her. She rolled backwards, lifting the male up and over her before pushing with her feet to flip him.

The attacker continued to hold onto his weapon. Sula was already back on her feet before he landed. Her gaze flashed to the weapon of the first attacker. She raced for it, hoping to reach the pistol before the male regained his feet. Sweeping the pistol up in her hand, she began to turned it on the male when pain exploded through her body, sending her stumbling backwards. A second shot echoed through the air, along with shouts in the distance.

Sula watched as the attacker fell back in slow motion, a small round hole in the center of his forehead. She twisted, stumbling awkwardly in time to see Beth falling wearily against the wall of the shed. The warm liquid running down her arm did little to stop the chill starting to set in.

"Beth," Sula whispered, staggering over to the other woman.

Beth leaned her head back against the wall of the shed, her eyes glazed with pain, and gazed up at Sula's pale face before moving to her shoulder. Sula followed Beth's gaze and paled, shivering with pain and shock. A pair of warm, strong hands grasped her around the waist when her legs suddenly gave out from beneath her.

"Tell Patch we are bringing in two wounded females now!" Cutter's strong voice echoed through the night.

"Destin…," Sula murmured, her head falling against his shoulder when Cutter swept her up into his arms.

"He's on his way," Cutter promised.

Sula nodded and closed her eyes. All around her, she could hear the sounds of voices. Lights swept over the area, sending shards of pain through her head when it flashed over them, and the hum of a ground transport echoed close by. Sula tried to open her eyes, but decided it took too much effort.

"Beth…?" Sula asked in a barely audible voice.

"She is safe," Cutter promised.

Chapter 18

Destin jerked awake when he heard a chime. Rising stiffly out of the chair, he stumbled around it briefly before striding toward the door. He laid his palm against the control pad next to the door, pulled it open, and blinked in surprise when he saw Tim and Mason standing on the other side.

"What is it? What time is it?" Destin muttered, glancing around for a clock.

"Three a.m. Get your shoes and jacket," Tim stated, stepping inside.

"What's going on? Three o'clock! Where's Sula? She should have been back before now," Destin groaned and ran his hands through his hair. "I fell asleep."

"Yeah, we kind of figured that. You're allowed to at times," Mason said, pushing past him. "Where are your shoes?"

"My shoes... Uh, by the chair, I think. What the hell is going on?" Destin asked, turning to follow them. "God, I need some coffee if you guys are going to ask me any questions."

"You can get it when we get there," Tim replied, grabbing Destin's jacket off the back of the couch while Mason grabbed his shoes.

"What the fuck is going on?" Destin demanded, standing still and frowning at the other two men before his face paled. "Sula...."

"Yeah, the blue... lady," Mason said, shoving Destin's shoes at him.

"Cutter just contacted us. Beth and your lady friend were attacked. Both of them are injured," Tim said. "We're going with you. Trig is checking the transport out and waiting for us."

"Shit! Do you know how bad they're hurt? What info do you have on who attacked them? How the hell could they have been attacked on the base?" Destin growled, pulling his shoes on and grabbing his jacket. He started for the door before he turned and glanced around the room. "I need a weapon."

"Troy and Richard are meeting us at the platform with some," Mason told him. "Come on."

Destin nodded and turned on his heel. They turned as the doors to the lift closed. Destin felt his stomach drop when the elevator quickly descended to the Launch Platform level.

"Cutter notified Trig of what happened and wanted to make sure that you were still safe. Mason and I were finishing up a last minute security check when we ran into him. I suggested we notify you while he checked the transport since he knows how to fly the damn things," Tim explained.

Destin nodded, stepping forward when the lift slowed. He turned sideways, exiting the lift before the doors had a chance to open all the way. Troy and Richard were talking quietly near a console. They both started forward at the same time. Troy was holding a small tote bag in his left hand.

"Destin, sorry to hear about your lady," Richard said.

"What else have you heard?" Destin demanded, taking the bag from Troy.

"Just that Beth and the Councilor were attacked," Richard said with a shake of his head. "We're still trying to figure out how that could happen right under the Trivators' noses."

"Yeah, well, I'm sure they are trying to figure it out, too," Tim retorted.

"We're ready to go," Trig stated from the platform.

Destin kept his features blank as he boarded the transport. The grim look on Trig's face showed he wasn't happy about what happened either. Destin reached over and pulled the straps over his chest. Through the windows, he could see Troy and Richard lift their hands in support. His throat tightened. He had been through a lot with these men over the last nine years. They all lost people they cared about.

"I'm sorry, Destin," Tim said quietly, leaning forward in his seat.

"For what?" Destin asked.

Tim was silent for a brief second. He glanced down at his clasped hands. Destin could see the muscle throbbing in the other man's jaw. Tim glanced at him again and released a deep breath.

"You really care about her, don't you?" Tim asked instead.

This time it was Destin's turn to be silent. He could feel both Tim and Mason's eyes on him.

Glancing out the front windshield, he debated if he should admit how much he did care. Hell, he had just accepted it today. The thought of losing her before he had a chance to tell her sent a shaft of physical pain shooting through his body.

"I love her," he finally murmured, turning back to look at the two men he considered to be friends. "She... She's strong and loyal... and has an incredible sense of humor when you get to know her." Tim sat back, his face reflecting his shock. Destin looked at Mason. The big man surprised him. Mason had a crooked grin on his face. "What are you grinning at?" Destin demanded, frowning at the big man.

"I kind of thought you might have fallen for her when you came close to whipping my ass earlier in the conference room. You deserve love, Destin. If the blue lady makes you happy, I'll stand by you," Mason promised.

Destin pressed his lips together and nodded. He saw Tim give him a nod in agreement as well. Destin refocused on the scene outside the window. They were beginning their descent over the base. He could see the markings of the landing pad. His left hand clenched on the small tote bag that Troy gave him. He unzipped it and began removing the weapons inside, checking each, and fitting them around his body. As far as he was concerned, whoever in the hell attacked Sula and Beth made a critical error. It was personal now.

* * *

Prymorus stared at the report coming in from the vidcom attached to one of the men on the team. As if in slow motion, he saw the human woman with her arms raised, a weapon held firmly between her hands. A moment later, the man wearing the recorder fell back and Prymorus could only see the dark sky and the flashes of light from the Trivator transports. With a press of a button, the vidcom shut down and the circuits dissolved when he activated the self-destruct sequence programmed into it. He had assigned the men to retrieve the Usoleum Councilor, and once again, an elite team was defeated as if they were unskilled civilians.

Earlier in the day, he instructed the Raftian to install a surveillance module in the Councilor's living quarters when the male told him he would be on the Trivator base doing some electrical repairs. Rising out of his seat, he walked around the desk. Retris stood at attention. Prymorus walked by him and out of the building they were using. If Retris was not so good at what he did, Prymorus would have taken his frustration out on the man. Instead, he drew in a deep breath and glared up at the stars.

Retris silently followed him, standing a short distance away. Prymorus didn't know if Retris instinctively knew to give him the space he needed, or if it was because the other male realized it would be safer. In the distance, Prymorus could hear the sounds of construction continuing throughout the city.

"Find the Raftian and the Jawtaw. Bring them to me," Prymorus ordered.

"Yes, sir," Retris replied, turning to order one of his men to complete the task.

"Personally, Retris," Prymorus stated. "I want you to find them and bring them here."

"Sir… Your safety," Retris began, remaining still when Prymorus swirled with an unexpected savagery. The male next to Retris raised his hand to touch the long blade protruding from his throat, a low gurgling sound escaping him before he collapsed on the ground next to Retris. "I'll leave immediately."

"See that you do," Prymorus replied, walking over and pulling the blade from the dead male's throat as he passed.

The sense that time was running out struck him hard. It had taken a very long time, and a great deal of coordination, to join the Waxian and Drethulan forces together. While the Drethulans were the ones to approach the Warlords, he was the only one that had recognized the full potential of their becoming allies.

The Drethulans were to enter this part of the galaxy within hours from the opposite side of the sun, using the huge mass and its radiation to help cover their arrival. It was one reason he sent the team in. He wanted Ikera and Parks alive. Once the Drethulans arrived, there was no guarantee they would survive the invasion. Unfortunately, the dead bodies of his team would alert the Trivators to the fact that a Waxian force was on the planet.

There was a tremendous military and psychological effect riding on the success of taking this planet. It would be the first test of the pods made from the unique ore mined on Dises V. If the metal proved to be impenetrable to the Trivator's weapons, it would allow the Drethulan and Waxian forces a superior edge in the battle against the Alliance. Even if the warships' shields failed, the hulls would not.

Prymorus had hired the former Usoleum Councilor, Badrick, recognizing the other male's weaknesses and using them against him. The Usoleum was instrumental in negotiating with the Disesians. The Disesians had wanted additional protection for their mining colony when a new ore was discovered. Prymorus realized the ore was instrumental if he wanted to negotiate with the Drethulans.

He had discovered the Drethulans' plans to seize control of the Alliance – and Prymorus wanted to be a part of it. The Waxians brought weapons, ships, and their mercenary services to the table, but they couldn't build enough without more ore, and no mining colony currently possessed a sufficient quantity to meet their needs unless he took over the running of the mines.

Getting enough ore to build the Drethulan pods took several years, in large part because of the resistance of several former military personnel on Dises V, including Commander Atlas, the former leader of the Western Region and the suspected leader of the rebel group on Dises V.

But the Drethulans needed more than just ore, mercenaries, weapons, and ships to take on the Alliance, they needed to learn the Trivators' weaknesses, and Prymorus was determined to make himself invaluable in this aspect, too. He was going to be a very important man in the new order.

Especially if he got that ring! There had been another discovery on Dises V that captured his attention besides the ore. A find that very few knew about. A tiny deposit of red crystals and a mummified body were discovered in one of the mines. The crystals fascinated Prymorus. The power locked within the blood red stones were incredible. That power, if he could harness it, would give him a decided edge over his fellow Waxian warlords, and the Drethulans. He had been furious when both the crystals and the mummy vanished.

Deep down, he suspected that damn Kassisan, Dakar, or perhaps even Badrick, was somehow involved in the disappearance. Ikera's comment earlier this morning about a ring possessing a blood red stone, possibly made from the same crystals found in the mine on Dises V, gave him hope that he might find the key to the missing energy crystals and the secrets to the unusual mummy.

* * *

Destin jumped out of the transport and jogged over to where he saw Cutter waiting. Tim, Mason, and Trig followed him. Cutter's face was grim. Destin nodded in greeting, matching Cutter's pace when he turned on his heel and began walking across to a land transport.

"How are they?" Destin asked, sliding into the front next to Cutter.

Cutter briefly glanced at him before focusing on activating the transport and pulling away from the landing pad. "They will heal," he replied in an abrupt tone.

"How could there be an attack here – on the base?" Destin demanded, his knuckles almost white from his grip on the side of the transport. "There used to be better security."

"A section of the shield was rerouted and the fencing was cut near the Councilor's living quarters. We are assessing who had access to the power grid to do that. This was done from the inside," Cutter stated, turning onto a long road that led to the main buildings. "I accept responsibility. Councilor Ikera stated she only needed to gather a few things from the residence that was assigned to her. Both she and the human female insisted they would be safe since they were on the base and would not be long. Another issue required my attention. I thought they had already returned to the tower," he added in a low tone.

"What do you know?" Destin asked, glancing at the dark buildings they passed.

"There were three intruders, all Waxians," Cutter stated. "It was obvious they were not expecting to encounter the resistance they did. Remind me never to upset the human female, Beth. In fact, I have learned it is better to never upset any of them," he muttered, releasing the steering long enough to absently rub at his right hand as if remembering something.

"What did Beth do?" Trig asked, leaning forward.

Cutter briefly glanced over his shoulder at Trig's tight face. "She killed two of them," he said, slowing the transport to a stop in front of the medical building. "Patch is with both females at this time."

Destin slid out of the transport and strode to the front door. A warrior standing near the entrance opened the door for the group. He paused inside, unsure of which way he should go. Cutter nodded for them to follow him through the doors and down a long corridor to the left.

"Councilor Ikera said she found a surveillance device in a lighting fixture. They realized they were in danger and were leaving when they were attacked. From the little Councilor Ikera related, they were sent to bring her to a Waxian called General Achler. I assume she was referring to Prymorus Achler," Cutter explained.

"Prymorus!" Trig hissed, slowing to a stop in the corridor.

"You know who that is?" Destin asked, turning to face Trig.

Trig grimly nodded. "Yes, he was on Dises V. He's the one that attacked the medical compound and kidnapped Taylor Sampson, Saber's *Amate*," he explained.

"That's where I heard the name before," Destin muttered with a frown.

"Destin, do you mind telling us what the fuck is going on?" Tim asked, resting his hands on his hips.

Destin closed his eyes and ran a hand over them before dropping it and looking back at Tim and Mason. He started to explain before Trig went ballistic earlier today – or was it yesterday? Hell, he was so out of sync with his days at the moment he wasn't sure which was which.

"I'll explain if you like, Destin," Cutter said. "I know you would like to check on the women."

"I want to see Bethany," Trig stated, the muscle in his jaw working.

Cutter looked startled for a moment before he nodded. "We'll be in the break room down the hall and on the left," he said.

"Sounds good," Destin replied. "Which rooms are the women in?"

"The Counselor is in the third room on the right. Beth is in the room straight across from it," Cutter replied.

Destin turned and headed down the hallway. He stopped, torn by what he should do and what he wanted to do. He wanted to see Sula first, but knew once he was with her, he wouldn't be able to leave. He paused, watching as Trig opened the door and stepped into the room. Beth was chatting with the Trivator healer.

"Patch," Destin murmured, glancing from the man to Beth. "Hey, Beth."

"Hi Destin," Beth greeted him with a tired grin. "I got shot by an alien. Grandma is going to have a fit."

"Yeah, I know. I didn't even think to tell Mary about this," Destin admitted, stepping into the room.

Trig had moved to the end of the bed where he picked up the tablet to read the medical report. Destin's lips twitched when Patch leaned over and pulled it out of Trig's hands with a raised eyebrow. Beth's tired laugh told him she did not miss the move either. Destin watched her lay her head back against the propped up pillows.

"I'm glad you didn't," Beth admitted with a weary sigh. "She wold be jumping all over me for getting hurt."

"No, she would be proud of you," Destin murmured. "These aliens have some pretty good medicine. You'll be kicking butt before you know it."

"I know whatever Patch gave me for the pain is some good shit," Beth grinned, her gaze moving to Trig when he walked around to the other side of the bed. "Are you giving Destin trouble again, big guy? Don't make me have to 'open a can of whoop ass on you', as Grandma likes to say."

Destin grinned, relieved that Beth would be fine. He glanced at Patch when the healer murmured he would return later to check on Beth. Following Patch out of the room, he closed the door and glanced across the hall at the room where Sula was located.

"How is Councilor Ikera?" Destin asked, sliding his hands into his pockets.

"As Chelsea would say, 'lucky to be alive'," Patch commented. "She took a blast to her shoulder. I was able to repair most of the torn tissue. She'll need a few weeks of rest before she is fully recovered. I would suggest that someone in her condition avoid getting shot."

"Someone in her condition? Is she ill?" Destin asked in concern, glancing at the door again.

"Being pregnant is not an illness. She can carry on with her daily activities as long as they don't involve almost getting killed," Patch stated in a dry tone.

"Did you... did you say pregnant?" Destin asked, a wave of shock hitting him with the force of a tsunami.

"I am not familiar with Usoleum anatomy, but I would suspect from the readings that she isn't far along," Patch murmured, glancing down at the tablet in his hand and touching it. "I'll have to access the database to be sure."

Destin pulled his right hand out of the front pocket of his jeans and ran it over his face before rubbing the back of his neck. His mind swirled with the knowledge. In all honesty, he did not even think of the possibility of Sula getting pregnant. He did not know why he thought it would matter that they were two different species. After all, so were Kali and Razor, and they had Ami.

"Does she know?" Destin asked, looking at Patch again. "Does Sula know she's pregnant?"

"Yes," Patch replied with a pained expression. "I left Chelsea with her when she burst into tears.

Chelsea thought having another female with her would be better than my attempts to quiet her."

Destin swallowed and absently nodded. He slowly walked toward the door. Pausing with his hand on the doorknob, he turned to Patch again.

"Will the baby be alright if the father is human and not Usoleum?" Destin asked in a quiet voice.

"Human…. Ah, yes, well… I'll do some research to be sure, but I suspect there shouldn't be an issue, otherwise she would not have been able to conceive in the first place," Patch said with a curious expression. "I assume you are the father?"

"I think it is safe to say that," Destin muttered. "Thanks for taking care of her."

Patch bowed his head and strode down the hallway. Destin watched the other man disappear into a room down the hall before he turned his attention to the door again. He ran his hand through his short hair then drew in several deep breaths and released them to calm his stomach.

He knocked on the door and opened it when he heard a woman's voice. He immediately recognized the cheerful, dark face of Chelsea, the resident human nurse and motherly figure who kept the Trivators, particularly Patch, on their toes.

"I…," Destin started to say, but his voice died when his gaze locked with Sula's watery one. His heart melted when he saw her swollen face. "You are the most beautiful woman in the world," he whispered, stepping inside and closing the door behind him.

"Now you're going to make me cry again," Sula wailed, burying her face in the small towel she was holding.

"Honey, you just keep on telling her that," Chelsea said, walking around the bed and patting Destin on the shoulder. "Go give that girl a hug, she needs it right now, but be gentle with her shoulder."

Destin nodded, walking slowly toward the bed. He heard Chelsea quietly exit the room, closing the door firmly behind her. He sank down on the edge of the bed and lifted a hand to slide it along her jaw. She sniffed and looked at him, her eyes red and her nose a dark blue.

"Destin…," Sula sniffed. "I… We… I'm…."

"I know," Destin murmured, leaning forward. "I love you, Sula."

He caught Sula's soft gasp with his lips. He gently teased her lips, waiting for her to open for him. A soft whimper escaped her and he immediately released her, afraid he had hurt her.

"No," she whispered, lifting her good arm and wrapping her hand around his neck to pull him close again. "Don't stop."

Destin's soft chuckle filled the room. This was his Sula – his alien mermaid. The woman with eyes of fire and skin the color of glacier ice. A woman who could fire his blood faster than any other woman he had ever known, could fight like a warrior, and cried ugly.

"I love you," he murmured, caressing her cheek and gazing at her with passion-filled eyes.

"I love you, Destin Parks," Sula whispered, a teary-eyed smile curving her lips before it faded and she bit her lip. "I should warn you, though."

"Warn me about what?" Destin asked, lifting her chin and rubbing her bottom lip when she released it.

Sula gazed at him with a worried expression. "My father and brothers will probably try to kill you," she said with an apologetic look.

"Let them try," Destin murmured, leaning forward to kiss her deeply again.

Her family was the least of his worries at the moment. Drawing back, he twisted so that he could lean back against the pillows with her and hold her. Thankfully, the beds were designed to hold a Trivator warrior, so they were both longer and wider than a normal hospital bed. He carefully wrapped his arm around her when she sat forward enough for him to do so. Once he was settled, she lay back against him.

"How bad is your shoulder?" he asked, rubbing his chin against her hair.

"Patch said it would take a few weeks to completely heal," she murmured, yawning and rubbing her cheek against his chest. "The medication he gave me took all the pain away. I feel good right now."

Destin chuckled and picked her hand up in his. He leaned his head back. He wanted to know what happened tonight, but it would have to wait. He could feel her exhaustion. He suspected the pain medication they gave her also had a sedative in it to help her sleep.

"Can you scoot down and I'll hold you?" he murmured.

"Yes," Sula replied, yawning again, but not moving. "In just a minute."

In less than a minute, she was asleep. It took a little maneuvering, but he was finally able to slide them both down a little. Feeling for the control next to the bed, he lowered the head of it. He stopped when she whimpered in her sleep.

Wrapping his arm around her, he stared up at the ceiling. He would hold her for a few more minutes before he joined the other men. Only when her body totally relaxed did he carefully slide his arm out from under her and cover her up. He rolled out of the bed and stood gazing down at her. Her hair was lying across the pillow. Under the loose fitting gown she was wearing, he could see the bandage on her shoulder. He could tell her right hand was lying protectively over her stomach under the sheet. He didn't know if she had it that way because of her injured shoulder or if she was subconsciously protecting their child.

"I'm going to be a father," Destin whispered, shaking his head in disbelief. "I sure as hell didn't see this coming. Kali is going to love this."

Destin reluctantly turned on his heel and walked to the door. He paused when a wave of indecision hit him. He did not want to leave her alone. His gaze went to the window. Fear hit him, and in his mind, he saw all kinds of horrible scenarios where someone came through the window and took Sula while she was sleeping. He jumped back when a soft knock sounded on the door. A second later, Chelsea peeked in.

"I think Cutter and the others are looking for you," Chelsea murmured, glancing at the bed where Sula lay sleeping. "You go take care of what you need to do. I'll stay with Sula. My Thomas is sitting with Beth. We won't let nothing happen to these two girls. Congratulations, by the way. Patch told me about Sula."

"Thank you," Destin replied, glancing one last time at Sula before he quietly exited the room.

Trig was waiting for him in the hallway. Destin could tell from the other man's expression that he wanted blood – Prymorus Achler's blood. Trig wasn't the only one.

"Let's find the bastard and take him out," Destin said.

"I can do that," Trig replied, turning to follow Destin down to where Cutter, Tim, and Richard were waiting for them.

Chapter 19

Destin looked at the other men when he entered the room. Tim and Mason started to rise, but Destin waved for them to remain seated. His eyes lit up when he saw the coffee pot in the corner. It was one of the old fashion kind, not the alien version.

"Thomas just made a fresh pot. He said he thought we might need some," Tim said. "Cups are in the cabinet above."

"Thanks," Destin replied. "Trig, do you want any?"

A disgusted expression flashed across Trig's face and he shook his head. "No. Beth gave me some yesterday. It takes like *shewta*! That means shit in your language," he said with a shake of his head. "I don't know how you humans drink the stuff."

Richard chuckled. "I kind of figured that was what it meant. It's an acquired taste. If you spend enough time up at night, it can be a life saver," he replied, lifting his own cup toward Destin for a refill.

"I'd like to know what happened, from the top," Destin requested in a quiet voice, pouring the coffee into Richard's cup and replacing the carafe in the coffee maker. "I also want to know everything you know about this Prymorus Achler guy."

* * *

An hour later at the former Usoleum Councilor's residence, the men were retracing what happened. It was obvious that someone had searched it – thoroughly. It was doubtful that it had been the men sent to kidnap Sula, so it could only mean one thing; Sula and Beth were searching for something. He turned when Cutter walked into the back bedroom where he was standing.

"We have a possible target," Cutter stated, angling his tablet so Destin could see.

"Who?" Destin asked, walking over to get a closer look at the image on the tablet. "What's that?"

"That is a Raftian. He was doing some electrical repairs today. One of the buildings was this one," Cutter replied in a grim tone.

"What did you find?" Trig asked, peering over Cutter's shoulder. "*Shewta!* Cartis!"

Cutter turned to face Trig. "You know the Raftian?" he asked with a frown.

Trig nodded. "It looks like Cartis. He worked with Cannon, Sword, and Jordan to help free Razor, Dagger, and I on Bruttus. Cannon knows him. If that is Cartis, there will be a Jawtaw named Omini not far from him. They work undercover together on the intergalactic slave market – to break it, not supply them with more."

"The missing women…," Destin said with a frown. "Is it possible they would know what happened to them?"

Trig ran a tired hand through his hair and nodded. "If Cartis is here with Omini, there has to be something going on. If there is, they would know. So much for thinking the Waxians and Drethulans were going to be our only issue," he said with a shake of his head.

Cutter released a muttered curse and glanced around the room. Destin saw the suspicion in Cutter's eyes. His gut clenched when Cutter turned to him.

"Badrick was involved before with transporting human females off this world. What is to say that Councilor Ikera has not decided to continue her predecessor's work?" Cutter asked.

Destin's fist clenched and he took a step closer to Cutter. "Sula has nothing to do with the missing women. Might I remind you that they disappeared before we ever arrived? Badrick was a bad apple. What proof do we have that it isn't a group of Trivator warriors behind their disappearance – or you for that matter? After all, this is all happening under your watch and Alissa was last seen talking to you about it!" Destin retorted in a low, angry tone.

"I think we all need to get some rest," Trig muttered, casting a wary glance at Cutter and Destin. Both men were standing toe to toe. "As much as I hate to tell you this, Cutter, my orders are to protect Destin at all cost. If you two come to blows, I'll have to defend him."

"I don't need protecting or defending, Trig," Destin growled under his breath, not breaking eye contact with Cutter.

"She will be confined to the base until I know what is going on," Cutter replied in a tone edged with steel. "If nothing else, her remaining in the medical unit would ensure her protection if she is innocent."

"Like hell," Destin said with a shake of his head. "She and Beth were under your protection when they were attacked here. She'll return to the tower with me. My team and I will protect her."

"Destin...," Cutter started to say.

"She goes with me. I'm not leaving her here, especially now," Destin stated with a wave of his hand, barely missing Cutter's chest.

"Maybe it would be best, Destin. Patch and the human nurse can make sure her wounds heal properly," Trig suggested.

"It isn't just her wound. She's pregnant," Destin said, his voice tight with determination. "I trust my guys to protect her."

"Pregnant!" Cutter and Trig muttered in shock at the same time.

"This is the end of this discussion. Tim! Richard! We're returning to the medical unit now," Destin called out to the other two men as he pushed past the two stunned Trivator warriors.

* * *

Sula awakened slowly. Her hand instinctively moved down to touch the arm wrapped around her waist. She winced when a shaft of pain reminded her of everything that happened last night.

"I'll get Patch or Chelsea," Destin murmured, his voice thick from sleep.

"No, not yet," Sula whispered, closing her eyes and enjoying the feel of him pressed against her.

"How are you feeling?" Destin asked.

A small smile curved Sula's lips when his hand moved down to cover her stomach. Fresh memories washed through her. She couldn't squeeze his arm without pain, but she rubbed her foot along his jean clad leg.

"I don't feel quite as good as I did after Patch gave me whatever he did for pain. How is Beth?" Sula asked, carefully rolling over when Destin moved so she could turn. "Did you see her?"

"She's fine. She suffered a graze to her arm. She's already peeked in on you," he murmured, leaning up on one elbow to gaze down at her.

"I was so frightened. Those men... they were going to kill her," Sula whispered, blinking rapidly when tears filled her eyes. "I never cry and now I appear to do it frequently. It is very irritating."

Destin chuckled and raised a hand to wipe the tear that escaped. "Hormones – I guess even aliens have them," he teased before sobering. "What were you and Beth searching for, Sula? It was obvious you two were on a mission."

Sula swallowed and nodded. Her head turned and she gazed around the room, an expression of worry on her face. Looking back up at him, she licked her dry lips.

"I don't want to tell you here," she whispered. "After last night... I don't trust the security here."

Destin looked up when a soft knock sounded on the door. A moment later, Chelsea stuck her head in and brightly smiled at both of them. She clucked when she saw the dampness on Sula's cheeks.

"Now, now, everything will be alright," Chelsea said with a compassionate expression. "Destin, why don't you go next door and get cleaned up. I had Thomas get you fresh clothes and a toothbrush from the supply store. I guessed at the size, so don't blame him if it's the wrong one. I'd like to check Sula's shoulder and I'll help her get cleaned up. I bought her some clothes, too."

Destin glanced at the white plastic bag that Chelsea held up and nodded. He bent and brushed a tender kiss across Sula's lips before rolling out of bed. Bending down, he picked up his shoes, grabbed his jacket off the chair next to the window, and stepped around the bed.

"Let me know if she needs anything," he ordered in a soft but firm voice when he passed Chelsea.

"Honey, you'll be the first to know. Sula is in good hands, don't you worry about her," Chelsea promised, shooing him out of the room.

Sula couldn't keep the amused smile hidden. Chelsea was a force to be reckoned with when she was on a mission. Sula discovered that when she was sick. Struggling to sit up, she couldn't quite hold back the hiss of pain that escaped her.

"Here now, let me help you," Chelsea admonished, dropping the bag onto the end of the bed and wrapping an arm around Sula's back to help her sit up. "I'll give you something for the pain and then we'll get you into the bathroom to get cleaned up for Destin."

Chelsea fluffed the pillows behind her and Sula carefully leaned back against them while Chelsea pulled a small kit from her pocket. Less than a minute later, Sula breathed a sigh of relief when the sharp pain radiating from her shoulder faded. She smiled her gratitude to the other woman.

"Thank you, Chelsea. Once again, you have come to my rescue," Sula murmured.

"Well, a head cold is a lot less painful, even if you do feel like you are dying at times," Chelsea laughed. "The pain medication I gave you will take the edge off, but it won't stop it from hurting if you try to move your arm too much. Pain is a good thing. It lets you know when you are doing too much."

Sula laughed and relaxed while Chelsea scanned her vitals. Her hand fluttered over her stomach and she bit her lip. She looked at Chelsea when the other woman gently lifted her hand and held it.

"Do you... You have a daughter, don't you, Chelsea?" Sula asked in a hesitant voice.

"Thomas and I have three of them, all married. The middle and youngest have kids," Chelsea replied. "You'll be fine, Sula. I don't know much about alien babies, but I suspect it isn't much different from human ones. Come on and let me help you get in the shower and you can ask me all the questions you want."

Sula's eyes filled again and she groaned in annoyance. "Will I cry the entire time? I do not remember if others of my kind cried," she sniffed, sliding her legs out from under the covers and sitting up.

"Sweetheart, if you feel like crying, you cry all you want. If you feel like ice cream at two in the morning, you tell Destin he better make sure he has it, otherwise there will be hell to pay," Chelsea chuckled, sliding an arm around Sula's waist and steadying her when she stood up. "My Thomas learned real quick which stores were open all night and which aisle my current craving was on. Trust me, when the baby decides to come, they'll be thankful they did."

"What is ice cream?" Sula asked in curiosity.

Chelsea's laughter filled the small bathroom. Sula was soon learning all the hilarious and frightening things about pregnancy and wondering if half the tales were true. She also made a mental list of all the foods that Chelsea was telling her about – like fried pickles, tacos, and chocolate covered potato chips.

Chapter 20

Destin stepped out of the shower next door and dried his hair and body off before quickly dressing. He was just slipping his shoes on when there was a knock on the door. He called out for the person to enter, expecting it to be Tim or Mason. Instead, he was surprised when Cutter stepped inside and closed the door.

Destin's features hardened into a controlled mask of calm. He finished tying his shoes and stood up, then grabbed his jacket off the back of the chair, and slid it on. Cutter watched him in silence until he straightened.

"She's not staying here," Destin started to say.

"I know," Cutter replied in a curt tone. "I talked to Beth this morning."

Destin drew in a deep breath and his eyes narrowed in suspicion. He had not thought about the fact that Beth might mention what she and Sula were searching for. He should have debriefed her last night.

"What did she say?" Destin asked, folding his arms across his chest.

Cutter shot him a frustrated glare. "That she only talks to the boss and since I'm not him, she couldn't tell me anything other than my security measures sucked big time and that I'd better not mess with Sula," he replied in a dry tone.

Destin's lips twitched and he dropped his arms to his side in relief. Beth was smart and creative, but most of all she had a way of dealing with others. He could just imagine her telling Cutter that he wasn't the boss of her with an infectious smile that would have Cutter agreeing. In many ways, Beth had helped fill the gap in his life left by Kali's absence.

"Good for her," Destin murmured, shoving his hands in his front pockets. "Is there anything else?"

Cutter's lips twitched and he shook his head. "I really hope Kali is as much of a pain in the ass to Razor as you have been to me," he muttered. "I've sent Trig out with Tim to find the Raftian and Jawtaw. Tim knows the city, but Trig knows the Raftian."

"Sula isn't involved in the disappearance of the women," Destin asserted.

"I know," Cutter acknowledged with a grim expression. "Thomas made another pot of coffee. General Baker has requested a meeting after this morning's incident and I've asked Jag to join us."

Destin nodded. Cutter gripped the door handle behind him and pulled the door open. Destin followed Cutter out of the room and back down the hallway. He was surprised when Cutter returned to the breakroom instead of leaving the building. Cutter must have sensed his surprise.

"We're meeting in here?" Destin asked, stepping into the room.

Cutter nodded. "Family is very important to a Trivator. We can only hope to one day be gifted with our *Amate*. You have found yours. I respect your protectiveness of her," he explained.

Destin knew he had a skeptical look on his face. It was strange listening to another guy, even if he was an alien, talk about gifts and protectiveness. It was obvious from Cutter's face that he wanted to be done with this part of the conversation as well.

"And that's that?" Destin asked.

Cutter shrugged. "Yes… and the fact that Patch wouldn't release her from his care yet. I want to ask her what she was searching for before the attack," he added.

"Now that I can believe. I need some coffee," Destin muttered.

"Make that two," Mason replied, walking into the room rubbing his eyes. "I'm getting too old to keep up with this shit."

"Old my ass, I've got three years on you," Mary Clark stated, sweeping in behind Mason with Beth following after her grandmother with an apologetic smile.

"You weren't up all fu—Ouch," Mason muttered, rubbing his arm when Mary smacked him.

"You can use any word but the f-one," Mary stated in a firm tone. "A good curse word is necessary at times to relieve the tension, but the f-bomb should never be spoken in front of a lady. I'll take care of the coffee if y'all want to find a seat. None of you can make a pot worth drinking and I think you'll need more than one before this is finished."

Destin chuckled when he saw the pained expression on both Cutter and Mason's faces. Mary was sweet, but kept the lot of them in line with an iron fist. She knew how to handle the less than polished men that had become a family to her and Beth over the last seven years. He was just grateful Mabel did not come along with Mary. Then, they would all be in trouble.

"Sorry about this, Destin. I contacted Grandma this morning to let her know I was okay. She insisted on coming. I had Mason go get her. It was easier than fighting with her," Beth muttered, sliding onto the chair next to him. "How's Sula doing?"

"She's doing better this morning – still in some pain," Destin replied, smiling his thanks to Mary when she placed a cup of coffee in front of him.

Destin looked up when a man in a uniform entered the room, followed by Jag, the commander of the *Star Raider*. The modest-size room was becoming a little cozier as it began to fill up. Destin recognized the human man as General Baker.

"General," Destin greeted with a nod. "Jag."

"Destin," Jag responded, glancing at the two women with a raised eyebrow.

"This is Beth and Mary Clark. They are part of my team. Mary handles communication and logistics for me," Destin responded. "Beth works with my security team."

"Cutter debriefed me on what happened last night. We are already on high alert due to these other possible threats," General Baker stated. "The human military forces are mobilized and ready around the world. I've been in contact with the Joint Council in New York City. After receiving an unusual transmission that was verified as authentic, they agree that the threat is real."

"I received the same transmission," Jag added, stepping forward and placing a vidcom device in the center of the table. "Play transmission."

A holographic image flickered for a moment before a man's face appeared in front of it. The man smiled into the video recording before stepping back. He started to speak before he stopped and frowned. They could tell he was glaring at someone on the other side of the camera.

"How do you expect me to warn them if you do not have the sound working?" a thick, accented voice demanded. "IQ, you are supposed to know how to operate this machine, oui?"

"Jon Paul, you better hurry. Jarmen will not be happy if he discovers we are sending this," another voice muttered. "He swore he would eject us into space if we mess up again."

"How is this messing up? We are simply sending a small message," Jon Paul argued.

"Technically, any interference with history could potentially change the course of it," another voice replied.

"Bah! Jarmen has been messing with your programming again," Jon Paul replied with a wave of his hand. "I will be careful."

"The video is currently running," a robotic voice stated.

"What? Oi! People of Earth…," Jon Paul began before he was interrupted when another man stepped into view and waved his hands in the air.

"Non! Non! If you say it like that they will think they are doomed. You must give them hope, Jon Paul. Not make them believe they are about to encounter the War of the Worlds! Oi! You must say it like this… My friends, there are very bad aliens coming on…. What is the date again, IQ?" Destin listened in disbelief when a voice called out the date. "Oui, yes, they are coming. We cannot tell you more for fear our uptight friend will eject us into space, but we felt a need to share with you the dangers. And now, we must go."

"Luc, you believe that is supposed to be a better transmission than telling them that a species called the Drethulans are coming?" Jon Paul stated, looking at the other man in disbelief as the vidcom faded.

Destin sat staring at the center of the table. He looked up, frowning at the others sitting around the table before his gaze focused on Cutter. He returned Destin's look with a grim one of his own.

"That's today… If the video is for real," Destin said.

"We are currently accepting that it is," General Baker stated.

"Why?" Mason asked with a puzzled frown. "It looked like a couple of Frenchmen who've had a bit too much wine to me."

General Baker glanced at Mason, then around the room. "That video was placed in the alien archives nearly a century ago. It was programmed to arrive in our mainframe and automatically play today," he replied in a quiet tone.

"When I search the properties of the transmission, I discovered the same thing. It was placed in the Trivator archives and set to automatically transmit on the *Star Raider*. The *Star Raider* was not part of the fleet until shortly before we were ordered to this planet," Jag stated.

"I received a transmission, but it was fleeting," a soft voice stated from the doorway.

Destin turned in his seat and rose. Sula stood in the doorway with Chelsea standing behind her. His breath caught when he saw her long hair was braided over her good shoulder. She was wearing a soft, button-up red plaid shirt, a pair of jeans, and a pair of black tennis shoes. She was pale, but composed.

"What did the transmission say?" General Baker asked.

Sula shook her head. "There was no audio, just a brief visual. It was so fast that I thought I imagined it," she said.

"What was the image?" Destin asked, stepping around the chair to walk over to her.

He grasped Sula's hand when she lifted it toward him. He could feel the tremble in it. Her eyes were dark and shadows appeared under them.

"I saw the tower where we are living in flames and the city burning," she replied, closing her eyes for a moment, trying to remember every detail. "It was so fleeting. I didn't recognize the city at first." She opened her eyes and looked at the small, portal vidcom Jag had placed on the table. A frown creased her brow as she remembered what she had seen. "I dreamed about it last night and it dawned on me that the tower and the city looked eerily familiar. The transmission reminded me of it."

"Last night you were searching for something. What was it?" Cutter asked.

Sula turned to look at Cutter. "I've been searching for more information about the missing women. I found a cache of Badrick's files that had not been deleted. It took a while, but I was finally able to access them. I discovered that Badrick compiled video documentation of most of his encounters. There was one with Destin in particular that drew my curiosity."

"What was it?" Destin asked with a frown.

"I noticed Badrick was wearing a ring with an unusual blood red crystal in it," she said. "I have seen the ring before, but I could not remember where. I sent a message to my brother, Andric. He replied shortly before I came in here. Many years ago, Andric left Usoleum on a quest of self-discovery. He traveled to many different worlds, some unknown to us at the time. One world was called Elpidios. I have the message."

Sula pulled the small disk out of her pocket and held it out to Jag to place in the vidcom.

* * *

Sula, I do not know where you found this ring, but it is the one stolen from me many years ago. The ring was given to me as a gift by a tribal leader on a distant world called Elpidios. It is a desolate world that appeared to be dying when I was there.

I landed in a desert not far from a range of mountains. I had been exposed to radiation poisoning when one of the power modules failed on my ship and was deathly ill. I ejected the module into space, but I knew I could go no farther. Elpidios was the nearest habitable planet. In truth, I expected to die on that inhospitable world.

I abandoned my spaceship and set out across the sands. On the third night, a small group of native inhabitants came upon my camp. They could not understand me nor I them. While our skin was similar in color, my eyes and hair were a novelty to them. I was finally able to configure my translator to decipher a portion of their language. The group led me back to their elders, where they placed stones similar to that of the ring around me and over my body. Over the course of several days, I began to feel better. I stayed with them for nearly a full lunar cycle before I explained that I had to leave.

The night before I left the settlement, one of the elders gave me the ring and told me a story. They said one day the great Empress from an unknown world would come and unlock the blood in the stones that would give life back to their planet. The elder told me the ring is said to have belonged to one of those that struck down the creatures that attacked centuries before. It was found in a city hidden beneath the mountains. He hoped giving the ring to me would lead the Empress to their world.

The stone is known as a blood stone and contains a tremendous amount of energy that absorbed the radiation. You can imagine my surprise when I learned that the Elpidiosians had joined the Alliance a few years ago. I would like to return it to the Grand Ruler."

* * *

"I don't know if the ring is of any relevance to what is happening or why the human females have been kidnapped, but something told me it was important," Sula murmured when the transmission ended. "Beth and I searched everywhere for it. There was no record of the ring in the inventory of items returned with Badrick's body. It was also not on his body during the autopsy. I thought for sure Badrick hid it in his living quarters somewhere. I was able to get the computer to recreate the ring and this is what it looks like."

"Shit!"

All eyes turned to Mason, who stood against the back wall. He groaned and ran both hands down his face. He dropped them to his sides and shook his head.

"I know where it is," Mason said with a grimace. "I forgot all about the damn thing."

"What are you talking about? How can you have it?" Destin asked.

Mason shrugged. "It was a crazy day. It was the day Kali was taken by Colbert. We were going in after her. If you remember, the place lit up like hell having a party. I was helping clean up the bodies. I caught one of the guys stripping valuables off the dead. I made him empty what took and kicked his ass to the curb. One of the items was that ring. I guess it got stuck in the bottom of my jacket because I found it a couple of months later. I tossed it in a box. It's been in the top of my closet ever since," he explained.

"But what does that have to do with the missing women?" Mary asked.

"I don't know – maybe nothing," Sula said with a sigh.

"I can go get it," Mason suggested.

"That would be….," Sula's voice died when the sound of an alarm went off. "What…?"

"We're under attack," Cutter stated, pushing past the group.

The rest of the group headed out the door. Patch strode out of his office and down the hallway. Chelsea came out of the room down the hall. Destin gently steered Sula toward Chelsea.

"Beth, Mary, I want you to stay with Chelsea and Sula," Destin ordered.

"Destin," Beth started to protest before she pressed her lips together at his fierce expression.

"Protect her, Beth. She's hurt… and she's pregnant. I need you to keep her safe for me," Destin stated in a quiet yet urgent tone.

"You go on and keep yourself safe. We've got Sula covered," Mary said firmly. "Come on, honey. We've got to find a safe place."

Sula watched Destin hurry after Jag and Cutter. Fear gripped her when she remembered the brief glimpse of the tower on fire and the city in ruins once again. Her eyes moved back to the portable vidcom Jag placed on the center of the table. She blinked when it flickered again.

Stepping away from Beth, Mary, and Chelsea, she walked back into the room. A frown creased her brow. For the first time, she saw the enlarged image of the ring. Staring at it, she stepped closer and peered at the image. Her lips parted in a gasp when she saw the small rectangular object in the side.

"What is it?" Beth asked above the sounds of the sirens.

"It is a microchip," Sula whispered. "Badrick liked to capture vidcoms of his meetings. There is a microchip in the ring. He would only have done that if it contained vital information that he didn't want anyone else to know about."

"But… What kind of information could he have?" Mary asked.

Sula turned and looked at Mary with wide eyes. "He was on Dises V. One of the reports I opened made a brief notation of it, but more importantly, it may have information on where the missing women were taken," Sula whispered with a growing urgency.

"Once we know what is going on, Mason can give you the ring," Mary said.

Sula shook her head. Her mind swirled with fear. What if this was the only chance there was of finding the women? What if there was information that could help against the Waxians and the Drethulans?

"I saw the tower in flames," Sula replied, gazing at the other women. "We have to get the ring before the tower is destroyed."

"But, how will we get there? Neither Grandma or I know how to fly one of those space transport things," Beth replied.

"I can, but I don't know where Mason's living quarters are or how to get in them once I find it," Sula said.

"Now that I know how to do," Mary stated with a smug, determined smile. "If there is a chance of finding those girls and bringing them home and defeating an alien species – the bad ones, darling – I can pick a lock to a flea's locker."

"I do not know what a flea's locker is, but I will trust you can pick the lock to Mason's living quarters," Sula responded. "I need my weapon."

"I'll get it. I'd love to go, but Doc Patch is going to need help when the wounded start coming in," Chelsea said, regretfully.

"You stay here," Mary said with a nod. "Beth and I will protect her."

"There is a transport in the third building to the left. It was given to Patch and me as a medical transport," Chelsea instructed.

"Maybe you should stay here, Sula," Beth said, biting her lip. "Grandma and I can go. I can take one of the jeeps. We know what we are looking for and you… well, honestly Destin would kill us if anything happened to you."

"I like that idea even better," Chelsea replied.

Sula started to protest, but Beth had placed the idea in the other two women's minds, and in all honesty, she knew she would be more of a liability with her injured shoulder. All three women winced and ducked when an explosion hit near the building and it shook.

"Go, find the ring and get back as soon as you can," Sula said.

"Find cover," Beth instructed. "Come on, Grandma."

Sula bit her lip and watched Beth and Mary hurry down the corridor. They both turned when Patch came out with a grim expression. This was not the healer from last night. This was a warrior.

"I've got reports of casualties coming in," Patch stated. "Get the operating beds ready."

"Right away," Chelsea said with a curt nod. "Sula…."

"Go, I will help any way I can," Sula promised.

Chapter 21

Destin watched the shuttle lift off the ground carrying Jag back to the *Star Raider*. High up in the sky he could see large flashes of light even through the clear blue skies. General Baker and Thomas jumped into a jeep that pulled up. The general was barking out orders. All around him, Trivator warriors moved with the skill of years of training.

"I don't know about you, but I feel like kicking some serious ass," Mason said, glancing up at the rain of pod-shaped vessels descending through the air. "Shit! It looks like a fu—a damn horror movie."

"Yeah, well, I've already lived through one. I don't want to live through another," Destin retorted. "You drive, I shoot."

Mason's eyes lit up when he saw where Destin was looking: an armored Humvee with a .50 caliber machine gun mounted to the top. The two men ran to the vehicle. Destin climbed inside, followed by Mason.

"Here, put these on," Mason said, tossing a pair of headphones to Destin. "This way we can communicate and you'll still have your hearing when we're done."

"Thanks," Destin replied, sliding on the headphones and turning them on. "Can you hear me?"

"Loud and clear," Mason replied, starting the vehicle. "I love being on a base where they are always ready. Do you remember how to work that thing?"

"Shut up and drive. I've got this," Destin retorted, locking the clip in and releasing the safety.

Destin braced himself in the swiveled seat. There was a short protective barrier around him. The seat allowed a full three hundred and sixty degree rotation with his body, giving it motion while his feet operated the brake and power to that made it rotate. Destin aimed at a pod and fired.

The force of the bullets didn't penetrate the metal capsules, but it was enough to knock it off balance. Realizing he was going to need more fire power or a better strategy for destroying the falling capsules, he continued firing until the one he was aiming at struck another capsule. The two careened out of control and crashed into the ground.

It was when they stopped spinning that Destin noticed an opening in the bottom, probably part of the capsules way to slow down before it struck the planet. Destin aimed at the engine opening and fired. The capsule exploded in a brilliant flare of flaming debris.

"Oh, yeah! Now that is what I'm talking about," Mason yelled.

Destin didn't need any more encouragement. He quickly fired on the second capsule just as a metal panel exploded and a creature unlike anything he had ever seen crawled out. Destin immediately fired multiple rounds, striking the creature and the vessel it had exited. The horrific sound of screeching reverberated through the air before it was cut short when the capsule exploded. Mason and Destin watched the fiery remains of the creature burn for several seconds before they refocused their efforts on the fight above them.

Transports flew low overhead, firing with precision at the capsules. They were discovering, like Destin had, that the metal was too dense to penetrate. He needed some way to communicate with Cutter or General Baker so he could let them know where to strike the capsules.

"We need to find Cutter," Destin growled.

"I saw him heading for the command center," Mason replied. "Hang on."

Destin swiveled around in his seat. He aimed upward at the incoming capsules. Mixed with them were additional fighters. These did not appear to have the same type of metal as the egg-shaped pods. The problem was the Trivator fighters were engaging with the attacking forces and not the pods.

Destin destroyed four more of the pods before one of the alien fighters realized what he was doing. Adrenaline poured through him when they turned toward him and Mason. Gritting his teeth, he continued firing at the two pods.

"We've got company," Destin said, wincing when Mason turned the corner between two buildings.

"I see them," Mason replied, accelerating.

"Yes!" Destin shouted.

"Ouch! What the hell happened?" Mason asked, taking another corner. "Bogies at eleven and two."

"The Trivators are figuring out what we are doing and two of their fighters took out the Drethulan fighters heading for us," Destin replied, swiveling to eleven o'clock and firing before turning to the one at two o'clock. "We're making progress!"

"Don't count your eggs yet, boss man. It looks like the alien chicken just hatched a new batch," Mason said, watching in dismay as the sky filled with the falling pods. "I hate fucking alien chickens."

* * *

Prymorus threw his vidcom across the room. Retris still had not returned with the Raftian and the Jawtaw, and the Drethulan commander refused to listen to him. He told the male that he didn't have troop placement yet, but the Drethulan was overconfident.

"Sir, what are your instructions?" one of the warriors asked, standing at attention.

"Bring the human child you found to me," Prymorus ordered.

"Yes, sir," the warrior said, turning on his heel.

Prymorus walked over to the opening and stared out. Drethulan pods fell through the atmosphere. He watched several explode before they reached the ground. His fingers tightened on the doorframe and he stepped back when two Trivator fighters flashed low overhead. The building shook from the explosions outside. Dust and loose debris rained down from the ceiling.

He watched the warrior walk back from the freighter. A struggling human boy fought to escape. Loud curses escaped the boy and he flashed a look of resentment at Prymorus.

The moment the boy was within striking distance, Prymorus backhanded him across the face. The force of the blow knocked the boy off his feet and he fell several feet away, stunned. Pulling his laser pistol free, he pointed it at the boy's leg.

"Struggle again and I will blow your leg off," Prymorus stated in an icy tone. "Do you know a human named Destin Parks?"

The boy raised a trembling hand to his busted bottom lip and nodded. Prymorus reached down, gripped the front of the child's shirt, and yanked him back to his feet. Dirty tears streaked the boy's face and his eyes shone with fear.

"You will lead me to him," Prymorus ordered. "If you try to escape, I will kill you slowly, do you understand?"

"Ye... Yes," the boy whispered. "He's... Destin isn't at the tower. I heard... I heard talk that he went to the base."

"The Trivator base?" Prymorus asked.

The boy nodded. "The one near the lake," he replied, pointing a shaky hand in the direction of most of the explosions.

Prymorus glanced toward the east. He started to turn toward the warrior when the male jerked in surprise and fell forward, dead. Prymorus' gaze locked on a human male holding a weapon against his shoulder. Next to him was a Trivator.

He started to reach for the boy to use as a shield, but the Trivator and the human male both opened fire at the same time as the boy fell to the ground and started crawling for cover. Prymorus lifted his laser pistol, returning fire at the two males who dove behind a partially collapsed wall. He briefly caught a glimpse of two of his men lying near the building across from him.

The other members of his team returned fire only to be cut down in the crossfire as more humans rose up out of the rubble. Prymorus quickly realized that his forces were outnumbered when additional explosions peppered the building and the freighter. He turned and dove through the entrance of the building behind him.

* * *

Beth gripped the wheel and turned it sharply, sliding around the corner. She fought the grin when she heard her grandmother release a line of swear words that would have almost made the men blush. She took the next left, then crossed between two buildings under construction and across the deserted roadway.

"Well, there's one way to clear the roads. All you need to do is have the aliens attack again and even they clear out," Mary said in a dry tone as she held onto the armrest. "Killing us before we get to the tower won't help the cause, Beth."

"Yes, ma'am," Beth replied, easing off the gas pedal. "Do you see any more of those pod things?"

Mary leaned forward and tried to see through the windshield. "The Trivators are picking them off pretty good now. I don't think there are quite as many falling as there were before."

"I hope they get them all," Beth replied, taking the next right and an immediate left. "We made it."

Beth turned right into the underground parking lot. The tires screeched on the smooth concrete when she followed the line around to the bank of elevators. She pulled to a stop and slid the gearshift into park before turning off the engine.

"Well, at least your driving is getting better," Mary remarked, opening the door and stepping out. "You didn't hit anything this time."

"Richard and Troy have been helping me," Beth replied with a grin, opening the driver's door and getting out.

"Mason's apartment is this way," Mary said, turning and hurrying to a set of doors with a sign stating authorized entrance only.

"I never understood why he wanted an apartment in the subbasement of the building," Beth remarked, waiting while her grandmother pressed her palm to the access panel.

"He hates heights and said he has a better chance of rising from the rubble than falling to the pavement," Mary replied with a wave of her hand for Beth to go ahead of her after she opened the door.

"How do you know that?" Beth asked with surprise.

"I may be old, Beth, but I'm not dead, and Mason is a very good-looking man," Mary replied with a twinkle in her eyes. "What do you think I do when you're working nights, sit at home and knit?"

"You don't… Oh!" Beth hissed out in surprise, staring at her grandmother's back with her mouth hanging open.

"You're catching flies, honey," Mary retorted, opening the door to Mason's apartment.

Beth snapped her mouth closed and shook her head. How could she have not known that her grandmother and Mason…. She blanched and shuddered.

"That's just nasty," she muttered at the thought of them getting it on. "I didn't think old people could still – and with Mason! Wow!"

Beth hurried into the apartment. It was sparsely decorated, but Beth could see small signs of her grandmother's touch. Releasing a long breath of air, she turned and strode down the hallway.

"Can you reach the top shelf?" Mary asked when Beth walked in the door.

"Let me find something to stand on," Beth replied, spying a chair in the corner. "Move aside."

Beth grabbed the chair and dragged it over to the closet. Climbing up on it, she turned and looked along the shelf. A neatly folded blanket, a couple of hats, a shoebox, and….

"Massage oil?" Beth asked, glancing down at her grandmother's upturned face.

"Don't look under the blanket," Mary instructed with a straight face. "That's where he keeps the sex toys and the bondage straps."

"Yew, Grandma!" Beth replied, grabbing the shoebox and thrusting it into her grandmother's outstretched hands before jumping off the chair. "You know you have totally damaged me for life."

"Well, it's about time you learned about the birds and the bees," Mary sniffed, not bothering to hide her grin.

"I don't ever remember seeing any bees or birds with massage oil and sex toys," Beth muttered under her breath, shaking her head in disbelief.

Mary took the box over to the bed and opened it. She briefly rummaged through the box before she held the ring out to Beth. "You hold onto this," Mary said. Beth nodded and slid the ring into her pocket while Mary put the lid back on the box. She handed the box to Beth as well. "Here, if you can put this back up on the shelf."

Beth took the shoebox, climbed back on the chair, and replaced it on the shelf. Jumping off the chair again, she returned it to the corner while Mary closed the closet door. Beth strode back toward the front door, wincing when the muted sound of an explosion nearby shook the building.

"Let's get out of here. Sula said she saw the building in flames. I don't want to be buried in it," Mary replied, pulling open the door to the apartment and motioning for Beth to go through first.

Beth stepped out into the hallway and turned when she heard frantic footsteps. Jason was running down the corridor toward her. Behind her, Mary closed the door to Mason's apartment.

"How bad is it?" Beth asked when Jason drew to a stop in front of her.

"Bad," Jason responded, reaching out to grip her arm. "What are you guys doing here and where in the hell have you been?"

Beth winced in pain when Jason grabbed her sore arm. "Ouch, let go," she muttered, pulling her arm away from him. They all hurried down the corridor, talking as they went. "Sula and I were attacked at the base last night by a couple of badasses known as Waxians. I took a minor hit, but Sula was hurt pretty badly. Anyway, there was a meeting this morning; Sula was looking for something important, Mason had it, some weird French dudes predicted the attack, and the tower is supposed to become the next inferno so we've all got to get out."

Jason stopped, looked at her with a strange expression, then shook his head, and began moving again. "Troy and Justin are up on the roof. We have weapons set up there. Richard's organizing the ground troops. I was heading to join him when I saw you enter the garage area," he explained.

"We've got to get back to the base," Beth said. "There may be information that can help defeat the Drethulans."

"I thought you said they were Waxians. Who the hell are the Drethulans?" he demanded, pausing at the door leading out into the garage.

Beth tossed back the long braid that was starting to come loose and sighed. Trying to explain this was almost as bad as learning about all the different countries when she was in elementary school.

"The Waxians attacked us at the base, but the pod things are the Drethulans. They are supposed to be working together," Beth explained as she opened the door.

"All I know is they are aliens and I'm fucking tired of them pissing on us," Jason retorted with a disgusted expression. "Sorry about the f-bomb, Mary."

"I'll let it slide this…," Mary started to say before her voice faded on a shocked hiss and she staggered backwards, clutching her chest.

"Grandma!" Beth cried out, reaching for the older woman when she started to slide down against the wall.

"Shit!" Jason said, lurching to the side as laser fire swept past them. He slammed the heavy metal door shut. "There are two of those creatures in the garage."

"Lock… Lock the garage down," Mary whispered in a pain-filled voice. "Key… The keypad. Hit nine-one-one."

Jason turned and punched in the code. The door immediately locked and he saw the large, thick metal door to the outer entrance that led to the street lower as well. The aliens didn't realize until it was too late that they were trapped. Beth knelt next to her grandmother, trying to stem the flow of blood from her chest.

"Oh, shit!" Jason whispered with a touch of horror in his voice as he stared through the thick glass window in the door.

"What is it?" Beth asked, glancing at him with tears in her eyes.

"These things... they... they're changing. We've got to get out of here," Jason replied in a hoarse tone.

"We can't move her. We've got to get help for her," Beth said with a shake of her head.

Beth was vaguely aware of Jason glancing down at her and her grandmother. Her blood-covered hands trembled as she put pressure on the wound. Her grandmother reached up and gripped her hand.

"Go, child. I'm not going to make it," Mary whispered.

"No!" Beth cried out in a shaking voice. "I won't leave you. Jason, you've got to help me get her up. We can go out through the service elevator at the end to the infirmary."

Jason jerked back when the door started to glow when one of the Drethulans fired on it. The other creature was trying to burst through the outer door to the street. Beth watched him shoulder his weapon and bend to slide his arm around Mary's waist.

"No," Mary hissed in pain.

"You heard Beth, Mary, we aren't leaving without you," Jason stated.

Mary pressed her hand against Jason and shook her head. "I can feel death coming for me, Jason," she whispered in a strained voice. "Get my granddaughter out of here and keep her alive."

"Mary...," Jason muttered, but he could see the light beginning to fade in the older woman's eyes.

"Do you have one of those little bombs you like to carry with you?" Mary asked in a barely audible voice.

"No, Grandma, please... no. You can't leave me," Beth cried. "Please... Oh, god... please...."

"Take her, Jason. Promise me...," Mary whispered as Jason slipped the small, round explosive into her hand. "Promise me...."

"I will," Jason murmured, sliding his arm from around her waist and touching her cheek in sorrow and regret. "You're an amazing woman, Mary."

"We've fought hard. Don't give up," Mary replied, leaning weakly back against the wall. "Go, Beth. I love you, honey. I always will. I'm in here if you ever need me." Mary weakly pressed her hand to Beth's heart.

Beth sobbed, clutching her grandmother's hand that was weakly pressed against her heart. She shook her head violently when Jason reached down and wrapped his arm around her waist. She wanted to fight him. Instead, Beth held onto her grandmother's hand until it slipped free.

"Noooo!" Beth cried, sobbing as Jason half carried, half dragged her down the corridor to the service elevator. "Noooo!" she screamed in pain, her gaze still locked on her grandmother's peaceful face. "No!"

Pain and grief tore through Beth. She would have never made it to the elevator without Jason. She stumbled, her eyesight blurred by tears. Jason activated the lift and pulled her inside. They both watched in grim horror as the door at the other end broke free from the hinges and long tentacles retracted and reformed until the two Drethulans were once more in an almost humanoid form.

She watched her grandmother's head move slightly before Beth closed her eyes when a brilliant flash, and then an explosion, shook the corridor. The doors to the lift closed before the wave of heat could hit them. When they did, Beth collapsed to the floor in uncontrollable sobs.

Chapter 22

Sula applied another bandage to one of the human soldiers that was brought in. All around her, she could hear explosions and feel the building tremble. She ignored the fear pulsing through her. It had nothing to do with her and everything to do with Destin.

Patch and Chelsea were quickly overwhelmed when the wounded started coming in. Sula took over the waiting room, working on helping those that were not in critical condition. She turned when the door opened and another man staggered in, his arm wrapped around a wounded soldier that looked too young.

"Mason!" Sula exclaimed, hurrying over to help him when he lowered the man into the last available chair. "Where is Destin?"

"Fighting," Mason replied. "We came upon this kid and he needed help."

Sula nodded, relieved to know that Destin was still fighting. She looked at the young male when he moaned and leaned his head back. A thick piece of metal protruded from his upper thigh. This one would have to go to Patch and Chelsea.

A pod landed not more than two hundred meters away and the door burst open. "Ah, shit! Damn it! Another one's hatched," Mason groaned, staring out the doorway.

Sula watched in horror as the Drethulan spilled out of the capsule. Instead of being in a humanoid form, it was in its natural one. It immediately started digging, trying to disappear beneath the soil to escape the gunfire aimed at it. Mason swung the gun on his shoulder around, and with a loud yell, he burst through the door after it, firing as he went.

Her heart in her throat, Sula hurried over to the door. She gripped the handle and stared out the doorway. The sky above them was difficult to see for all the smoke. The building across from medical had been hit and was on fire. Trivator fighters were still engaging the Drethulans. There were fewer pods opening. Most were destroyed before they made it to the ground.

Horror made everything feel hazy for a moment. Sula refocused when Mason and two Trivators aimed a burst of gunfire at a section of ground that was moving near the pod. Mason and two Trivator warriors turned in a tight circle when the ground stopped moving. Sula's lips parted when she saw the ground buckle a short distance from them. One of the Trivators twisted around as the Drethulan erupted from the ground behind them. Sharp tentacles struck out, hitting the man in the side.

"No!" Sula cried out, seeing the man fall and the Drethulan strike him again. "Mason, look out!"

Sula started forward. She was unaware of even moving until she was running toward Mason. Her hand wrapped around the Mylio-batoidei baton stuck in the back of her jeans. Another creature suddenly appeared and Sula flung out her arm, shooting out a wave of energy from the baton just as the creature struck Mason in the back.

The wave sliced through the creature's tentacle, severing it. As if in slow motion, Sula watched Mason's large body stiffen for a moment before he fell forward. Swinging the baton around, she snapped the band of energy across the creature's neck, nearly decapitating it. The lone Trivator turned his weapon on the first Drethulan, riddling its body with a burst of laser fire until it collapsed.

Sula fell to her knees next to Mason. Hot tears streaked down her face as she tenderly looked down at his blank eyes. Her fingers trembled as she ran them down over his cheek. Pain and grief engulfed her at the senseless death of a good man. Looking up, she gazed through the smoke at all the destruction.

"Why?" she whispered, blinking through the haze of tears.

"The fall of this planet would just be the beginning of a new era," a voice behind her said. "Drop your weapon, Councilor, or I will remove your hand from your body."

Sula turned, falling to the side in surprise. Her eyes widened and she stared at the twisted face of a Waxian. He held a laser gun in each hand. Her gaze followed the direction he was pointing one and she saw the body of the Trivator lying on the ground next to the Drethulan she had killed. Her fingers relaxed and the Mylio-batoidei baton dropped to the ground next to Mason.

"You are my way off this world," the Waxian stated, motioning for her to rise.

Sula pushed off the ground and slowly stood up. Her gaze locked on the male pointing the pistol at her. A shiver ran through her when she realized who he must be.

"You're the one called Prymorus," she said more than asked.

"This way, Princess," Prymorus ordered with a wave of his gun. "Where is the other human?"

"Other human...?" Sula asked.

"The one called Destin Parks. Where is he?" Prymorus demanded, sliding one of the pistols he held in a holster at his side before grabbing her arm and pulling her close.

Sula couldn't keep the cry of pain from escaping her when he roughly jerked her arm with the wounded shoulder – intense pain radiated down from the wound into her arm. His fingers bit into her through her long-sleeve, plaid shirt. She stumbled on the uneven ground, biting back another cry when he shook her.

"I... I don't know," she said. "I've been working in the medical unit while he is fighting."

"Do you have a communicator?" Prymorus asked.

Sula reluctantly nodded. "Yes," she admitted when he squeezed her arm in a crushing grip. "Yes, I have a communicator, but I don't know if it will work."

"Contact him. Tell him to meet us at the body of water near here with an off-world transport,"

Prymorus ordered, jerking her to the left and standing still next to a building as several Trivator and human soldiers ran by. "Now or he will find your body in pieces."

"How can you expect him to bring an off-world shuttle? He is human. He does not know how to operate such ships," Sula started to argue before she closed her eyes in pain when he jerked her around, pressing his thumb into her shoulder and the gun under her chin.

"He'll find a way," Prymorus murmured. "Now contact him."

Sula whimpered softly when he pulled his thumb away. Her knees felt weak and nausea threatened to overwhelm her. For a moment, she was tempted to give up on controlling it and just throw up all over the Waxian ignoramus. She opened her eyes and reached into the front pocket of her trousers to remove the small communicator.

Slipping it into her ear, she murmured the command to connect her to Destin. It took several tries before he finally responded. Sula felt a fierce wave of protectiveness and love sweep through her, threatening to choke her when she heard the sound of his slightly breathless greeting and deeply drawn in breath.

"Sula…." Destin greeted.

"Destin… Destin…." Sula had to swallow before she could continue.

"Where are you? Are you in danger?" Destin demanded.

"The lake... Yes, Prymorus... Destin, Mason is dead," she whispered brokenly.

"Tell him," Prymorus ordered, shaking her hard.

"The lake... Prymorus wants you to meet us at the lake with an off-world transport," she forced past the thickness in her throat. "He said... he said if you don't that you'll find me in pieces."

"On the lake, where?" Destin demanded in a voice devoid of emotion.

Sula looked at Prymorus for instructions. Fear gripped her when he didn't say anything at first. It took a moment to realize that the other man was unsure of the area.

"Tell him the old planetarium," Destin finally said. "You'll need a transport to get there. Go due east until you get to the lake, then north along it. It will be on an island by itself. It is a dome-shaped building. It will take me a while to get the type of transport he needs."

"Proceed with caution, human. I have no fear of dying," Prymorus warned. "I would not say the same for the Councilor."

"Sula...," Destin said.

Sula closed her eyes again and tilted her face away from Prymorus when he reached up and removed the communicator from her ear, effectively cutting Destin off. She turned her head toward him when he stepped away. Swallowing down her fear, she turned back to him and defiantly met his eyes.

"Move inside," Prymorus ordered, nodding to a door nearby.

Sula slid past him and slowly walked to the door. This was the building where Chelsea's transport was stored. She opened the door, and stepped inside. The interior was dim. The first three bays were empty. The fourth bay contained an air transport.

"You will pilot the craft," Prymorus said, motioning for her to move forward.

Sula hesitated. Her feet felt like they were filled with the heavy ore of the Drethulan pods. She started to shake her head, but stopped when he shoved her in the center of her back.

"Why do you want Destin?" Sula asked in a thick voice.

"Because I am a force to be reckoned with! The Alliance will fear me, not just the power of the Drethulans and the Waxians – me! They need an example of what is still to come. He will be the first," Prymorus replied.

Sula swallowed and opened the door to the pilot's seat. She climbed into the front of the transport while he climbed into the back. Pressing the power, she waited while the doors of the transport closed and the one to the building opened.

"Why involve a human? He is not part of the Alliance Council. Why would they care about you killing a human male?" Sula argued.

"Chancellor Razor's *Amate* will care," Prymorus replied in an icy voice. "Move slowly and do not engage any other fighters."

"This is a medical transport. The Trivators will give it clearance. I can't say the same for the

Drethulans," Sula snapped, guiding the transport carefully out of the storage bay and into the yard.

She carefully maneuvered the vehicle clear of the building and rose. Once again her throat tightened when she saw Mason lying among the other dead. Swirls of smoke danced around the transport and she refocused on the distant shoreline. Pressing the accelerator, the transport shot forward, away from the Trivator base and toward Lake Michigan.

She was forced to keep the transport low. There were no more Drethulan pods falling from the sky, but the Trivator fighters were still locked in combat with the few remaining Drethulan fighters. Her hands tightened on the controls and she turned the transport sharply to avoid colliding with an escaping Drethulan fighter.

An explosion behind them rocked the transport and she almost lost control of it. Her shoulder protested the strain she placed on it, but she ignored the pain. Instead, she used all of the calm she could muster to focus on a plan of attack that wouldn't leave Destin or her dead. Leveling the transport out, she moved away from the battle to the tranquil waters in the distance.

Chapter 23

Destin stood frozen, staring across the open area of the base where he had been fighting. Smoke, fires, bodies, and the destroyed remains of both Trivator and Drethulan fighters littered the area. The remains of the burning Drethulan pods covered the area.

The acrid smell was so overwhelming that Destin had removed his outer T-shirt and wrapped it around his nose and mouth. He didn't bother replacing it after talking to Sula. His gaze locked on Cutter. They had been fighting together for the last several hours.

"What is it?" Cutter asked.

"Mason is dead. Prymorus has Sula," Destin replied. "I need your assistance."

Cutter grimly nodded. "Where are they?" he asked.

"The old Adler Planetarium," Destin responded. "Prymorus wants an off-planet transport."

"I know where one is and I know a good pilot," Cutter replied with a sharp-tooth smile.

"I won't jeopardize Sula's safety," Destin said.

"He will kill you both if he takes you. I promised Trig I wouldn't let that happen," Cutter retorted, pushing past him to one of the hangers several hundred meters away.

Twenty minutes later, Cutter guided the off-planet transport in the direction of the planetarium. Destin sat beside him. He removed all weapons except for the knife he kept in his boot, untied the black T-shirt from around the lower half of his face, and pulled the shirt back on over his dirt and blood streaked white one. He discarded his jacket hours ago and had no idea where it was.

"Waxians are mercenaries. He would sooner cut your throat than negotiate with you," Cutter was saying.

"I pretty much already figured that out," Destin replied. "I've dealt with men like him before."

Cutter shook his head. "They are ruthless, without compassion or caring for life – even their own if they discover there is no way out alive. To make the situation worse, Prymorus is a Waxian Warlord. They earn that position by killing their predecessor, which is no easy feat, believe me. Take into account what happened to Dagger and the situation on Dises V, and the likelihood of you and Sula surviving is *very slim*. There has to be a way to do this other than walking right up to him and giving yourself over."

"It better not be one that puts Sula in more danger," Destin said, shooting the other man a determined glare. "Her safety comes first."

"Trig—" Cutter said, breaking off when Destin sharply turned to him and gave him a savage look.

"I," Destin bit out in a slow, measured tone, "don't give a flying fuck about what Trig, Razor, Ajaska, or some mystical message from the past or future says. Sula comes first. Do you understand?"

Cutter gave Destin a sharp nod in acknowledgement. Destin returned his focus on the scenery in front of him. They were approaching the planetarium. There was a grassy knoll where Cutter could land the shuttle. Destin saw a small medical transport in what used to be the parking lot.

"I'll come around and land facing south," Cutter said, making a wide circle over the water before swinging back around and coming in for a landing.

Destin jerked when the communicator he was wearing pinged. He touched his ear, and nodded to Cutter when the other man tapped into the communication so he could hear what was being said.

"Exit the shuttle when you arrive. If anyone remains on board, I will relieve Councilor Ikera of a body part," Prymorus instructed.

"I understand," Destin replied in a terse tone. "Release her and I will go with you."

"You will go with me regardless of whether I release her or not," Prymorus responded, ending the transmission.

"They are generally not very talkative either," Cutter muttered, shutting down the power to the shuttle. "You go first and I'll follow you."

Destin nodded. He didn't say anything. There wasn't a lot to say – Prymorus held all the cards at the moment. All they could do was hope that by some miracle the other man fucked up somehow. Swallowing down the bile that threatened to choke him, he unstrapped from his seat and rose. Walking through the shuttle, he glanced around at the strategically placed weapons he and Cutter had hidden. If there was a chance to escape and kill the bastard, he would do it.

Drawing in a deep breath, he placed his hand on the release. The platform in the back slowly lowered. When the platform hit the ground, Destin strode down toward Prymorus, who was standing about twenty meters from the platform with Sula held firmly in front of him.

Destin stopped almost ten meters from the other man and returned the man's assessing gaze. His eyes narrowed when he saw a hint of fresh blood on Sula's shoulder. She gazed back at him, her heart in her eyes.

"Release her," Destin said in a quiet voice.

Prymorus' lips curve up in an ugly smile. "You are not the one giving orders, human," he stated coolly. "Where is the pilot?"

Behind him, Destin could hear Cutter's footsteps as he descended the platform. An oath escaped him when Prymorus raised his arm and fired. The impact of the laser hitting Cutter in the chest sent him flying off the side of the platform.

Sula turned in Prymorus' grasp, brought her knee forcefully up into his groin, and tried to get the gun out of his grasp. The blow startled Prymorus, and he groaned in pain, but held onto the gun. Destin didn't wait. Sprinting forward, he tackled Prymorus around the waist.

This time Prymorus released the gun when his hand was slammed against the concrete as the two hit the ground and rolled several times. Prymorus landed on top and Destin elbowed him in the mouth when the other man tried to hit him. The blow, combined with the pain he was still experiencing from Sula's unexpected attack, knocked Prymorus off of him. Destin jumped to his feet and reached for the knife in his boot.

"Stop!" Sula ordered, holding the laser pistol at Prymorus.

Prymorus shot Sula a venomous glare and rolled to his knees. He breathed deeply, the sound hissing through the air, and spit out a mouthful of blood.

"This is just the beginning, human. The Drethulans and Waxians have joined forces. This will not end here," Prymorus said, slowly pushing up off the ground.

"It will end here for you, though," Destin quietly replied.

Prymorus laughed and ran his arm across his mouth, smearing the blood covering his split lip. Destin felt a chill run down his spine at the other man's laughter. Prymorus glared back at him. The flat sheen of his eyes was eerie, his gaze gleaming with a hint of insanity.

Destin was about to take the weapon from Sula when he saw a flash out of the corner of his eye. Destin wrapped an arm around Sula and fell backwards just as a blast struck a small bush behind where Sula had been standing. Prymorus took advantage of the distraction and darted up the platform. Destin rolled onto his stomach and released the knife in his hand. Prymorus stumbled when the blade embedded in his right shoulder, and started to fall, but caught one of the supports on the platform and flung himself inside the shuttle.

Destin covered his head when additional blasts struck the ground a few centimeters from his head. Sula rolled onto her side and released a series of defensive blasts. The move was enough to give them time to run to the seawall that outlined the property, and hop over it into the soft sand on the other side. They crouched down in the sand, their backs to the hard surface of the wall.

"I've got to stop him," Destin muttered.

"Take this," Sula said, handing him the laser pistol.

Another round of fire forced them to sink lower behind the concrete wall. Destin glanced down at the gun and shook his head.

"No, you keep it," Destin ordered, closing her fingers around the grip and pressing a hard kiss on her lips. "I love you."

Destin could see the answer in her eyes. He didn't need to wait to hear it. Staying low to the ground, he ran along the wall, keeping it between him and the thick row of trees their attacker was using for cover. He needed a distraction so he could jump the wall and use the cover of the trees to work his way around to the location where the laser fire was coming from.

He got his wish when Sula and another shooter opened up on the man. Destin could only guess that Cutter must have somehow survived the blast. Destin gripped the top of the wall, pushed off with his legs, and launched himself up onto the wall. He immediately sprinted to the row of trees that lined the sidewalk and led up to the planetarium.

In the distance, he caught a brief glimpse of their enemy shooter when he retreated back in the direction of the planetarium. Destin ran along the line of trees, looking to see where the male was aiming his shots. He hoped to hell that Sula kept her head down.

The sound of the shuttle's engines engaging helped add to the distraction. The male, realizing he was about to be left behind, gave up on firing and focused instead on reaching the top of the building on the off-chance that he could escape.

Destin followed him, jumping a low wall and running up the long, curved support that led to the glass roof. The male in front of him jumped off the support, swung his legs, then twisted and grabbed the edge of the roof and pulled himself up and over the side of it. Destin picked up speed and did the same. The muscles in his upper arms strained as he pulled the weight of his body up until he could roll over the edge and onto the glass.

He used his momentum to surge to his feet and race after the man. The shuttle was beginning to rise off the ground. Destin could see that the back platform was still down. A quick glance showed Cutter's body half lying, half leaning down against the sun-bleached steps leading down to the water. From here, he couldn't see Sula.

A fierce determination swept through Destin along with a rush of adrenaline. Destin surged toward the shuttle a second after the man did. They landed on the metal platform hard, one after the other, when the shuttle swung around. Their bodies slid with the force of the teetering swing and they went over the edge, each grabbing for whatever support they could find.

Destin grunted when the man kicked him in the ribs. His fingers slipped and Destin struggled to keep his grip on the platform. Twisting his body, he scissored his legs around the man. The other male fought to break free of the hold Destin had on him.

Both men's heads jerked up when the platform moved upward, beginning to close in preparation for flight. Destin glanced down. They were just moving over the water. If he fell into the shallow water from this height, he would either die or be permanently injured. His gaze jerked to the opening. They were running out of time.

* * *

Sula watched in horror from the shoreline as Destin's body flew through the air. Her hand rose to her mouth and she pressed her fist against it to keep from crying out. She reached out to steady herself when she saw he made it onto the platform – for what good it did him when he slid off the side after the shuttle wobbled dangerously.

She moved along the uneven sand, keeping Destin's hanging body within sight. She cursed softely when she realized she would have to climb over the rocks if she wanted to keep him in view. Stumbling, she braced her hand on one of them and scrambled up.

"Don't let go. Please... I can't lose you. Hold on for just a few more seconds," Sula whispered, unable to look away.

A loud cry escaped her when she saw the two men's bodies falling. Without thinking, Sula dropped the gun in her hand and kicked off her shoes. Running across the stones that were placed like steps to stop shoreline erosion, she dove off the end of the concrete embankment.

In her natural element, she opened her eyes wide and struck out in the direction she had seen Destin hit the water. Her body rapidly cut through the frigid waters, even with the resistance of her clothing. Sula ignored the pain in her shoulder. Her body felt numb to anything but her search for Destin. In the murky distance, she caught a glimmer of white. She sped toward the faint glow.

Sula grabbed the familiar hand that was drifting upward. Destin's eyes were closed and his body relaxed as he plunged toward the bottom. Her fingers closed around his, and she pulled his body up against hers, kicking her powerful legs to slow his descent. Holding him tight against her, she reached up to pinch his nose while her lips covered his in a life-giving kiss.

Breathing air into his lungs, she stared at the crescent shape of his lashes lying against his skin, willing him to accept the gift she was giving him and be alright. Her body strained to supply the needed oxygen for both of them.

Several long, precious seconds passed before she felt his body stiffen. His eyes snapped open and he gazed back at her in confusion. His arms swept around her, allowing her to release her grip on him. She continued to breathe in and out in slow, steady breaths as they both kicked to the surface. Only when they broke through the surface did she release his nose and lips.

"My siren," Destin whispered, gazing at her with a slightly dazed expression. "You can breathe under water."

"Yes," Sula answered, her face crumbling and her arms wrapping around his neck. "Don't you ever scare me like that again!"

"I probably will, but it won't be intentional. The other man?" Destin asked, pulling back enough to glance around.

"He fell, too. Dead for all I know," Sula said, gripping his hand in hers. "Come."

Together they swam back to shore. Cutter was waiting for them. Sula smiled in appreciation when the Trivator helped them both out of the water. She sat on the warm concrete while Destin lay on his back, staring up at the sky. High overhead, they could see the bright flashes as Jag's forces fought against the remaining Drethulans in Earth's orbit.

Destin turned his head to look at Cutter. He was standing, looking out over the water. Sula reached over and cupped Destin's hand in hers, unwilling to release him. There had been enough death and destruction today. She wanted to hold onto the living.

"How the hell did you survive a direct hit to the chest?" Destin asked, sitting up.

"I grabbed a piece of the metal from a Drethulan pod and shoved it under my shirt," Cutter replied, turning to look down at Destin and Sula. "I need to return to base."

Destin nodded, rising to his feet and holding his hand out to Sula. She rose, shivering when a breeze blew across the water, chilling her even more. There was so much to do. Regret and sorrow filled her.

"I'm so sorry about Mason," Sula whispered, tears filling her eyes. "I know he was a good friend to you."

"He was a good man," Destin agreed in a thick voice, looking out over the water. "Mary will be devastated. We've already lost so many."

"I know," Sula murmured, standing in silent memory of the missing women, the senseless deaths, and the difficult future ahead of them.

"Let's go," Cutter finally said, breaking through the silence. "We have a lot of work to do."

Chapter 24

A week later, a small group consisting of both aliens and humans gathered in the Northshore Gardens cemetery. Sula held Beth's hand on one side while Trig stood at Beth's other side. Sula was thankful for the arm Destin wrapped around her waist.

This was the first human burial ceremony she had ever attended. Two caskets, side by side, were gently lowered into the ground while Beth quietly sang. The melody of the words wrapped around Sula and she could feel the tension gradually drain from Beth.

"Life is for the living," Beth said, gazing down at the coffins. "I'm never alone because as long as I remember her, I know that she is here." Beth lifted her left hand and touched her heart.

Sula stepped back when Beth released her hand and drew in a deep, calming breath. She gazed around at the men who had become her family over the years. Sula couldn't help but notice that Beth was avoiding looking at Trig. She wondered what that was about.

"First round is on Grandma, all the ones after that you guys are on your own," Beth declared. "Let's go party."

Loud, whooping yells filled the air and everyone started talking at once. Sula watched in amazement as Beth laughed along with some of the tales being shared. Destin held her close as they walked out of the cemetery and down along the sidewalk. Once again, the city came alive and the builders were back at work, repairing the damage and continuing with the existing plans.

"I like that your people celebrate the life of a loved one and not their death," she murmured, reaching up to tuck a long strand of white hair behind her ear.

"Oh, there will be plenty of tears still, but tonight is a celebration of Mary and Mason. I expect Beth will experience her first hangover before the night is over," Destin replied, watching Richard, Troy, Jason, and Justin tease the young woman who had lost the last of her family, but would never be alone. His gaze followed the bemused Trivator trying to keep up with everything going on. Beth must have sensed Trig's hesitation because she suddenly turned, wrapped her arms around his neck, and jumped up so he was forced to pick her up.

"That way, big guy! You are going to learn to party tonight!" Beth ordered, pointing down the road to the tall tower that was still standing.

Sula giggled when she saw the pleased grin on Trig's face. It was hard to believe, but she was beginning to understand some of the terms the humans used – including the one about having a big strong warrior wrapped around her little finger. At the moment, she was happy to have his arm wrapped around her waist and if the night went well, there would be even more.

She slowed to a stop when Destin fell behind the others. Puzzled, she looked at him with a raised eyebrow. Her eyes briefly closed when he ran his palm against her cheek.

"I have a surprise for you," Destin murmured.

"What?" she asked, tilting her head into his palm.

"It's a surprise! Come on," he said, sliding his hand down to grab hers.

Sula giggled and followed him. She jerked to a stop when he paused in front of a strange transport with two wheels. He picked up a hard hat and carefully slid it over her head, attaching a strap under her chin. A few seconds later, he threw his leg over and straddled the seat. He motioned for her to follow him.

Sula carefully slid on behind him. She wrapped her arms around his waist, careful of her still tender shoulder and placed her feet on the short metal bars sticking out of the sides. A startled squeak escaped her when he started the machine. It was loud and vibrated under her.

"Hold on. I won't go too fast," he shouted above the engine.

All Sula could do was nod. The head device felt heavy and strange. She wasn't sure why she was wearing one and he wasn't, but it would be too difficult to ask him about it at the moment.

Her arms tightened when the transport suddenly moved. A gasp of delight escaped her and she rested her chin as much as she could on his shoulder. She laughed when he weaved through the streets.

Thirty minutes later, they pulled up in front of the planetarium. Destin cut the noisy engine. They gazed out over the water for a few minutes before he kicked a bar down, and they both slid off the transport. He stepped closer to help her remove the protective headgear and placed it on the transport before turning back to her to soothe the wayward strands of silky white hair that came loose.

"Why are we here?" she asked, unable to control the shiver of memory from the recent events that occurred.

"This place can be magical, Sula," Destin murmured, threading his fingers through hers and walking toward the sea wall. "Kali and I loved to come here. We sneaked in when we were little by telling the guard that our parents were inside. When we got older, we'd find other ways in. We never got caught, but it was close a few times."

He stepped behind her and she leaned back against him. Her hands folded over his and they gazed out across the water. In the distance, patrols flew overhead, searching with special sensors for any Drethulans that might have escaped underground. Her fingers moved over the ring on her thumb. Beth gave it to her earlier. Both of them had forgotten about it during all the confusion and grief.

She lifted her hand, turning it until she could see the small object in the side. Running her fingernail against it, she was surprised when it slid deeper into the slot and a list of holographic images appeared. Destin's loud intake of breath told her he was just as startled by it as she was.

"That looks like one of the missing women," Destin exclaimed, reaching out to touch the image of a woman. "What the hell?"

Destin's soft exclamation echoed through the air when the video of the woman began to play. They watched it for several seconds before touching another holographic file, and then another. Each one played, giving detailed accounts of what was going on. In the background, they could hear Badrick's mocking voice.

Sula reached up and touched the last one. It looked like the two men in the vidcom that Jag had played. She bit her lip when the video started. The two men were once again arguing with each other.

"But... what if he finds it?" Luc argued. "He might remove the disc."

"Who... Jarmen?" Jon Paul argued in a thick French accent with a touch of indignation. "He is too busy with Jane to know what we are doing. Humans need all the help they can get. Who is to say we are not to have done this anyway? Perhaps it is what makes the world the way it is supposed to be and if we do not do it – boom, it all blows up!"

"IQ, what do you think?" Luc asked, looking at someone they couldn't see.

"That it is above my pay grade. Ask Numbnuts; he might know," IQ replied in a dry voice.

"Numbnuts!" Luc hollered.

"Hush! Do you want Jarmen to come see what we are doing again? Think!" Jon Paul snapped, slapping his forehead.

"I have found that anything I say is irrelevant to a conversation with both of you because you refuse to listen anyway. But, if you want my calculations... We are all going to die. Now, if you don't mind, dinner is served," Numbnuts replied in a slightly stuck-up tone.

"You must work on his programming. I do not like his tone of voice... *And*, we are not all going to die!" Jon Paul snapped in irritation.

"You are the one who wanted to make this ship grander," Luc argued.

"Grander, oui, but not...."

Sula giggled when the video of the two men suddenly faded, as if the person recording realized that this was not something others should see. She turned in Destin's arms and wound hers around his neck. Her lips parted and she kissed him deeply. Whoever the mysterious men were, they had given them hope of finding not only the missing women, but additional information on the Waxians and the Drethulans... and a missing Trivator named Edge.

* * *

Destin ran his hands down Sula's sides to her hips. The videos helped lift yet another cloud from over their heads. Tomorrow, he would meet with Cutter and they could go through each video and learn everything that they could. Lifting his head, he tenderly gazed down into Sula's eyes. He brought her here because it was a place that meant something to him – and to celebrate.

"I want to show you something else," he murmured, stepping back and holding her hand again.

They walked in silence around the curved walkways to the front of the planetarium. The front doors were boarded up and chained, but that didn't stop him. He pulled free the lock he had picked earlier in the week and opened the door. Sula stepped through with a puzzled smile and waited for him to follow her inside.

He closed the door and looped the chain around the inside of the doors, sliding the lock back on the chain, but not locking it. Turning, he led her through the foyer and to the center section where a set of large, double doors stood open. Love filled him, heating his blood when he saw her lips part in wonder when they passed through into the domed theater of the planetarium.

"You did this for me?" Sula whispered as if afraid of breaking the spell he had cast.

Destin released her hand, watching her walk down the aisle to the center. On one side, he set up a small table and two chairs. A battery operated flameless candle in the center of the white table cloth softly lit the table. He cut a dozen roses from a rose bush he discovered in the central gardens and placed them in a vase in the center of the table. There was a cart next to the table that Destin begged for Chelsea and Thomas' help with. Thomas made a nice Italian dinner and the couple had slipped it into the building late this afternoon.

Tim and Richard helped him repair the Planetarium projector and Cutter made sure that the power was installed. It took some teamwork to get it done this quickly, but Destin wanted tonight to be perfect for Sula.

He looked up, staring at the array of glittering stars. He would never look at them in the same way. He had traveled through them to a distant world and discovered a siren that captured his heart when he kissed her under the water.

"Destin, this is… You are a very unusual and amazing man," Sula whispered, her eyes glittering with the same stars that filled the room.

"Sula," Destin grasped her hand and slowly knelt down on one knee on the floor in front of her. He cleared his throat and gazed at her. "Princess Jersula Ikera of Usoleum, would you do me the honor of becoming my wife? I don't know the traditions of your people or how they form a union, but here on Earth, it is through marriage – like the ceremony Saber and Taylor celebrated on Rathon. I promise to love, honor, and worship you for the rest of my life, in sickness and in health, till de—"

The rest of his words were captured by her lips when she bent and pressed them against his. Her lips parted and her tongue slipped against his, tangling and dancing until their breaths came fast and heavy. He rose, never releasing her. His arms swept around her, lifting her off the floor and he carried her over to the king size air bed he made up so they could lie under the stars and talk about their future after dinner.

He gently laid her down, his hands greedily running over her even as she tugged at the buttons on his shirt. He shrugged out of his jacket, tossing it with one hand onto a chair. He gasped softly when her fingers quickly unbuttoned his shirt and he felt her fingers tangling in the hair on his chest.

"Yes," she whispered, brushing tiny kisses along his jaw while her hands pushed his shirt off his shoulders. "The answer to your question is yes. I will be your wife, Destin Parks."

"God, Sula, I love you," Destin moaned, kissing her again as his hands ran over her.

The heat from their kisses could have rivaled the stars over their heads. Their hands slid over each other, pausing, learning, exploring, and worshipping each other. Their breaths mixed with whispered words of love and the wonder of their child growing in Sula's womb as they made love far into the night.

It was after midnight when Destin reached for the small box he had hidden under the pillows of their makeshift bed. Destin's fingers trembled slightly when he slid the ring he made for Sula onto her finger. Swallowing, he gazed at her, his throat tight at her beauty. Unable to resist, he traced her face, letting his fingers skim down over her neck and shoulders to her breasts, memorizing the feel of them and letting this memory burn into his heart and soul. He now understood the two faint lines on her neck were not scars, but an evolution of her species. He vaguely wondered if their son or daughter would be able to breathe underwater like their mother.

"I will need to talk to your father," Destin murmured, threading his fingers through her hair and watching it fall back over her bare shoulders. "Do you think he will be upset? I'm not exactly royalty."

"You are giving him a grandchild. He will love you forever," Sula laughed, resting her head on his shoulder so she could stare up at the stars overhead. "What will happen, Destin?"

"What do you mean?" Destin asked, his stomach clenching with worry.

"What will happen with the missing women – both here and the ones on the vidcom?" Sula asked, tilting her head to look at him. "There was also the Trivator called Edge. I have not heard of him before."

Destin relaxed and smiled into the darkness. His hand came up to caress Sula's arm, being careful of her shoulder. These kinds of worries he could deal with; it was the fear of losing her that he couldn't.

"I don't know about Edge, but I do know about the missing women here. The Raftian and Jawtaw were working undercover for Razor to find the missing women. One of their leads led them back here and to the Armatrux. Cutter is rounding the Armatrux up. The Raftian approached Alissa Garcia, seeking her cooperation. Alissa and a small group of other former police officers agreed to be 'kidnapped' by the Raftian and Jawtaw to find out where the missing women were kept before they were taken off world and, if necessary, to tag their spacecraft with a long-range locator. The Raftian and Jawtaw didn't anticipate Prymorus showing up and demanding their assistance. They discovered that Trig and Tim were looking for them and were able to lead them to Prymorus. Unfortunately, he escaped – both from them and the Trivator forces. Cutter has sent a request to the Alliance Council to have a bounty put on Prymorus' head. The attack on Earth has also increased tensions between the Drethulans and the Alliance, but Cutter said it might take a while for the Alliance Council to actually do something. In the meantime, there are still issues with them mining on Dises V. I have to tell you, I've learned more about alien politics in the past week than I ever wanted to know," Destin muttered with a dry laugh.

"I'm hungry," Sula suddenly exclaimed. She sat up and looked around. Her eyes lit up on the cart. "Do you think the food will still be edible?"

Destin laughed, leaning up and pressing a kiss to her shoulder. "If not, I know where the cafeteria is. I stocked some food just in case," he promised, sliding off the air mattress. He reached for his jeans and pulled them on.

Sula rose, wrapping the blanket around her. Together they walked over to the cart with the covered dishes. Lifting the lid, Destin frowned when he saw a neatly printed card folded on the plate instead of food. Picking up another lid, he found another card. Each of the five covered dishes had a plate and a card with something different written on them. He picked up the sheet of paper in the center of the dishes and silently read it.

"What does it say?" Sula asked, glancing over his shoulder when he laughed.

"It says 'We figured you two would be distracted and didn't want a perfectly cooked dinner to go to waste. Instructions for heating each item are on the plates. Ice cream is in the freezer; chocolate sauce and the rest of dinner is in the refrigerator, chocolate covered potato chips are on the counter. Bon appétit, Hearts: Chelsea and Thomas.'"

"Oh, I think I am going to love this world," Sula moaned with delight. "I want to try the chocolate covered potato chips."

Destin's loud laughter echoed through the planetarium. His eyes landed on the stars shining overhead and he couldn't help but pause when he saw a replica of a shooting star. He had always wondered what it would be like up there and if life existed somewhere in those vast galaxies. Glancing back down at Sula, he had the answer to his questions and to the wishes he used to make as a child.

"I love you, Destin. Hold me and never let me go," Sula whispered, caressing his cheek as if she knew he needed her near him at that moment.

"Not as much as I love you, Sula, my beautiful alien mate. I could hold you forever and still not get enough," Destin replied, lifting her hand to his lips and pressing a tender kiss to her knuckles before drawing her into his arms and tightly holding her against his body. "I promise to hold you forever."

To be continued:
Edge of Insanity: The Alliance Book 6

Additional Books and Information

If you loved this story by me (S.E. Smith) please leave a review. You can also take a look at additional books and sign up for my newsletter at http://sesmithfl.com and http://sesmithya.com to hear about my latest releases or keep in touch using the following links:

Website: http://sesmithfl.com
Newsletter: http://sesmithfl.com/?s=newsletter
Facebook: https://www.facebook.com/se.smith.5
Twitter: https://twitter.com/sesmithfl
Pinterest: http://www.pinterest.com/sesmithfl/
Blog: http://sesmithfl.com/blog/
Forum: http://www.sesmithromance.com/forum/

Excerpts of S.E. Smith Books

If you would like to read more S.E. Smith stories, she recommends Touch of Frost, the first in her Magic, New Mexico series. Or if you prefer a Paranormal or Western with a twist, you can check out Lily's Cowboys or Indiana Wild…

Additional Books by S.E. Smith

Short Stories and Novellas

Dragon Lords of Valdier Novella
For the Love of Tia (Book 4.1)

Dragonlings of Valdier Novellas
A Dragonling's Easter (Book 1.1)
A Dragonling's Haunted Halloween (Book 1.2)
Night of the Demented Symbiots (Halloween 2)
A Dragonling's Magical Christmas (Book 1.3)
The Dragonlings' Very Special Valentine (Book 1.4)

Pets in Space Anthology
A Mate for Matrix

Marastin Dow Warriors Short Story
A Warrior's Heart (Book 1.1)

Lords of Kassis Novella
Rescuing Mattie (Book 3.1)

The Fairy Tale Novella
The Beast Prince
*Free Audiobook of The Beast Prince is available:
 https://soundcloud.com/sesmithfl/sets/the-beast-prince-the-fairy-tale-series

Boxsets / Bundles

Dragon Lords of Valdier Boxset Books 1-3
The Alliance Boxset Books 1-3

Science Fiction Romance / Paranormal Novels

Cosmos' Gateway Series

Tink's Neverland (Book 1)
Hannah's Warrior (Book 2)
Tansy's Titan (Book 3)
Cosmos' Promise (Book 4)
Merrick's Maiden (Book 5)

Curizan Warrior Series
Ha'ven's Song (Book 1)

Dragon Lords of Valdier Series
Abducting Abby (Book 1)
Capturing Cara (Book 2)
Tracking Trisha (Book 3)
Ambushing Ariel (Book 4)
Cornering Carmen (Book 5)
Paul's Pursuit (Book 6)
Twin Dragons (Book 7)
Jaguin's Love (Book 8)
The Old Dragon of the Mountain's Christmas (Book 9)

Lords of Kassis Series
River's Run (Book 1)
Star's Storm (Book 2)
Jo's Journey (Book 3)
Ristéard's Unwilling Empress (Book 4)

Magic, New Mexico Series
Touch of Frost (Book 1)
Taking on Tory (Book 2)

Sarafin Warriors Series

Choosing Riley (Book 1)
Viper's Defiant Mate (Book 2)

The Alliance Series
Hunter's Claim (Book 1)
Razor's Traitorous Heart (Book 2)
Dagger's Hope (Book 3)
Challenging Saber (Book 4)
Destin's Hold (Book 5)

Zion Warriors Series
Gracie's Touch (Book 1)
Krac's Firebrand (Book 2)

Paranormal / Time Travel Romance Novels

Spirit Pass Series
Indiana Wild (Book 1)
Spirit Warrior (Book 2)

Second Chance Series
Lily's Cowboys (Book 1)
Touching Rune (Book 2)

Paranormal Novels

More Than Human Series
Ella and the Beast (Book 1)

Science Fiction / Action Adventure Novels

Project Gliese 581G Series
Command Decision (Book 1)

Young Adult Novels

Breaking Free Series
Voyage of the Defiance (Book 1)
Capture of the Defiance (Book 2)

The Dust Series
Dust: Before and After (Book 1)

Recommended Reading Order Lists:

http://sesmithfl.com/reading-list-by-events/
http://sesmithfl.com/reading-list-by-series/

About the Author

S.E. Smith is a *New York Times, USA TODAY, International, and Award-Winning* Bestselling author of science fiction, romance, fantasy, paranormal, and contemporary works for adults, young adults, and children. She enjoys writing a wide variety of genres that pull her readers into worlds that take them away.

CPSIA information can be obtained
at www.ICGtesting.com
Printed in the USA
LVOW01s2148140217
524296LV00012B/741/P